Praise for
HOW TO SURVIVE A HORROR MOVIE

"*How to Survive a Horror Movie* by Scarlett Dunmore is a love letter to slasher films and the horror genre and a real page turner. Laugh out loud funny and heart-in-mouth thrilling!"
Gabriel Dylan, author of *Whiteout*

"Fast-paced and humorous and a homage to classic films like *Scream*, this is a delightfully fun and creepy read—perfect for reading in one sitting!"
Ravena Guron, author of *This Book Kills*

"An enormously fun love-letter to the horror genre, with all the gore, ghosts, and gay panic you could ask for, and twists that will leave you desperate for more!"
Leanne Egan, author of *Lover Birds*

"*Scream* meets *Fear Street*. Perfect for slasher fans, this book is packed with horror movie references, scares, and witty dialogue. It kept me guessing all the way to the end!"
Amy McCaw, author of *Mina and the Undead* series

"Packed full of laughs and gore in equal measure, this exhilarating slasher takes you along for an endlessly fun ride!"
Tess James-Mackey, author of *You Wouldn't Catch Me Dead*

"Toss some Skittles in your popcorn and settle in for the horror-comedy read of the season! Twisty and delightfully gory, *How to Survive a Horror Movie* is the perfect addition to any Halloween reading list."
Kat Ellis, author of *Harrow Lake*

HOW TO SURVIVE A HORROR MOVIE

HOW TO SURVIVE A HORROR MOVIE

SCARLETT DUNMORE

UNION
SQUARE
& CO.
NEW YORK

UNION
SQUARE
& CO.
NEW YORK

UNION SQUARE & CO. and the distinctive Union Square & Co. logo are trademarks of Sterling Publishing Co., Inc.

Union Square & Co., LLC, is a subsidiary of Sterling Publishing Co., Inc.

Text © 2024 Scarlett Dunmore
Cover © 2024 Little Tiger Press

All rights reserved. No part of this publication may be reproduced, stored in a retrieval system, or transmitted in any form or by any means (including electronic, mechanical, photocopying, recording, or otherwise) without prior written permission from the publisher.

First published in Great Britain in 2024 by Little Tiger Press.
First published in the United States and Canada in 2025 by Union Square & Co., LLC.

ISBN 978-1-4549-6333-2 (hardcover)
ISBN 978-1-4549-6334-9 (paperback)
ISBN 978-1-4549-6335-6 (e-book)

Library of Congress Control Number: 2024055017

For information about custom editions, special sales, and premium purchases, please contact specialsales@unionsquareandco.com.

Printed in China

2 4 6 8 10 9 7 5 3 1

unionsquareandco.com

Cover design by Little Tiger Press and Liam Donnelly
Interior design by Little Tiger Press
Additional images used under license from Shutterstock.com

For my big brother,
who showed me my
first horror film when
I was far too young.

Rule #1

TEAM UP

They stood before me, backs against the lockers, hands on hips—perfection from head to toe.

Gabrielle was wearing the cobalt-blue blazer I'd been eyeing in Zara over the summer, wishing the price tag would magically lose two digits. It was slightly open, revealing a top that was cut way too low for the teacher not to notice. Annabelle stood beside her—the eternally loyal sidekick, never doubting, never questioning, always following. She was the kind of girl that would run you down with her mom's car just because her friends told her to. She wore whatever was leftover in the wardrobe they dipped into, no matter if that wardrobe was her own. And leaning against the wall by the water fountain, perched in the lead position as always, was the feared *Rochelle Smyth*.

Her blood ran deep in these walls and in the very foundation of the boarding school. Her mother had been a student here, her grandmother, maybe even her great-grandmother. Rochelle's parents had been very generous over the years, lining the pockets of administrators. All for the sake of educational resources, of course, no one could—or would—accuse the Smyth family of anything other than that. Even if their daughter was suddenly now class president and captain of the volleyball and field hockey teams, and she and her friends were the only ones in our year who enjoyed back-to-back study hall periods after lunchtime on Fridays, which meant that come 1:05 p.m., they were done with school for the weekend. The rest of us mortals had our study period sandwiched between humanities and PE, which meant most of it was spent in the changing rooms sorting shoelaces and squeezing into too-tight sports bras in the fear that by the time we actually developed anything worth admiring in the chest region, it would already be stretched down to our kneecaps.

Rochelle looked particularly goddess-like today, compressed into an above-the-knee black-and-white floral dress, cut low enough to show off a glistening collarbone that even I was staring at. Thank God this was an all-girls boarding school; who knew what would be going on in this hallway if boys were here gawking too.

"Charley, you're gawking." Olive, who'd been my best friend since day one, nudged me.

I closed my mouth and diverted my eyes back to the classroom door, as we all stood waiting for Mr. Gillies to let us in for wood shop. "I wasn't gawking." I snorted. "I'm just stunned the Elles are allowed to dress like that."

"It's the last Friday of the month—lighten up. It's the only day we don't have to wear a uniform. They're just '*expressing* themselves.'" Olive grinned, pumping her fingers into exaggerated quotation marks.

"I can see Annabelle's belly button, and I dread to think what I could see if Rochelle dropped a pencil and bent over." I shuddered dramatically, shaking the skinny rose-gold bracelets on my right wrist, which were the only thing at all trendy or cool about how I dressed. Today, Olive and I wore matching cotton leggings with graphic sweatshirts emblazoned with images from our favorite horror movies. Mine had Christian Slater and Winona Ryder from the cult classic *Heathers* (such an underrated movie), while Olive confidently wore the face of Cujo. Only Olive could pull off a rabid Saint Bernard.

"I heard there's a party at Eden tomorrow night," Olive buzzed.

I groaned and rolled my eyes. Eden was Harrogate's counterpart, an all-boys boarding school about three miles along the coastline. Both schools were as secluded as was humanly possible, miles and miles from towns and even farther from cities, perched on a cliff edge overlooking a deadly plummet of dark blue waves and gray limestone caves that became completely submerged when the tide came in.

SCARLETT DUNMORE

We were isolated out here on Saltee Island until the holidays, when we were shuttled onto rickety boats and ferried back to the mainland, where parents would reluctantly let us crawl into their cars with bags of dirty laundry, knowing their child-free evenings and weekends were over until school resumed.

I wasn't always a student at Harrogate, and I wasn't always a boarding school resident. I went to a normal school once, where I awoke in my own bed at home and at three o'clock walked back there. I even had friends at that school—note the plural. And I had a girlfriend, but she was long gone. Now all I had left were memories and a thin gold necklace with her initial on it. Not that I was lonely now—Olive was a fantastic friend, and without her I'd have definitely packed a bag in the middle of the night and scaled a cliff to get out of here—but she was my *only* friend. At my last school I had been kind of—yes, I'll say it—*popular*. Not in a Rochelle Smyth kind of way, but definitely floating somewhere in that realm.

I twirled the necklace pendant between my fingers as I pushed back memories of the life I had before, some more painful than others. Suddenly the classroom door swung open and slammed off the lockers, sending a clanging echo reverberating down the tiled hallway. Mr. Gillies stood in the doorway, his eyes fixed on Rochelle's, Gabrielle's, and Annabelle's scanty outfits, which showed blatant disregard for school policy. Olive and I exchanged eager glances.

HOW TO SURVIVE A HORROR MOVIE

Mr. Gillies hated these girls, the loathing visible in his eyes and in the slight tremble of his grizzled hands. He parted his lips, and I waited hungrily for Rochelle's first-ever public telling-off, but then his eyes drifted to the floor and he closed his mouth, opting to brush aside whatever was left of his teaching ethics. He knew who ran this school, and if Rochelle complained to her parents about a staff member, then it was well known that person's position would suddenly pop up in the job ads the next day. Rochelle Smyth ruled the school, and I ruled . . . wood shop.

I had become fairly decent at crafting objects from wood in Mr. Gillies's class, so much so that I typically got a nod of approval from him and the occasional sought-after handshake. If only I could have fashioned a wooden bat to smack the Elles over the head with.

"Do you want to take a walk down to the cliffs after school?" asked Olive, who was gluing back together two pieces of wood that she'd accidentally hacked through. Her safety goggles slid down her face with the sweat.

I gave her a thumbs-up and went back to my disc sander, the wood beneath the machine thundering and vibrating in my hands. It was finished with a final buffing to smooth out any splintering sharp edges and a quick polish to make it shine. I stood back to admire my work, nodding with a grin.

Overhead, the bell roared, followed by the cheers of oppressed teen girls in dire need of a weekend of debauchery. Olive heaved her heavy book bag onto her shoulders, slightly tilting back with the weight, then sauntered over to my worktable. "Nice work, Sullivan . . . what is it?"

"A DVD stand." I smiled, running a finger over the crescent-shaped shelves. We had one just like it at home, where Dad had kept our home movies of days spent bathing in sunshine and salt air down at the beach by our old caravan. I didn't know where those videos were now, probably packed in a box somewhere in the attic or maybe even thrown out, discarded after I was sent away to boarding school to rectify an academic future I'd apparently thrown away the months after Dad's death.

"Fitting, considering that's the extent of our weekends usually." She sighed, heading for the exit.

"I thought you liked our horror movie nights. You're the one who nicknamed them Slasher Saturdays," I argued. "Or does partying with the Elles interest you more these days?" I playfully poked her in the ribs as I caught up to her.

"The partying not so much, but the *boys* . . ." She swooned. "*A* boy would be nice, for a change."

I laughed and opened the door, the smell of ocean and seaweed hitting our faces and tickling our noses. Hopefully we'd get some sun-filled days this weekend, meaning we could lie out on blankets, read Stephen King, and forget all about the mundane humdrum of high school life, where the most exciting conversational topic was the length of Rochelle's skirt. We headed toward the ridge, where tide met rock and cliffs formed underfoot, and seagulls squawked over crashing waves. The dry grass crunched and snapped beneath the soles of my sneakers, which were about ten years older than the minimum style needed to fit in here with this crowd. My mom used everything she had—everything my dad left us and everything my aunt could offer—to secure me a place here at Harrogate. There wasn't much left over for limited-edition Hokas or tailored Zara blazers. If only my mother had known just how much more fashion mattered here than education, she may have thought differently about sending me.

We trudged to the sea ledge, our toes balancing on the edge of the big rock formation that jutted over the cliffs below, allowing us to drop scraps of food to the gulls and the crabs. Olive gripped a bag of torn bread in her hands, letting it bounce off her hip as she walked. She reached in and grabbed a handful, opening her palm to the sky.

Hungry gulls squawked and gathered overhead. I tipped my head back and watched them.

Gliding.

Soaring.

Waiting.

Their wings sliced through the crisp September air. If I were one of them, I'd fly as far away from here as possible, and not look back. Away from the mean girls, away from restless nights in cold dormitory beds and lukewarm showers in communal bathrooms. Away from myself, from the girl who probably deserved to be here, isolated like this, because of who I was before.

In the distance a boat horn ripped through the gulls' feeding frenzy and they scattered, startled at first, then curious, searching for something more than bread scraps.

"Think that's a new girl?" I asked, pointing to the red-and-white vessel on the waters, fast approaching the port.

"Nah, you're the new girl." Olive shrugged. "Can't have more than one in a school year. Messes up the dynamic."

"I came *last* school year," I corrected, knotting my hair up in a bun.

"And now I can't get rid of you." She smirked, tossing the last of the bread to an empty beach down below.

"What are you getting from Shop this week?"

Shop was an antiquated system which allowed us deprived Harrogate girls one "frivolous" purchase a week, usually something not covered by the odd care package sent from the mainland. For those with money, Shop was usually a time to buy nail polish or a lip balm, and for those without money (example: me and Olive), Shop was a one-pound purchase of a bag of M&M's or a soda. The type of junk food neither of our moms would send us, for fear the sugar might distract us from our academic endeavors.

"Dunno," Olive muttered, gazing up at the gulls, who had returned to the skies above our heads, soaring and diving. "I might go crazy and buy a Snickers."

I gasped. "You daredevil! All those nuts!"

"You know I need the protein for all my gym workouts." She snorted. "How about you?"

"I might do something equally crazy. I might get . . . I can't say it . . ."

"Go on, tell me. I'm ready for it."

"I might get a bag of Skittles!"

She opened her mouth wide. "Shocking! Skittles?!"

"We're just too adventurous for this school," I said, shaking my head.

"That we are—Shit!" she wailed, covering her head.

"What?"

"I think a seagull just pooped on me!"

Rule #2

BEWARE OF STORMS AND ISOLATED ISLANDS

"Knock, knock."

I turned to see Olive standing at the dresser next to the curtain rod we'd hung between our two wardrobes when we'd first been paired up. We didn't have a door for privacy, but the curtain did its job when one of us had to get dressed. Out of all the rooms I could have been assigned, I was very lucky I ended up in Olive's.

If we stood side by side in front of the mirror, we were complete opposites in every way. I was awkwardly tall and lean, with gawky limbs and pin-straight hair. I had my dad's dark eyes and lips that always seemed turned down like I was perpetually sad. Olive, on the other hand, was short and had broad shoulders, wild curly hair, and contact lenses that made her eyes a fierce green. Her face was bright, and unlike me, her mouth was always turned up—she was a forever smiler and, unfortunately, a people-pleaser too. When I first arrived, she had been vying for the Elles' attention like all the other girls in this school. She even did their homework, although she denied that for a long time. But something brought me and Olive together on day one, during our first-ever conversation, while she watched me unpack my DVD collection.

"DVDs are defunct in the world of streaming platforms," she told me, which made me question my future at Harrogate. But when she skimmed through my collection, her fingers lightly grazing the spine of each box, she revealed the most desirable trait a roommate can have—a fondness for the horror genre. Actually, "fondness" didn't do it justice: it was a passion, a fervor, a *compulsion*.

We spent that first week watching the numerous Texas Chainsaw Massacre movies, discussing in great detail who played the best Leatherface, before moving on to the Halloween franchise (all thirteen films), soon establishing Slasher Saturdays, where our obsession with Romero, Cunningham, and Craven grew. We ate popcorn with melted butter; realized we both liked to mix Skittles into the kernels, just like they did in the movies; curled up on the floor with pillows and blankets; and talked horror. Sadie had *tolerated* conversations about horror, but I never really knew anyone who shared my enthusiasm for it, until now. It was what brought Olive and me together. It was what kept me from running for the ferry every morning after I woke up and remembered where I was.

SCARLETT DUNMORE

"How's Elizabeth Bennet coming along?" Olive asked now, leaning against the dresser.

I moaned loudly and pushed my laptop away. I had been frantically trying to finish an English essay on Jane Austen, when all I wanted to do was read another chapter of Stephen King's *Misery*. I gazed longingly at my stack of horror novels and anthologies, which sat on the edge of my desk tempting me to forgo Austen and the Brontës. Bram Stoker and Shirley Jackson were great, but Stephen King was literally the king. If I met him, I'd drop to my knees and kiss his shoes. Well, probably not, because that's incredibly unhygienic, but I would thank him for his very generous contribution to the world of literature and to my most favorite genre when it came to reading and watching and breathing.

"She's boring my brain cells into dust, even after the first page. Why are all her books just about a woman trying to find a husband? Nothing exciting ever happens, and there are always balls and dinners with fancy goblets. I want—"

"Heads in freezers? Bodies in cupboards? Serial killers in masks?"

"Excitement."

"Well, this will be as exciting as it gets at Harrogate—the coast guard is here. Big assembly in the school hall. We all have to be there."

"Why?" I asked, pushing out my chair and grabbing a warm cardigan to cozy into. The assembly hall was always freezing. It was like the headmistress purposefully turned on the cold air in there to keep us all alert and awake.

"Apparently there's a big storm headed our way."

"Storm? Isn't that normal?"

Storms were definitely not normal on the mainland, especially in the city, where the weather was milder than the people. But over here, the Irish seas were wild and the terrain was unpredictable. The islands were like another world entirely. There was a reason places like this had such low population numbers. Here, you only went to the mainland to go home for school break. Olive relayed a few occasions when she and the other students had stood on the rickety wooden dock in the freezing cold and peppery rain waiting hours for the ferry, which resembled an old fishing trawler. In the city, if the train was three minutes late, commuters would riot. But this was "island life," as Mr. Terry said, and "people move on island time and at island speed."

We were ushered into the assembly hall by Mr. Gillies, who regarded the sea of students woefully, probably wishing the storm would come and wipe us all out. We positioned ourselves at the back wall, where the axe and the "Use in Case of an Emergency" sign hung. Of course, I clocked the axe on my first day here and memorized its location. You never know when you'll need an axe at an all-girls boarding school, so it was best to be prepared. That was another one of my interests—recounting the survival skills taught to us by the best film directors. Craven taught us to never answer the phone when home alone, Hooper strongly encouraged us to refrain from exploring abandoned farmhouses while road tripping with friends, and Gillespie reminded us to always report a crime, particularly one that involved accidentally running over a vengeful fisherman on the road. Other rules were conveyed through the horror genre—such as always keeping the car topped up with gas, and avoiding crowded areas during a zombie outbreak—many of which were likely to keep us alive in most modern survival situations. In fact, I had been considering putting in a request to the headmistress for a new unit to be taught here at Harrogate. But perhaps I'd wait until after the storm passed to propose it.

I scanned the last few clusters of girls streaming into the hall. The whole school was here, all five hundred of us. At my last school there were *five thousand* students. Eden School for Boys, on the other side of the cliffs, apparently had only three hundred enrolled students, which meant that on this island, girls far outnumbered boys, much to Olive's dismay. For me, there were five hundred girls but only one that made me turn an embarrassing shade of coral every time I passed her.

Saoirse Quinn.

Even her name sounded amazing, with long flowing consonants and silent vowels.

She was in the year below, so we didn't have any classes

together or share the same study periods, and she was housed over in the Alexandria Wing, far away from our dorm. I didn't have much opportunity to talk to her and, so far, hadn't even tried. Every time I saw her, I froze. I wasn't used to feeling like that, so powerless in the grip of my emotions. Relationships were easier to navigate on the mainland. People were more open about their sexuality in the city; it was easier to be myself. But here I was suffocated by the isolation, the dark skies, and the waves of testosterone that transmitted across the island from Eden School.

I glanced quickly at Olive as she nibbled on her thumbnail like it was a ham sandwich, then gazed out at the sea of students sitting in chairs, looking for that familiar mane of red. But I couldn't see her.

On the stage, where Olive had auditioned for *My Fair Lady* with a Cockney accent that would certainly offend any Londoner, stood Headmistress Blyth. She was flanked by the entire faculty, who were all female bar Mr. Gillies. Two men in navy waterproof gear were up there, too. They must have been the coast guard officers, although one looked way too young to have already devoted his life to the abandoned seas and barren islands. Half the hall had already clocked him and were now twisting and curling their hair around their fingers and blinking abnormally fast. Beside me, Olive stopped chewing on her nails and started breathing heavily like a dog in need of water.

SCARLETT DUNMORE

Perhaps he was somewhat attractive, with spiky hair and a cheeky grin, in a Christian Slater/*Heathers* kind of way. But he was no Winona Ryder. The piercing dark eyes, that delicate jawline, and those cheekbones? *Swoon!* Everyone was so obsessed with her performance in *Stranger Things*, but for me, she totally smashed the role of Lydia in *Beetlejuice*.

"As you know," started the older coastie, "the weather is turning tonight. Nothing to be afraid of, just a little storm. Should pass over us in a day or two. But given our surroundings and our distance from the mainland, we'll be following some simple protocols. Windows will be boarded up to prevent any glass damage, the backup generator has been fueled and safety checked, and all shoreline activities such as fishing and swimming will be suspended until further notice."

Headmistress Blyth stepped forward, clearing her throat loudly so we all knew she was the speaker and we were the listeners.

"Just to expand on that last one, *all* outdoor activities will be suspended until I say otherwise. That means indoor PE and recess only, no outdoor recreation. And that includes walks along the coast, not just scheduled after-school clubs."

The whole school groaned in protest, my voice the loudest. Time outside, even just a few minutes of fresh air, was my only chance to get out of the school. For a moment I was back on vacation on the Devon coast with my mom and dad, with the wind in my face and the lapping of waves down below. Olive and I always went for a walk after school, and she'd feed the greedy gulls while I'd just breathe in the air, which was so thick with salt that it would crust on the sleeves of our coats. Now we were stuck inside *indefinitely*.

"Well, that sucks," whispered Olive.

"The power better not go out this weekend for Slasher Saturday."

She nodded. "Best keep the laptops charged up just in case."

"If we can't watch our Saturday horror flick, I'll kill someone."

"Use the axe in the assembly hall. That emergency box is gathering dust."

Rule #3
DON'T GO OUTSIDE TO INVESTIGATE

It was an unsettling wind, howling and moaning like voices calling out to us. It pushed the tips of the branches against the windows so that they scratched like claws trying to get in. We huddled in our beds, covers and blankets pulled up to our chins, and listened as the storm circled the island, watching and waiting like the hungry gulls.

By breakfast, the windows had been boarded up. Well, partially boarded up. Turned out Harrogate had less wood than they thought, or they'd just decided supplies were better allocated elsewhere. Ms. Blyth's office window was boarded up with three planks; of course, nothing would be getting in there. The Augustine Wing, where Rochelle Smyth resided, got two per window, and the rest of us got one horizontal plank for protection. Slap-bang in the middle of the window. I could still see the trees and bushes in the back garden where our dorms sat. Hopefully a smashed window from a flyaway branch wouldn't derail our beloved Slasher Saturday.

Harrogate was a former monastery, constructed in the thirteenth century. It had a sweeping facade and was considered of historical importance. The Old Building was a U-shape wrapped around a large gray-stone courtyard and a very ostentatious marble cherub fountain in the middle. On the right were the dorms, separated into wings that were named after saints, which the Harrogate girls were certainly not. The Elles, and anyone else whose family donated generously to the school, were housed in the Augustine Wing, where the rooms were single occupancy and each had an en suite bathroom and a TV. I'd heard one room over there was at least double the size of our shared rooms.

Along with about thirty other students whose families didn't line the pockets of the school council, Olive and I resided in the Edith Wing, which was considerably less opulent, while the other students were scattered around the Mary, Therese, and Alexandria Wings, which fell in the middle between the scholarship wing and the ridiculously rich wing. On the left side of the courtyard were the library, the infirmary, the assembly hall, and Ms. Blyth's office. That was the Elizabeth Wing. The Catherine Wing on the other side housed the dining hall, the gym, and the equipment rooms, and the classrooms were dotted around the Rose Wing and Clement Wing. There was a large indoor pool in what we called the New Building (even though it was built about forty years ago), along with a tennis court and a large communal space where students could gather for movies, games, and socializing after school and in the evenings. But most students, especially sixth years, tended to socialize in their own dorms. As Olive and I shared a room, our commute was nice and short.

Harrogate sat close to the island friary, where we were encouraged to attend mass on Sundays in staggered services. Fifth and sixth years attended together, and most of the girls went, but only because it was a mixed mass service with the boys of Eden School. The girls dressed up in the shortest skirts possible, smeared on lipstick, curled their hair, and went to church to pray. That was probably why the Eden boys went too. It was of great mutual interest to ogle persons of the opposite sex at the one place they were allowed to mix, and yet the one place where, by religious rules, they were forbidden to *mix*.

A priest came from the mainland on Sundays, ferried in by Mr. Terry, the all-around caretaker / boat driver / fisherman / deliveryman / plumber. On Mondays, Mr. Terry would ferry him back. There was no reason for us girls to leave the island, and if you wanted to you had to get special permission from Headmistress Blyth, which I'd heard was extremely rare, especially for those not living in the Augustine Wing. We were kind of marooned here on

HOW TO SURVIVE A HORROR MOVIE

Saltee Island, left to fend for ourselves. Well, maybe not "fend for ourselves," as we did have a chef. Even though we lived in a monastery and were encouraged to attend weekly mass, Harrogate was predominately nondenominational, much to the mainland's surprise and also disgust. Who opens a school in an old Franciscan monastery on a clifftop and declares it open to *all* religious groups? But it was true, Harrogate School and its admissions committee wanted students from all walks of life, in the religious sense of course. Assuming families could afford the hefty tuition fee, all were welcome, particularly those running from reputations or who blindly still believed in Harrogate's academic mission. And definitely those who could weather the frequent storms, the salty ocean winds, and the vicious attacks from hungry gulls and entitled princesses like Rochelle.

I belonged to the "running from" group. Running from the city, my questionable choice of friends, my bad decisions. My real name was Charlotte Ryan. When I lived in the city, I went by Lottie with my friends, but Mom convinced me to shorten it to Charley instead and take my aunt's family name, Sullivan, for the admissions form. Harrogate never checked; they didn't care. I wasn't that important to them. I was just another number. Aunt Rhoda filled out the sponsor form, and after that, she retreated to her usual life, which didn't involve Mom and me.

SCARLETT DUNMORE

Whatever. I was never a *Charlotte*. And *Lottie* was way too trendy for me, anyway.

"That rain is lashing down," Olive said as she peered over and then under the sole wooden plank. "Happy Slasher Saturday to us," she added with a groan.

"Has Harrogate ever flooded?" I asked, setting up for our movie night.

"Not Harrogate, because it's the highest point on the island, but Eden gets screwed every year. Serves them right for building a fancy modern building right down there."

Eden was pretty much a lesser version of Eton. They tended to get its rejects, but nonetheless the boys' school churned out future politicians, prime ministers, bankers, and everything in between. Their building sat on the other side of the island, about an hour's walk along the cliffs, encased in a pretentious modern dome. It looked more like a science lab or a space center. And glass, so much glass. They probably spent weeks boarding up that building for storms. Whoever came up with the design clearly had not known about the climate. I'd never been inside, but Olive knew many, many, *many* girls who had. Apparently, there was an indoor running track and a sports field bigger than a village, and their classrooms were equipped with the newest laptops for each and every student.

"So, we have *Fright Night*—both original and remake—*Queen of the Damned*, *Lost Boys*, or *A Return to Salem's Lot*," Olive said, plopping down on the floor on my arrangement of strewn blankets, pillows, and beanbags "borrowed" from the communal room in the New Building.

"Ooh, you went with a vampire theme this week." I grinned, shaking the bag of popcorn into a large red bowl. "Tough one." I sprinkled the Skittles on the top and then carefully mixed them in. Never shake, or the sweets just fall to the bottom.

"Should I have added in *Twilight*?"

"Absolutely not. I want to be scared, not eye-rolling my way through a love triangle." I handed the bowl to Olive and walked over to the light switch. "I think we should go eighties tonight—*Lost Boys*."

"Retro, I like it."

I plopped down beside her, tucking one leg in. She slid the popcorn bowl over to me. The first bite should always be the best, and with the correct popcorn-to-sugar ratio for ultimate eating pleasure. "I forgot how good the soundtrack is," I whispered as the opening credits rolled across the screen, a darkened ocean in the background.

The carousel turned slowly, revealing the laughing faces of teens as they gripped the horses and spun around and around and around. Suddenly, a young man appeared, his pale face and dyed golden hair emerging from the crowds. He moved effortlessly as if his feet didn't touch the ground, merely grazing it. He was floating—

A crack of thunder spun our heads around, the lightning flickering beyond the glass. We stared at each other, eyes wide, then slowly turned back to the small boxy TV on the dresser with plastic figurines of a bloodied Chucky doll and a fanged *It* clown beside it.

As he walked through the crowds gathering at the fair, the faces of his friends emerged, the hungry glint in their eyes shimmering in the moonlight—

"They are so obviously vampires—look at them! Hello! Doesn't anyone see this?" Olive shouted at the TV as she shoveled another mouthful of popcorn into her face.

The thunder cracked and snapped behind us.

They eyed a victim in the crowd, watching him as he moved, walked, breathed. They watched the rhythmic rise and fall of his chest, smelled the blood pulsating through his veins, his neck—

"I have to pee."

"Olive!" I groaned, pressing the Pause button. "It's been on for three minutes!"

"Sorry! It was all that cranberry juice at dinner," she mumbled, untangling her feet from the blankets. She sorted the waistband on her red *Stranger Things* pajamas and marched over to the door, tripping on a corner of the blanket. I pulled myself up and started following her.

"You have to go too?"

"No solo trips to the bathroom at nighttime. Survival skill number one, remember?"

She snorted and rolled her eyes. A flurry of voices echoed down the hallway as she swung open the dorm door. A group of girls walked past, completely ignoring us, of course, carrying thick bath towels and oversized shower bags.

"See, they're headed my way. No solo urinating for me tonight. You stay. Back in two."

I nodded and heard the door slam as I walked over to the window to watch the storm that churned and rumbled beyond, as if desperately wanting to get inside. That one plank of wood would do nothing to protect us if the window blew in. The darkness outside was thick, with tiny speckles of dulled moonlight poking through the trees and shrubs that cocooned us. A fierce rain hammered the earth, stabbing at the rocks and pounding the ground like heavy footsteps.

Thud. Thud. Thud.

A cold shiver seeped into my skin and snaked up my spine. I shuddered. The branches of the trees stretched out like growing limbs, all knobbly and knotted, reaching for our window. Above, the sky crackled and roared, angry and hungry. A streak of lightning lashed out and illuminated the trees.

Suddenly, a silhouette appeared, standing by the old hawthorn, partially hidden by the low-hanging branches. I screamed and stepped back, my breath catching in my throat.

I pressed my palms against the glass, frantically peering above and below the plank of wood that obstructed my view. The dark figure was definitely there, but it wasn't moving. It was still, stoic, solid. A deep sigh vibrated through my chest. It was just a shadow, maybe from a marble statue I hadn't noticed before. The old grounds of the monastery were full of them. Statues of monks, saints, or whatever it was that people prayed to, believed in. Summoned. I leaned closer to the window, my nose against the glass, searching for features on the shadow so I could identify the statue. My breath fogged the pane, and as I brushed a hand over the condensation to clear it, the statue *moved*. Slowly at first, walking, breezing past the low-hanging branches. Then it ran, fast, hard, swiping manically at the bushes and shrubs in its path, as if desperately trying to get away from a pursuer.

I screamed again.

The lights flickered in the dorm room, and before I could get to the door, everything around me was plunged into darkness.

Rule #4

NEVER WALK ALONE

The storm finally passed, and the air outside our window seemed calm and still with gulls absent from the skies. Ms. Blyth announced at breakfast that curfew was lifted and we were allowed outside, but not on the coastal paths. There were reports that a small section of the path between Harrogate and Eden had given way just above the docks. Mr. Terry would assess it later and determine whether it was still safe for students to use. If not, the students who frequently snuck out at night would need to be very creative with their commutes to Eden School for Boys.

"I still don't understand. Why didn't you go outside to investigate?" Olive said as she yanked on her boots.

"Investigate? It's a stormy night, thunder, lightning, the whole deal. I see a creepy dark figure hiding in the shadows staring right through our window, and you want me to pop on my raincoat and boots and just go outside to take a little look, maybe say hello, invite him in to chat about movies, over popcorn? Have you already forgotten our survival rules?"

"How do you know it was a him?"

"I suppose I don't know," I said, zipping up my coat, which would do little to protect me from the chill once autumn truly set in. I had no idea how I was going to survive winter here.

"'Him' implies it was one of the boys from Eden, which, now that I think about it, is very likely. I wouldn't put it past them to break curfew to come over and scare the life out of all the girls tucked into their dorm beds."

"Idiots," I muttered.

"*Cute* idiots," she said with a sigh.

We headed down the hallway, past the groups of girls huddled against walls, excited for Sunday mass. With our phones confiscated, this was the only real source of entertainment for many of the students here. Blyth's hope was that over time, we as a generation would become less dependent on social media and technology, graduating Harrogate with "an enlightened view of the world." But really, her rule just forced some of us to be a little more original with how we communicated. Sixth-year girls in particular were more skilled in other means of contacting the Eden boys, which included handwritten notes via messengers—a well-paid job at this school—not to mention the occasional exchange of drugs via empty water bottles and makeup cases. Olive once saw a drug trade where the pills were concealed in a face-powder compact. Very impressive.

Eden boys had better access to marijuana than us Harrogate girls, for some reason. I was pretty sure I could have proven otherwise, but any contacts I once had in the city were in the past, and I was very much a changed person. A *better* person. Or so I liked to tell myself.

"Sure you don't want to go to mass?" I grinned, playfully nudging Olive, who I knew was dying to attend the weekly ritual with her boy-starved peers.

"No." She snorted. "But we are headed that way, I suppose."

"We're not headed that way. In fact, it's the opposite way."

"OK, so we'll take a new route."

I smiled and shook my head. Suddenly, a dot of red pulled my attention back down the hallway and I froze.

It was *her*.

The *her* I had been trying to talk to, to say anything to, since I came here. But so far, I'd only managed a smile and a weird nod that looked more like a muscle spasm than a cool and casual greeting.

Saoirse.

I didn't even know if she felt the same way I did about girls, but there was something I just couldn't put my finger on about her. Something that made me immediately infatuated with her.

SCARLETT DUNMORE

OK, "infatuated" is kind of a strong word. Maybe "obsessed" is better?

She swayed toward me, her long red hair bouncing on her shoulders, the little freckles on her nose sparkling under the sun's early rays that shone through the window. I stepped forward, cleared my throat, and prepared myself. I parted my lips, felt my heart pounding, and started to speak. "S—"

"I borrowed your underwear," said Olive loudly behind me. I quickly shut my mouth.

Saoirse looked up, her eyes glistening, and then giggled with her friend. She passed me, the smell of lemon and oak from her shampoo lingering in the air between us.

"What?" I exclaimed, turning to Olive, who had her head down as she fished around in her bag for something.

"I said, I borrowed your underwear," she repeated.

"I heard you the first time but . . . but . . . what?"

She yanked her hand out, holding a rose-tinted lip balm. "I didn't have any clean clothes and you hadn't put your laundry away, so I borrowed a pair of underwear from the pile. I hope that's OK?"

I stared at her, mouth agape.

"Is that not OK?" she said, wrinkling her nose. "Is that really weird? Have I become too comfortable with you already? I have, haven't I?"

"No, that's fine," I spluttered. "Just maybe say these things a little quieter next time." I looked into the crowd, searching for a glossy mane of red, but she was gone. I sighed and roughly pushed open the double doors to the outside. Another opportunity gone.

The air was thick, warm with a slight musky woody scent like burning sage. I stood on the first step and inhaled deeply, smelling the remnants of the storm. All around were broken branches, torn shrubs, and pools of rainwater. The sky was still a gloomy hazy gray, but there were no dark clouds. It was just still, quiet, peaceful—

The door slammed into the back of me, throwing me to the wet dirt. "Watch it!" screamed Olive to the group of girls standing in the doorway.

"Well, who stands in front of a door?" snapped one. The voice was thick with a recognizable disdain, peppered with a touch of boredom. *Rochelle Smyth.*

I heard her friends giggling beside her as I extracted a hand from the mud. It was like gloopy wet concrete and almost immediately started drying on my skin, caking between my fingers. I sat back on my heels and assessed the damage. My mustard cords now had mud at the knees, and there were thick globs spattered up my coat, staining my favorite embroidered patch, which I'd attached to the sleeve with fabric glue only last week. I could even taste a little dirt in my mouth.

"Well, look on the bright side. I think I improved that outfit," she said, carefully stepping over me.

Olive pulled me to my feet and tried to smooth my hair

down. We watched the Elles navigate gracefully over the wet path in their suede ankle boots, floral tea dresses, and white denim jackets, swinging umbrellas like they were weapons. In their hands, they probably were.

"Thank you!" I screamed at them, throwing my arms up in the air. They didn't look back.

Olive tried to blot away the mud with a handkerchief she'd tucked into her dark denim overalls, which she'd bought in July just after we watched *I Know What You Did Last Summer*. "If it makes you feel any better, Rochelle has actually gotten nicer with age."

"That's her being nice? I'd have hated to see her in her younger years. Don't worry, Olive. I'll wash it later."

"Do you want to go back in and change?" She grimaced.

"No, it's fine." I sighed. "We'll miss the initial gathering of the sexes outside the chapel, and I know that's your favorite part."

Her cheeks blushed and a wide grin stretched across her heart-shaped face. She looped her arm in mine and we trudged away from the doors, over the puddles and fallen shrubbery.

"She was sad and bitter in first and second year—she wanted to attend secondary school with her friends back on the mainland—angry and cruel in third and fourth years, sarcastic and resentful in fifth year, and now she's just . . . well, I don't know what she is."

"All of the above?"

HOW TO SURVIVE A HORROR MOVIE

"You'd think she'd be tired by now."

"Girls like Rochelle peak in high school, and she probably knows that too," I muttered, wiping the mud off my chin with the only clean section of my sleeve.

"Let's hope that's true. She's made a lot of girls miserable here, myself included."

The path turned rocky as we slowly ascended the hill leading to the highest part of the island. From here, the views across the sea were breathtaking. Miles and miles of dark blue ocean. Had we not all been sent here like cattle to a farm, it would be an incredible setting, perfect for a vacation, a few days away from the bustling city life on the mainland.

The clanging of the bell broke through the heavy air, still thick with moisture, always thick with salt. It chimed once, twice, vibrating through the calm. We slowed our steps so as not to be noticed too close to the friary and risk being beckoned in by Ms. Blyth or the minister. I'd always wondered what a nondenominational service was like, especially one held in a formerly Christian building. No wonder it stormed and rained so much here. It was like the island was smiting us for our religious irresolution.

"Whoop-whoop, here we go," squealed Olive as a large group of Eden boys made their way up the hill toward the friary steps.

We watched as the boys tucked in their shirts, slicked their hair down, and practiced their deep, pensive stares, which were reciprocated by the Harrogate girls who tugged at the hems of their skirts, tousled strands of hair around their fingers, fluffed its roots, and smiled coyly.

"We could go in . . . maybe . . . just for a second?" Olive suggested, not taking her eyes off one boy with mousy blond hair and a zipped-up black jacket.

"No, absolutely not! I'm staging an intervention!" I giggled. "Fight your Harrogate fate: walk away from the boys!" I tugged on her coat and laughed, knowing my voice was drawing attention. Olive shooed and batted me away.

As I glanced back, a hand still on her sleeve, I saw a large man standing by the steps: broad shoulders, expensive tweed coat, tartan scarf draped across his chest. His umbrella leaned against the stone wall of the friary. He turned to face the students, his eyes dark, his face cleanly shaven but with a five o'clock shadow. He barked orders at the male students, gesturing to those haphazardly wandering around or with hands stuck lazily in their pockets. Then he turned slowly and stared at the Harrogate girls, his expression steeped in disdain. When he clocked Blyth, he nodded. She waved awkwardly, then hurried into the chapel.

"Who is that?" I whispered to Olive.

"That's Dr. Pruitt, Eden's headmaster. He was brought in from some posh private school in Surrey to take over from the last one, who couldn't hack island life. Rumor is, Pruitt wants Harrogate too. He wants to own this whole island, turn us all into creepy children from *Village of the Damned*."

"Great film. Not too sure about the sequels."

"I hate sequels, yet I can't stop watching them—oh, there she is."

"Who?"

"You know who." She grinned, her eyes glinting.

I turned, that familiar mane of red catching my eye as it bobbed and swayed up the steps to the friary. Saoirse went to Sunday mass? I felt so bewildered for a moment, maybe even a little betrayed.

"Miss Sullivan, you're blushing!" Olive squealed. I rolled my eyes. "Finally, we're talking the same language."

"Olive, I'm not talking your language, trust me."

She giggled and nudged me, knocking me off balance. "You can't possibly graduate high school without a crush. It's a rite of passage, or something."

"Well, it's lucky you have a new crush every week," I scoffed.

"Sure you don't want to go in?"

I gazed out at the crowd that gathered with each toll of the friary bell. Females on one side, males on the other, each clang of the bell bringing them one step closer. It was like watching an episode of an Attenborough nature documentary on the mating rituals of mammals. I shuddered, pulling my eyes away from the scene. "Nope."

The bell chimed one final time, and the doors thudded

closed. Inside, a voice bellowed, reverberating through the stone chapel and out onto the clifftop where we stood.

Olive exhaled defeatedly.

"You could just talk to him, you know," I said, pulling Olive away from the friary and down the coastal path.

"Who?"

"The blond guy you were staring at."

"Thomas? No, definitely not."

"Why?"

"Guys like Thomas Byrne don't talk to girls like me."

"Are you kidding?" I said, stopping in the middle of the path. "Olive, you're amazing!"

"You have to say that, you're my friend—my *only* friend." She snorted. "Look at us, literally covered in dirt, no offense, and look at the other girls, like Rochelle and Gabrielle and Annabelle, all clean and glowy and pretty and perfect. I'm not them."

"Thank God for that! Tell me something, then, if they're so pretty and perfect, why is the amazing Rochelle still single?"

Olive cocked her head. "Good point. I don't know . . . although I did hear she was dating someone over at Eden for a while. Ended badly too."

"Really? Please tell me more!"

"All I know is that he dumped her for someone else."

I grinned. "Savage. I love it." We crept closer to the edge

of the cliff, where we could get the best view of the sea stack and the lighthouse.

"I bet she hasn't forgotten about it. That girl holds grudges for life."

"Yep, hell hath no fury like a woman scorned," I muttered, gazing up at the hooded crows circling above our heads, watching us as we walked, squawking and swarming. A shudder climbed up my spine, prickling my skin underneath all the layers.

"There are a lot of crows today," Olive said, clutching a brown paper bag of scraps from her toast this morning. "Must be the storm that brought them in. I don't think I have enough bread."

"I don't know why you feed the birds. They pluck poor defenseless fish from the ocean, yanking them away from their families, and eat them alive."

"Says the person who had fish pie for dinner last night."

"Yes, but at least the fish was already dead before I ate it."

"Oh, how humane of you. You should join PETA." Olive snorted.

Even though it was calmer than usual today, the slight wind picked up as we got to the cliff edge. On the coast, everything seemed a bit colder and emptier than even the harshest winters in the city. We were barely into October, and I was already in my warmest layers. I dreaded to think what December and January would bring. I huddled into my thick green scarf, which had belonged to my mother before I bravely liberated it from her wardrobe over summer break, but the wind managed to squeeze in through the threads and prick at my collarbone. Up above the birds swooped and flocked and dived for the ground beneath us, where the ocean crashed against the rocks that jutted out from the cliff. "You're right, there's hundreds of birds today. It's like a Hitchcock movie."

"Do you know they're doing a remake of that?"

"I hate remakes. *Fright Night, Poltergeist—*"

"*The Fog, Witches of Eastwick—*"

"*Evil Dead, Prom Night, The Thing.*" I sighed. "Why are all of the best horror classics turned into CGI Hollywood blockbusters?"

A bird swooped down, its claws almost pulling at our windswept hair.

"Olive, it's your bread they want!" I yelled, cowering under my hands. Island wildlife was vicious and unpredictable. Much like the sixth-year girls.

"Maybe if I feed them, they won't try to eat us." She walked closer to the edge, her toes almost over.

My belly fluttered and swooped like the crows above us. She always did get a little too close for my liking. But it wasn't courage or adrenaline-fueled stupidity, it was just trust. She'd now spent six years of her life on this island. She'd walked these paths and around this coast hundreds of times over the years. She trusted the island and respected it, feeding its wildlife and protecting its seas, spending her school breaks campaigning against overfishing and ocean litter. And in turn, the island protected her, allowed her to explore just that little bit closer.

As she raised her arm to throw, she gasped and froze. Crumbs trickled from her hand and were carried away on the breeze. Her face was white, expression frozen in fear.

"Olive?"

She didn't respond. She just stared down to the rocks, to the hissing ocean. I crept up next to her, and followed her gaze.

Suddenly the air felt warm around us, stifling what little breath we had left. My stomach curdled, remnants of a heavy breakfast rising up my throat.

"Is that what I think it is?" spluttered Olive.

"I . . . I . . ." The words were stuck in my throat, because at the bottom of the cliff, splayed on a rock at an angle that twisted my intestines, was a *dead body*.

I stood frozen, eyes fixed on the sallow face, seaweed hair, and blue-tinged lips. Then the corpse's lips suddenly trembled and parted, like she still had some life within her. I reached for Olive's arm with hope, but when I looked again at the dead girl's lips, out crawled a crab, walking across her lifeless face and scurrying off to the sand.

I heard the thud of Olive's body hitting the ground beside me before I even realized she'd fainted. Then I turned around and vomited up my bacon and eggs.

Rule #5
WEAR FOOTWEAR YOU CAN RUN IN

The school courtyard looked like a cheap wedding venue. Lilac fall crocuses, baby-blue dahlias, and rainbow begonias were arranged to form a kind of aisle, scattered with white pillar candles. There were even a few balloons tied to the door, an inappropriate color too—ruby, sanguine, bloodred.

There wasn't much else the school could do to honor the death of Hannah Manning at such short notice. Any kind of formal floral arrangements would have to be ordered and shipped over from the mainland, which could take days, perhaps even weeks. The priority would be getting her body back to the city for a proper burial, not bringing across floral wreaths for a school vigil. Most of the paper trimmings that hung from the courtyard lanterns were leftover decorations from school dances and festivities.

"Headmistress Blyth will be raging," whispered Olive as she nudged me in the side. I hadn't even heard her come up.

"How so?"

"All of those flowers were pulled from the school garden. See over there—someone even yanked out herbs from her greenhouse."

At the foot of the large wooden easel displaying a very small poster of Hannah with her friends was a generous sprinkle of heavily fragranced cooking herbs.

"Nothing says 'Rest in Peace' more than Italian basil," giggled Olive, half-heartedly putting a hand over her mouth to stifle it. It didn't work. A couple of students turned around to glare their condemnation of our disrespect.

All around students were gathering, many crying, some holding candles or each other. I didn't know Hannah well as we didn't share any classes, and she lived in the Augustine Wing. The rich wing.

Mr. Gillies leaned against the wall, his head down and his jaw tightly clenched, while Ms. Evans from the English department wiped tears away with a blue handkerchief. Headmistress Blyth glared furiously at the easel as if someone had ripped out and displayed her organs instead of the herbs. Even Mr. Terry was here, his green rubber boots accidentally crushing the head of a dahlia. He was a big man, but formidable only in size. He had soft eyes and a wiry black beard laced with gray. He kept his head down and his arms crossed.

"He's bringing her body back to the mainland later today," whispered Olive, nodding toward him.

"Really? She was just found."

"What are they going to do—pop her in the freezer with the fish fingers?"

"Yuck, Olive."

"Shh!" urged a student beside us.

Olive ignored her. "I don't want her body here on school grounds. It was bad enough I saw it. I can't get her face out of my head."

"Me neither."

"Do you think she fell?"

"Of course, did you see her choice of footwear? She was breaking a major survival rule of horror movies."

"Some people are saying she jumped."

"*Jumped?!*" I yelled, the words spilling from my throat.

The crowd around us turned and stared, their mouths open in disgust.

"Sorry," I said, raising my hands in submission. I turned back to Olive. "Why do they think she jumped?"

"We were on strict storm curfew, and Hannah wasn't the rule-breaking type. Do you really think she was innocently taking a walk at night, by herself, along the cliff edge during a storm? She was either visiting a boy at Eden and fell, which, like I said, doesn't really fit the straight-A profile, or . . . well, she *jumped*."

"Her poor family," I muttered.

Someone in the back started humming, softly at first, then rapidly escalating into a high-pitched croaky attempt at singing. We all turned to match the face with the unfortunate voice. It belonged to Rochelle Smyth. Of course.

"Is she singing Ed Sheeran?" I asked.

Olive squinted and looked up. "Hmm, I think this song is about drugs and prostitutes."

Headmistress Blyth clapped her hands loudly, silencing Rochelle, who looked absolutely furious. "OK, students. Back to your scheduled classes. Officer Farrell and I will be going classroom to classroom asking anyone if they saw anything. We just want to ascertain why Hannah was out walking by the cliffs during a lockdown. We want to be able to tell her parents something to answer the many questions they probably have."

"Do you think I should mention that I saw someone outside our window on Saturday night?" I whispered to Olive.

"Shh!" urged Mr. Gillies, scowling at us. He turned back to the easel poster of Hannah, his jaw tightening again.

Ms. Blyth continued, "Hannah Manning was a loved and popular student at this school and will be deeply missed by us all. We'll be having a *silent* vigil . . ."

She looked at Olive and me when she said that, then continued.

". . . at the friary tonight after dinner. Everyone at Harrogate and Eden is expected to be there. No exceptions. I want us to move slowly and with purpose today so we can truly consider the gravity of such a loss of life." She bowed her head, then quickly straightened up. "Also, I know these herbs came from my organic greenhouse, so I will be following up on that and handing out punishments as I see fit." She glared at everyone, her eyes burning with rage. "There is no excuse for ripping out rosemary! No excuse!"

Olive and I exchanged glances, then walked slowly with the rest of the school, back through the courtyard, over crushed dahlias and the mangled crocuses, and around the candles, which were still flickering. The air was weirdly still and the ocean was calm behind us, which I'd heard was quite common after a storm. There would be more. Autumn was apparently storm season here on the island. I glanced back at the ocean, at the cliff edge where we'd walked yesterday, where we'd found her. A large lump caught in my throat, and I inhaled deeply, forcing away images of limbs splayed and broken on rock. When I looked up, I saw Olive's eyes fixed on the cliff point too.

"I know I've asked a dozen times, but are you sure you're OK?" I asked.

She nodded slowly, then started walking toward the school doors. "Please, let's just pretend it never happened."

"Deal. Pushing it to the back of my mind now."

"Meet you at the kiosk for a coffee after school?"

"I've got English, then I need to go to the library to try

to finish this paper on nineteenth-century literature. I've still only written one paragraph."

"Dinner, then?"

"Dinner, yes. Meet you back at the dorms at five thirty to walk there."

We never walked to the dinner hall alone; that was social suicide. Not even the strongest could survive entering those doors by themselves, with social groups already established, the odd one turning to stare mid-bite, mid-conversation.

"Can't wait until the vigil tonight." Olive smirked.

I smiled back, knowing what was coming. "And why's that, Miss Montgomery?"

"Because there will be *boys*!" she cooed, turning down the hallway.

Olive and I shared a room, all of our mealtimes, all of our free time outside of Harrogate, and sometimes a bed too if one of us got freaked out by our horror pick, but what we didn't share was an academic schedule. We took wood shop together and our classes joined for PE once a week. Unfortunately the Elles' class joined us too.

"Hey, Charley?" she called out.

"Yeah?"

"Maybe don't say anything about what you think you saw on Saturday outside your window. It sounds . . . well, a little crazy. And no one will believe us, anyway. OK, see ya."

SCARLETT DUNMORE

I watched her go, her backpack swaying and bouncing off her hip as she strode toward the science rooms, one part of the school I would never see. Students marched up and down the hallway beside me, single file and perfectly matching. We were carbon copies of one another from the collarbone down to the socks—forest-green Harrogate-crested blazers, crisp white shirts, pleated skirts, and white socks. Thankfully, footwear was a personal choice, which surprised me when I found out. While most girls opted for pumps or other heels, sometimes ankle boots, basically any kind of footwear most intelligent people would deem inappropriate for rural island life, Olive and I both wore comfy but sturdy sneakers. Always wear footwear you can run in. Perhaps someone should have told Hannah that.

When I got to room 3B I could hear the headmistress's voice seeping out from under the classroom door. I turned the knob slowly, generating the high-pitched squeak of old brass in need of oil. Everyone turned to stare at me. Ms. Blyth stood beside the desk while a scruffy police officer in a disheveled uniform sat on it, his right bum cheek on Ms. Evan's academic planner. He lazily rested a dirty boot on the chair in front of him. Ms. Blyth's eyes burned.

She looked up finally and gestured me in. I dropped into the chair behind Gabrielle and immediately became cocooned in a cloud of perfume. I coughed, choking on sandalwood and flowers and something horribly warm and sickly sweet. Gabrielle turned and glared at me, her lipstick-smeared mouth curved into a pout. I coughed again and swatted away the perfume before it could trickle inside my nostrils and cause brain malfunction.

"Charley," warned Ms. Blyth.

"Sorry," I spluttered, the heavy perfume hitting me once more like a fist.

The officer cleared his throat, probably also digesting Gabrielle's perfume, and continued on. "So, as I was saying, we won't know the exact details until we get the coroner's report on the mainland, but we're estimating her time of death to be between eight and ten p.m. on Saturday. Can anyone try to explain why Hannah Manning was taking a walk outside alone in the storm?"

"Is that what preliminary findings are suggesting, that Hannah fell while taking a walk?" I blurted out.

"Preliminary findings," repeated Rochelle from the front, not even trying to hide her annoying smirk. She sat sideways, facing the class, her shirt unbuttoned way too far. A hint of lace shimmered through, suggesting she was wearing a camisole underneath. A thin gold necklace adorned her neck. That was two rules broken right there—visible jewelry and non-school clothing—but I doubted she'd be written up for it.

The police officer smiled too. "Uh, yes, preliminary findings, well, *my* findings are suggesting that. What else would it be?"

The class fell silent. Ms. Blyth's eyes were on me, burning

a hole right through my skull. "Well," I muttered. "I just thought . . . um . . ."

"Speak up, Miss Sullivan," snapped Ms. Blyth.

I cleared my throat. "I just thought we perhaps shouldn't rule out foul play just yet."

Some of the class snickered.

"Foul play!" snorted Gabrielle, the perfume killer.

"Is there something you want to say?" asked the officer, sliding his other boot onto the chair in front of him and leaning back lazily.

"Actually, yes, um, well . . . between the hours of eight and ten p.m. on Saturday I saw something strange outside my window." A chair shifted, and the dragging of metal on tiles startled me. "I saw someone standing there."

"Hannah?" asked the officer, taking his shoes off the chair and sitting up.

"No, not Hannah. I don't think so, anyway. The person was wearing a dark coat with the hood up and was just standing next to the tree by my window, staring at me."

The officer glanced at Ms. Blyth, but her face was unreadable. Emotions hidden from me, from all of us.

"And what were you doing between those hours yourself?" the officer asked me.

"I was watching a movie with my roommate."

"A stupid horror movie, no doubt." Rochelle sighed.

"Is that true?" he asked me.

"Well, yeah, but—"

HOW TO SURVIVE A HORROR MOVIE

A couple of students laughed quietly. They stifled the sound in their hands, but I knew what they were thinking.

"Yes, I was watching a scary movie, but I wasn't freaked out. I saw what I saw. And I just thought no detail is too small when it comes to police investigations."

"No one is saying Hannah's death is suspicious. There will be no investigation as such. This was nothing but a very sad and tragic accident because of a storm and clifftop erosion," he said with finality. It seemed there would be no more questions.

"Of course, the horror nerd wants it to be a *murder*," cooed Rochelle, crudely mimicking a strangulation. More laughter.

Olive was right, I should have stayed quiet.

Rule #6
BEWARE OF STRANGE NOISES THAT FOLLOW

Everyone was talking about Hannah Manning's fall—or, should I say, *suicide*. She was the main topic of conversation at Harrogate, even among the teachers. Her name could be heard behind the staff-room door at lunchtime, was murmured in the hallways, and was openly discussed in the courtyard outside. Some said she jumped because she'd met someone on the mainland over the summer and couldn't bear to be apart from them any longer, while others said she took her own life because Headmistress Blyth confiscated her antidepressants during a routine drug search. There were reasons flying around ranging from alcohol abuse to academic pressure. It could have been anything: bullying, abuse, fear. Perhaps she just couldn't get her head around the social politics of Harrogate, any more than I could. Truth was, if Hannah did jump, we'd never truly know the reason why. But what unnerved me was that word "if," because what if she *didn't* jump?

HOW TO SURVIVE A HORROR MOVIE

Even though I wasn't hungry, I wolfed down my cottage pie, glazed carrots, and rhubarb crumble, just so I could excuse myself for a few moments of non-suicide chat before the vigil, maybe even read more of my Stephen King novel. I was promptly told to sit back down. At six thirty, we were finally excused and allowed back to our dorms for a quick refresh before the vigil. A quick refresh for me was a visit to the bathroom and maybe a small handful of Skittles from my bedside dresser. A refresh for the rest of the Harrogate girls was not so quick, and after about twenty minutes, Ms. Blyth sounded the assembly bell so we knew to start walking. Olive and I zipped up our coats and wound our scarves around our exposed necks, fluffing them up to our chins to warm our breath. The sun had set, and a crisp nighttime chill was already setting in. The friary bell tolled, and students spilled out all around us, applying the last touches of makeup and hairspray. We were told to come in uniform, as were the boys of Eden.

When we finally made it up the hill, the stone turret of the friary came into view, then the thick wooden doors, the archway, and finally the steps. We trudged up the stairs, our legs aching before we'd reached the top, and followed the rest of the girls. Inside, the friary was packed, students pressed against each other, breathing the same stale air, filled with sweat and teen hormones. Just how Harrogate and Eden students liked it. After about ten minutes, the side doors were eventually opened to let in a much-needed breeze and allow students and staff to spill out onto the evening grass, some holding candles.

The service began with a reading from the minister, then Headmistress Blyth stepped forward to give what felt like a thirty-minute eulogy on a student whose name she probably hadn't known until her untimely death. All around me, whisperings of suicide trickled through the crowds, down the pews, and up to the altar, until Blyth told everyone to be quiet.

"And now for a reading by one of Hannah's friends, Rochelle Smyth," she continued.

I frowned and nudged Olive beside me. "Now I know why Hannah jumped."

Olive burst out laughing. When students and staff turned around in disgust, she ducked her head.

Rochelle took to the podium with a devilish grin and a flick of her curls. Her smile faded as she gazed out at the pews. Then the real performance began. "I have . . ." She gasped and dramatically placed a hand over her heart. "I mean, I *had* known Hannah for five wonderful years . . ."

"Did she even ever speak to Hannah?" whispered a girl to her friend in front of us.

". . . The tragedy that has struck Harrogate School for Girls is unimaginable. But we are strong, and we will support each other through this like we always have here. My friends Annabelle, Gabrielle, and I have set up a grief counseling group on Wednesdays for anyone needing to talk, or to share, or for anyone who just feels blue . . ."

A couple of girls snorted in the pews.

". . . I'm here for you, Harrogate!" Rochelle proclaimed, holding her hand up like she was the saint her wing was named after.

After a long silence from the audience, Gabrielle and Annabelle finally clapped, looking around and encouraging everyone else to do so as well.

"Wow, how touching—the mean girls at school offering to counsel those they've bullied," Olive said, rolling her eyes.

Rochelle's speech was thankfully followed by a reading from a girl named Lisa who actually did seem to have been close friends with Hannah, and wasn't just vying for a little of the spotlight thrown by her death. It was then that we heard more about who she really was: academically strong, a violinist, a kind person who had spent last summer in Cambodia building a well for a village while the rest of her class had holidayed in the South of France or idled away the weeks binge-watching Netflix. She was shy and reserved and spent a lot of time in her dorm room alone. We listened to anecdotes from another friend after that and a glowing commentary from one of her teachers. Then, we were asked to bow our heads in silence. I dropped my chin to my chest and closed my eyes, faintly remembering doing this in church after my dad died.

The air was thick inside the friary, with almost zero

circulation due to the students that jammed the open doorways. The one-minute silence felt like three hours, broken by coughing and other bodily noises. I could hear my own breathing, the way it hitched and scraped the back of my throat before I exhaled through my nose. I could hear someone in front of me biting their fingernails, which was driving me insane, and an incessant scratching of skin. I shuddered and tried to zone out.

It was then I heard it. A dull crackle. A loud twisting and a pop like crushing a plastic juice bottle. It was so loud I lifted my head and looked around for the brave student who was about to face Blyth's wrath. But everyone still had their heads down, and no one else seemed bothered by it. I dropped my head again, hearing the ticking of someone's watch and . . . and that noise again, that cracking of plastic and popping. It was like someone was twisting a Coke bottle or bending the neck forward and back. I jerked my head up, staring around, but again no one else seemed to have noticed. And my hearing was just OK, not like Superman sensitive. Other people must have heard it, surely? Who was making that noise?

I skimmed the crowd: the students in the pews, those standing with candles at the sides, those beside me, behind me, in front of me. Suddenly, green eyes stared back me. Green eyes with that familiar mane of red and those freckles that tickled the bridge of her nose. While everyone else was facing the podium, their heads down, Saoirse was looking right at me.

I quickly averted my gaze and went back to the prayer-silence thing. But I could feel my cheeks reddening, my skin burning, my belly churning. When I glanced up again, she was smiling. I looked to either side. Was she smiling at *me*?

I looked down again. She couldn't have been. Why would she be looking at me? One of her friends must have been standing behind me. Or, if it was me, then shouldn't I smile back or wave? I wouldn't want to seem rude, or not interested. OK, I was going for it. I looked up confidently, flicking my hair back, and beamed my brightest smile. But she was facing front again. I'd missed my chance.

"Why are you smiling like that?" whispered Olive.

"I'm not smiling," I said, shaking my head.

"You're definitely smiling, and it's, like, creepy Chucky-doll smiling."

The smile slipped quickly from my face. The bell clanging to signal the end of service startled me, and a strange high-pitched scream escaped my lips. A few people turned, Rochelle included. She rolled her eyes and started following the crowds who shuffled down the pews, past us, and out into the evening air. The Eden boys walked slowly, very slowly, back up the hill, exchanging a few glances and brief words with the girls as they passed them.

Soon the friary and the grounds outside were filled with excited voices, giggles, and definitely some flirting.

"Shh!" roared Blyth. "Remember, boys and girls, this is a vigil for the dead."

The crowds dispersed quickly after that. I stayed to look for Saoirse, but she wasn't there. My shoulders slumped a little lower. We started the short walk back to Harrogate's stone walls. And as Olive droned on about Thomas and his "super-shiny hair," I drifted in and out of the conversation, distracted by Saoirse's smile, the crashing of the sea, the swirling beacon at the top of the lighthouse that shone into the sky above our heads, and that *sound*. That cracking, twisting, popping sound that echoed over the cliffs and followed me all the way back.

Rule #7

DON'T BE THE LAST ONE IN THE GYM

I didn't sleep for a moment that night, all hope of dreaming or deep REM cycles thwarted by that vexing plastic sound. In the early morning before dawn had set in, it was accompanied by a new, equally disturbing and annoying sound, like moaning, or maybe more like groaning. *Loud* groaning. But every time I sat up and turned on the lamp, the room was empty apart from Olive and the hallways were quiet. I heard the sound in the bathroom in the morning while brushing my teeth, while dressing, while eating my breakfast in the dining hall. I could even hear it as I changed into my PE uniform of boring green-and-white shorts and a striped T-shirt.

The noise was everywhere.

"I am so tired," groaned Olive as she collapsed on to the changing-room bench, one shoe on, the other discarded by her gym locker.

"Sorry about that," I said, scrunching up my nose.

SCARLETT DUNMORE

"Light on, light off, light on, light off . . . I felt like I was back sharing a room with my little brother when he'd just discovered the magic of light switches."

Everyone shuffled down the hall, Olive and I pale and ashen from our lack of sleep, and into the gym, which had been divided into four sections with a large white net and rackets in each one. Olive froze at the doorway, holding up the other students behind her. "Oh no," she moaned. "Doubles tennis."

I groaned too. I was not a doubles tennis kind of girl. I was more of a solo PE participant than a team player, especially when there was a risk of injuring others with my questionable hand-eye coordination.

Our PE teacher, Ms. McDonald, was a slim woman with bulging muscles in her legs that looked ready to pop. As a former Team GB relay runner, she was not about to let any of us sit this one out. To her, we were all athletes, but some of us just needed more training than others. A lot more training. And that definitely referred to Olive and me.

"Yes, ladies, it's Wimbledon here at Harrogate!" she exclaimed heartily to the students.

"Isn't Wimbledon in June?" called out someone from the back.

"We'll be playing in doubles today, so I'll assign you a court after your warm-up. Once around the building, meet back here."

"Around the *whole* building?" spluttered Olive.

"Yes, Montgomery—the whole building. Come on, there's a runner in all of us!" Ms. McDonald cooed, pushing open the side door.

Olive nudged me. "There's not one in me, and there's definitely not one in you. I've only seen you run to get the popcorn from the microwave."

I snorted and followed the group outside, where a gust of cold sea air smacked me hard in the face. Now I was awake. The waves crashed and tore through the wind, calling to us from down below. And then it started again, that popping, cracking, snapping. I stopped and gazed out at the ocean beyond the cliffs; it was louder out here, much louder, and it pierced my ears and dragged up my spine.

"Oof!"

Someone whacked into the back of me, stumbling down.

"Why did you stop?!" Rochelle screamed from the ground. "Idiot!" She pulled herself up, a scowl smeared across her already bitter face.

"Sorry, Rochelle, I—"

"Hurry up, girls!" yelled Ms. McDonald as she circled around us. I think that was her third time around the building.

Rochelle grunted and moved past me, leaving me standing on the path outside, the popping, cracking, and snapping still resounding in my ear.

Olive's hands wrapped around my shoulders and pulled me into a walk. "Come on, we're already last."

SCARLETT DUNMORE

We hopped and skipped a step, walked another five, tried a light jog again, and went back to walking. My body just didn't work like the other girls'. It wasn't springy and it didn't lift off from the ground effortlessly. In fact, my body stomped and thudded like a hungry baby elephant. By the time we made it all the way around the very long and very wide building, we were frozen to the bone and shivering with the salt air. Our warm-up would have been much more efficient had we just stayed inside. We barreled through the doors to get out of the cold, then stopped. Everyone was already paired up into doubles and had started their games. Or were they called matches?

"Welcome back!" called Ms. McDonald from the first court, waving a racket like it was a machete. "Last court. Your opponents are waiting."

We limped to the back of the gym, blistered and broken from the warm-up. "Shit," tutted Olive.

I looked up and saw Rochelle and Gabrielle sitting on one side of the court, their rackets on the floor beside them, their legs straight out, talking animatedly about Hannah's apparent jump from the cliffs.

A cold shiver tickled down my back.

"Finally! PE's almost over," Gabrielle sneered at us.

"Good," moaned Olive, bending slowly to pick up a racket.

Rochelle grinned. "This will be an easy game."

For once I thought she was probably right.

She threw the ball up in the air, then whipped it right at me. I screamed and ducked. They laughed. I hated PE. She swung again.

"Is it not our turn now?" asked Olive. The ball hit her arm. "Ow!"

"Hey!" I yelled across the court.

"What's going on here?" asked Ms. McDonald, popping up behind Rochelle.

"I served and she turned away and started having a conversation with her friend. It's not my fault it caught her in the arm."

Before Ms. McDonald could respond, a loud clatter of metal falling and rope unwinding was heard from down the court. "Watch the nets, ladies!" she shrieked, marching down the hall.

"Your serve." Rochelle sighed, bouncing a ball to me. It soared right past me and hit the wall. I scrambled to get it, somehow managing to stumble over the bag of rackets in the process, and hurried back to the net.

"Serve!" I called out, startling Olive beside me. I bounced the ball and swiped the racket as hard as I could, completely missing.

Gabrielle giggled.

I fumbled on the floor for the ball, but I could hear the sound again.

Pop. Crack. Snap.

SCARLETT DUNMORE

I tried to block it out. "Serve!" I missed the ball again. "Serve!" And again.

"Come on, you don't get that many turns!" Rochelle argued, throwing her arms out. "Ms. McDonald, they're cheating!"

Pop. Crack. Snap.

I couldn't take it anymore. My head was throbbing.

Pop. Crack. Snap.

"It's our turn now!" wailed Gabrielle.

Pop. Crack. Snap.

I bounced the ball angrily, growling in pain as the noise pierced my eardrums, slicing into them. Why wouldn't it stop?

Pop. Crack. Snap.

I swung.

The racket finally collided with the ball and it soared through the air, barreling over the net and past Rochelle. And right into Gabrielle's face. A howl cut through the air, and the courts fell silent. I dropped my plastic racket and it thudded against the floor.

Oops.

Ms. McDonald came rushing over as Gabrielle collapsed and rolled around, screaming and moaning. Rochelle knelt beside her, gently touching her arm, feigning concern. When Gabrielle pulled her hands away from her face, a small trickle of blood oozed out of her nostril and dripped onto the floor.

Olive made a gagging sound beside me.

"It was an accident," I whimpered.

"You did it on purpose!" Gabrielle howled, the blood now spilling down onto her hands.

"Rochelle, bring her to the nurse. Ladies, that's it for today. Quick shower, then on to your other classes."

The students dispersed, a few staying to watch Gabrielle crying and bleeding on the gym floor. Olive tugged at me, and we started walking away too. I felt in need of a cold shower.

"Not you, girls," snapped Ms. McDonald. "While I'm filling out the accident report form that I get the pleasure of sending to her parents, you both are tidying up."

"All of this?" Olive groaned, gazing down the four courts. "But it's recess next. We only get twenty minutes."

"Then you've got twenty minutes to get this all cleaned up and downstairs to the equipment closet."

The last of the students filed out, along with an injured Gabrielle, who was now limping as if her foot had been struck too. Olive and I exhaled loudly. We detached poles, chased after balls, and wound rope into loops we deemed acceptably tidy for storage. I checked my watch. We had about five minutes left of recess, which meant by the time we hauled all this down the stairs to the closet we'd probably not have time to change and have to attend our next class still in our sweaty gym clothes. Great.

SCARLETT DUNMORE

"Sorry," I said as we dragged the balls and nets down the first set of stairs, the metal poles banging off each step.

"It's fine. Actually, it was really funny. I didn't expect that."

"Me neither." I scoffed.

"That was some serve. You really whacked that thing!"

"I hope her nose isn't broken."

"She'll be fine. Mommy and Daddy will get her a nose job— Oof!" Olive collided with someone and staggered back against the stair railing. One of the metal poles dropped to the ground, rolling and clanging along the floor.

"Careful, ladies," Mr. Gillies grunted, quickly shifting around us. He leapt up the stairs two at a time, his oversized tweed blazer bouncing off his back.

I bent down and caught the pole before it escaped any farther. "What's he doing down here?"

"Don't know. Exercising?"

I handed the pole to Olive. When she tried to grab it, she lost her grip on the others, sending them all clattering to the ground. Olive muttered a string of words I didn't know she had in her vocabulary, then started gathering them up again with an air of defeat. She balanced each one impressively in a different position until she was walking like a character from *Hellraiser*, the sharp edges of the poles scraping along the wall.

HOW TO SURVIVE A HORROR MOVIE

We finally reached the bottom of the second set of stairs, then began lugging the gear down the hallway, screeching and trailing, scraping and scratching. Sweat dripped down our faces. The storage closet was at the end of the corridor, the only section the overhead lights didn't reach. Olive dropped everything she was carrying, the sound echoing through the empty hallway. She tugged on the door, once, twice.

"I think it's locked. Did Ms. McDonald give you a key?"

"No." I pulled on the door handle, feeling it shift slightly. "I think it's just stiff, like everything else in this school, including the students." I pulled harder. Olive placed her hands over mine and tugged with me. The door popped and finally released, flying open as we stumbled backward.

The smell hit us first. The stench of rot and urine, mixed with a sickening sweetness like vanilla. Then it was the sound of Olive's screaming and the thumping of my own accelerated heartbeat. There was a heaviness on me, something dangling from my shoulders. When I looked up I saw gym shoes, then white socks, and finally bare gray-tinged ankles. I staggered backward as the whole image came into focus—the expressionless face, the wide-open eyes, the bulging tongue hanging out of the mouth, the bent, crushed neck with the rope tied around it. And the creaking sound of Sarah Keenan's body hanging and swaying off a ceiling beam.

Rule #8
EXPECT STRANGE THINGS IN A LIBRARY

We spent the rest of the day in Headmistress Blyth's office, bombarded with questions from her and Mr. Gillies, whose eyes darkened the more we described Sarah's lifeless hanging body. Ms. McDonald was immediately granted sympathetic leave from the school and from the island.

Like Hannah, Sarah Keenan had been an avid athlete, and she was captain of the school netball team. Many of Ms. McDonald's photos in the gym hallway were of either Sarah or Hannah, or both together. Of course, having two girls take their own lives in the same week, with Ms. McDonald being the only common factor, was bad for school business, and by the end of the day Blyth had spent more time crafting a letter to parents than consoling us. There was also the question of why the gym equipment closet—full of rope and ties—*wasn't* locked. Needless to say, Ms. McDonald probably wouldn't be returning to Harrogate after her leave.

HOW TO SURVIVE A HORROR MOVIE

When the weather allowed, a police officer would be ferried in from the mainland to ask us more questions, but until then, there wasn't much any of us could do. Olive and I had just been unlucky to find her body in the closet. We didn't know her, hadn't heard any strange sounds, and hadn't seen anyone while we were down there. Other than Mr. Gillies.

Harrogate labeled it another "tragic accident." They were becoming common here on this island.

Finally, Olive and I were excused and went our separate ways, both needing some time to process what had just happened, again. I took a walk up to the lighthouse, the gulls swooping overhead thinking I had bread for them, which I didn't. And Olive, well, I didn't know what Olive did that afternoon. We didn't say too much to each other for the rest of the day. Around five o'clock, we meandered to the dining hall together, slow and stiff like zombies from *Night of the Living Dead*, moving mindlessly in a horde. We slid trays off the metal rack and joined the line, pointed to whatever we saw in the metal containers behind the glass, and collapsed down at the first empty table we found. No one joined us, naturally enough. We were the girls who had found two dead bodies in the past week.

Olive's fork dropped clumsily to her tray, clanging off the plate and making me jump. I looked up at her gray face, her sunken eyes. Her *Fright Night* T-shirt hung loosely on her torso, the sleeves dipping into her gravy.

"Did you know Sarah Keenan?" I eventually asked.

"Not really. She spent most of her early years with the Elles. I think she was friends with Clara Richardson and that lot, after."

I glanced over at their table. Clara and her friends hadn't touched their dinners either. Some sat with their faces in their hands, others staring off blankly.

"Do you think it was suicide again?"

"What else would it be?" she asked me.

"I don't know. It's just weird. Two suicides in one week?"

"Maybe it was like a suicide pact. I saw that in a horror movie once."

"I thought Hannah and Sarah didn't hang out, outside of sports stuff?"

Olive shrugged. "Who knows? We don't really keep up with the social goings-on of sixth years."

"True," I muttered, the sound of breaking plastic so familiar to me now, it was more of a dull annoyance than a distraction, like tinnitus. "Don't you think it was odd that Mr. Gillies was down there? Wood shop is a long way from PE."

"I don't know, Charley," Olive said softly, resting her head in her hands. Her wild curls covered her face like a thick blanket.

"Come on." We returned our trays, barely touched, to the rack and walked out of the dining hall, clocking the stares that followed us.

HOW TO SURVIVE A HORROR MOVIE

"I'm skipping the vigil tonight," Olive announced as the wooden dining-hall doors closed heavily behind her.

"Me too. I can't handle another remembrance service and Rochelle speech."

"I can't handle another dead body," she whimpered, her bottom lip trembling.

"I know." I wrapped an arm around her shoulders and squeezed gently.

She brushed a tear away from her eye with her sleeve. "Movie and popcorn tonight?"

"I'd love that, but my English essay is due tomorrow and I still can't get past that first paragraph."

"Want me to just do it?" she scoffed. Olive probably passed advanced English when she was ten.

"As much as I want to say yes, I should say no because knowing our luck at the moment, we'd get caught."

"Good point. Well, I'll come with you, so you're not in a creepy library all by yourself," she said, following me down the hall.

We reached the library at the back of the Elizabeth Wing by the time the assembly bell had rung, giving students time to quickly finish and return their dinner trays, layer up, and head for the friary. Ms. Blyth's office was in darkness. She was probably already standing in the friary, preparing a second remembrance speech. I hoped this would be the last. With the Eden students and Harrogate girls, plus staff, it was unlikely our absence would go noticed, unless someone was looking for us specifically.

We pushed open the stiff doors to the library, relieved to find it empty. The lamp was still on over the librarian's desk, which was strewn with open volumes, dust covers she'd been cleaning, and an old coffee mug with the question "Too Many Books or Not Enough Bookshelves?"

The rugs on the dark mahogany floors were old and frayed at the edges. The library was small compared to the ones in cities on the mainland, but well preserved and picture-perfect with iron staircases spiraling up the sides to balconies that held rare editions and classics. Our class textbooks were stored downstairs. Anything we wanted to read for fun had to be specifically ordered in from the main catalog and sent over with Mr. Terry on the boat. I'd requested the new Stephen King when I returned after the summer, but after two months I had yet to receive it. Island post at its finest.

"I'm going to look for a book on thermodynamics. Let me know when it's movie and popcorn time," Olive said, heading off toward the catalog computers.

I nodded and carried on walking into the belly of the library alone, treading lightly, just in case we weren't the only ones skipping the vigil tonight. My shoulder bag was heavy with a gigantic volume of Jane Austen's collected works, so I set it down on one of the tables. All the reading lamps were still on, as they were operated by a general switch behind the librarian's desk. It was peaceful in here with everyone else gone. The silence and calm that only libraries offered. I could see the warm amber lights from the friary flickering through the large stained-glass windows at the back, the old masonic building on the hill still visible through swirls of red, blue, and green glass all intersecting and eventually merging together to create the outline of the Virgin Mary. The stained glass was original to the thirteenth-century building, and the school council had thankfully kept it, preserving it well. Movement flickered on the rocky ascent up to the friary, all the students now on their way to the vigil. From here they looked like little ants marching up their mound.

The screech of a chair broke my trance, and I spun around, startled. It was just Olive, who grimaced as she glanced toward the door, waiting for a staff member to barrel through and reprimand us for being there. But no one came. Thankfully the hallways were quiet, empty. I exhaled loudly and sat down, unpacking my things from my bag. I opened the anthology and began skimming with my finger, determined to jot down some bullet points on something. Anything. Soon the scraping of my pencil melded harmoniously with the pecking of branches at the windows, swaying and shaking in the wind—*scrape*—*peck*—*scrape*—*peck*—like little crows looking for food.

I quickly became aware of another sound joining the

symphony of tapping and pecking, adding its own disturbing rhythm: *crack—snap—pop.*

I shuddered. I hadn't heard it since this afternoon, but now it was back, taunting and tormenting me as I tried desperately to finish a sentence about Mr. Darcy.

Crack. Snap. Pop.

I sighed and dropped the pencil. How could I concentrate with that going on? The catalog computers by the main desk sat empty, one of them still alight with Olive's recent search. I glanced around for her, but the aisles were empty, illuminated only by the lamps in the center of the tables and the moonlight, which cast pools of red and green through the stained glass over the library. I pushed back my chair and went to the science section, heading down the first aisle I saw. My steps were heavy and reverberated around me. "Olive?" I whispered. The library sat quiet, only the wind outside answered me. "Olive?"

Crack. Snap. Pop.

There it was again, but this time there was something else too, a second sound. A muffled gurgling and choking. It didn't seem far away or outside anymore. It was coming from *inside* the library. From beside me.

My aisle was completely empty, only the books on shelves and the odd clump of dust. I turned slowly to the shelf and shimmied out a thick hardback so I could stare into the adjoining aisle.

HOW TO SURVIVE A HORROR MOVIE

Bloodshot blue eyes appeared through the gap in the stack.

I stifled a scream and fell back, slamming against another bookcase.

Hands, white and gnarled, fingernails long and bloodied, reached through the shelf, through the books, toward me. Soon a body emerged from the bookcase—dark matted hair, an expressionless face, wide eyes, a bulging tongue hanging out of the mouth, and a bent, crushed neck with a rope tied around it.

Sarah Keenan.

But she wasn't dead. She was here, in the library, reaching for me. She opened her mouth to say something but all that came out was gurgling and choking. Bile rose to my throat, burning my insides. I turned to run and saw another figure at the bottom of the aisle, blocking my path. Chestnut-hued hair clumped with sand, twisted limbs, half a face, the other side completely mangled, chunks of flesh hanging on by skin. A small crab perched on her shoulder.

"Hannah?" I gasped. I stumbled backward again, landing hard on my hip.

She edged toward me, her arms and legs contorting and snapping as she moved. And then it dawned on me, the truth hitting me hard in the gut. That cracking, snapping, and popping was the sound of Hannah Manning's bones breaking when she'd fallen to her death.

Rule #9

IF IN DOUBT, SEEK MEDICAL ADVICE

I huddled on my bed, gripping a mug of hot tea as steam wafted up. The cup trembled in my hands as I shook, droplets of creamy brown spilling onto my quilt. Olive draped a blanket around my shoulders. I wasn't cold, but I couldn't stop shaking.

"Should I get the nurse?" she asked, sitting down on the other side of the bed.

"No," I whispered, straining to get the word out. My throat was raw from screaming the library down.

"What happened in there?"

"I can't say," I muttered.

"Why? Tell me."

"It sounds . . . crazy."

"The past week has been crazy—dead bodies, police. I can handle crazy, trust me."

I took a deep breath, my shoulders sore from tensing. "I saw . . . *something*."

"In the library?"

I nodded.

"What?" She edged closer.

"I saw . . ." I trailed off, not quite sure how to say what I was thinking. "I saw . . ."

"Just say it."

"I saw Hannah Manning and Sarah Keenan," I blurted out.

Olive sat back, her forehead scrunching up into little lines. "You mean you saw them last week?"

"No, I mean I saw them *today* in the library."

"But they're dead, Charley. Like officially dead."

"I know, and how I saw them today was exactly how we found them. Hannah's body was all broken from the rocks—"

Olive swallowed hard.

"And Sarah had a crushed neck, with the rope still attached—"

"I'm going to be sick," she announced, rushing for the sink in our room. Up came a dinner of spaghetti and meatballs.

"Sorry," I said, sliding off the bed. "I didn't mean to be so graphic. I just wanted to explain what I saw."

She washed her hands and face, patted them dry with the towel, and staggered to her bed. "I'll clean that up in the morning."

I grimaced, then plopped down on my bed, hearing

footsteps and voices in the hallway and outside our window. "Vigil must be over," I murmured, gazing out at the cliffs behind the trees where Hannah fell, or jumped. I didn't know.

Olive lay spread-eagled on her bed, still in her clothes. "Look, see how you feel in the morning, then maybe visit the infirmary before breakfast. See what Nurse Clare has to say."

"Yeah, that's probably a good idea." I slipped under the covers, too tired to change into my pajamas, and stared up at the white ceiling. Olive turned off the lamp between us and sighed deeply.

"Mind if I sleep with you tonight?" she asked.

Without saying anything, I slid over to one side, then lifted the covers for her to join. She scooted over and wriggled in, pulling the quilt up to her chin.

"Do you think they were scared, you know, before they did it?" she asked, huddling into the back of me.

I could still smell her vomit, both from the sink and her breath. "Probably."

"I wonder why they did it. Sarah had a boyfriend, good grades, seemed happy. Hannah too."

"I don't know."

"Do you see them now? I mean, are they here?"

"No," I lied, looking right at them. They were standing side by side at the bottom of the bed. Eyes vacant, faces gaunt and stretched, hair matted. Their twisted bodies curled around each other as they stared at me.

"Good night, Sullivan."

"Good night, Montgomery," I whispered, gripping my pillow in fear.

I watched them the whole night, terrified that I had a brain tumor and wouldn't wake up if I closed my eyes, yet also wondering whether, if this was all real, the ghosts might try to possess my body, like in *The Amityville Horror*. But they didn't move. They just stood there, making cracking and choking sounds. I rose at dawn, scuttled past them with my head down, and quietly left the room. I closed the door as gently as I could so not to wake a snoring Olive. Her spaghetti and meatballs were curdling in the sink as I left.

The hallways were quiet, the soft light from the windows spilling in and washing the walls and floors around me. I hadn't brought a coat, so when I crossed the courtyard to the Elizabeth Wing, the morning wind hit me, seeping in through the weave of my sweater and leggings. The ground was cold underneath my slippers, and I regretted not bringing some better footwear for the walk to the infirmary. I didn't know if Nurse Clare would be in this early, but wondered if, since it was a Friday and we'd had two suicides this week, she would perhaps be here already.

SCARLETT DUNMORE

But when I arrived her door was locked and her room was shrouded in blackness. I sat on the floor, back against the wall, and waited for her. And waited and waited. Apparently, Nurse Clare didn't start until after breakfast, which I was now missing. By the time she arrived I had dozed off. I startled awake when I felt a hand lightly squeezing my shoulder.

"Are you waiting for me?" Nurse Clare asked. She was younger than I imagined, not appearing much older than some of the girls in my year. She had light brown hair and a thick accent that I couldn't place but made some of her words hard to identify out of context.

I nodded and clambered to my feet, following her into her office.

She flicked on the lights, illuminating the large medical cupboard and fridge in the corner and the posters on the wall describing early signs of sexually transmitted diseases. I suddenly felt queasy.

"How can I help you?" she asked, gesturing to the chair beside her.

I collapsed into it, feeling heavy from the lack of sleep. "I think I have a brain tumor."

"Why do you think that?"

"Well, I'm hallucinating, seeing things that aren't there."

"OK. Mind if I turn down the lights?"

I shrugged and watched as she sat down opposite me,

edging in close. She gently shone a light into my pupils. "Any discomfort? Headaches?"

"No."

Then she felt the glands in my neck. "Fever? Nausea?"

"No."

"Any problems with your speech lately or with your vision? Any trouble remembering things?"

"No."

"Muscle aches, throbbing, tingling sensations?"

"No, none of that. I'm just seeing things."

"What kinds of things?"

Outside, the first bell went, echoing through the hallways. "Dead people," I whispered, suddenly feeling like the creepy boy in *The Sixth Sense*.

She sat back in her chair. "Ghosts?"

I nodded.

"What kind of ghosts?"

"Um . . . the regular kind?"

"Ghosts of whom?" she clarified.

"Oh, well, ghosts of dead students."

She inhaled sharply, then stood up to turn the lights back on. "What did you say your name was?"

"Charley Sullivan, sixth year."

"You're one of the girls who found them, Sarah and Hannah?"

I nodded again.

SCARLETT DUNMORE

Footsteps echoed on the tiles outside as students hurried to class, no doubt grateful that it was Friday. In two weeks it'd be the Halloween formal, when the school would open its doors to the Eden boys and pretend this was the only time boys were ever seen inside Harrogate. Formals, proms, social gatherings of any kind weren't my thing, not anymore, but Halloween definitely was. And as I hadn't yet plucked up the courage to ask Saoirse, Olive was my date. Costumes were optional, but I was going as the eponymous protagonist from *Carrie* and Olive was Freddy from *Nightmare on Elm Street*. She'd slashed up an old striped T-shirt with a pair of scissors, but she was yet to figure out how to simulate razors for her fingers. All of her ideas so far were grounds for expulsion or immediate police arrest.

"Charley," started Nurse Clare. "What you and your roommate witnessed would break even a teacher, let alone a student of your age. You found the deceased bodies of your classmates, two in one week! What you're experiencing is completely normal."

"It is?"

"It's a form of PTSD, because what you saw was very traumatic. It's normal for your body to still be reeling from that, to be experiencing oddities like hallucinations, insomnia, and so on."

"But it feels so . . . real. I feel them beside me, I can hear their choking, and their bones breaking. I can *smell* them, Ms. Clare."

HOW TO SURVIVE A HORROR MOVIE

"What you're describing isn't too dissimilar to what a veteran might say after a war."

The hallways were once again quiet, empty of footsteps. The light spilled through her window, washing over the wooden floor and the stack of student files by the fridge.

"Next time you see one of these ghosts, I want you to look it square in the eye and say, 'You are not real.'"

"OK."

She smiled, the first real smile I'd seen from a staff member at Harrogate, and it reminded me strangely of my mother. As if she knew what I was thinking, she frowned. "I think I should call your mom."

"No, please don't. She'll panic. I just want this year at Harrogate to go smoothly."

"OK, but please check in with me regularly. I can organize grief counseling for you and your roommate at any time."

"Will do," I said, sliding off my chair.

"And I'm writing you a note excusing you from classes today. It is my medical opinion that you need a day in bed, in your pajamas, with movies and junk food." She opened her drawer and handed me a small chocolate bar from inside it.

"That I can definitely do." I smiled at her and took the chocolate, repeating, "Ghosts are not real."

Rule #10
AVOID ROOFTOPS IN THE RAIN

Ghosts were real.

In fact, Half-Broken Hannah and Strangled Sarah were sitting opposite me at the table in the dining hall as my bowl of cornflakes grew soggy and inedible. I was having breakfast with dead people.

"Happy Slasher Saturday," shouted Olive, popping up from behind my shoulder.

I startled and nudged my bowl, slopping cornflakes and milk all over the table beside me.

"Sorry, didn't mean to scare you," she murmured, quickly mopping up the mess with her napkin.

"It's fine. I'm just jumpy this morning."

"How are you feeling today?"

I looked down at my bowl, at the soft flakes soaking up the creamy white liquid, slowly expanding and creeping toward the edges. "Um . . . not great."

Olive touched my shoulder softly. "Look, Charley, we've

had a crazy week. We found two dead bodies! Most people go their whole lives without ever seeing one, and we saw *two*!"

Yep, and now they were sitting with me at the breakfast table.

"No one would blame you for . . . seeing things," she continued.

"I'm not hallucinating. They're *here*."

Her eyes darted around. "What do you mean? Like *here* here?"

"Yes, *here* here. They're right there," I whispered, pointing to the empty chairs opposite me.

Olive jumped up and walked around to the other side of the table. "Here?" she said, waving her arms through Hannah's broken neck, while she slumped forward, softly wailing.

I gulped, a clot of bile warm in my throat.

Olive collapsed down in the chair, right into Sarah's strangled, blue, lifeless body. "Charley, there is nothing here. These chairs are empty. Those girls are D-E-A-D, never coming back. They're decomposing in a pile of earth somewhere on the mainland." She paused. "Or they're in the freezer out back with the fish fingers."

Hannah turned to her, her face alight with anger. I sat forward, my skin prickling into tiny goose bumps. Could they hear us?

"Hello, Charley?"

"Sorry," I said, shaking my head, my mind heavy. "I think I'm going to go to the service tomorrow morning."

Olive stopped mid-bite, her toast hanging limply in her fingers. "What?"

"I think it might be good for me."

Olive sat agape, a piece of crust poking out from her mouth.

"No, really. I think I just need to, I don't know, pray or something," I added.

She pushed the rest of her toast into her mouth, globs of butter oozing out onto her chin, and swallowed hard. "You're not going to join a new religion or start a cult or anything, are you?"

"No, I think I have enough going on at the moment."

I downed the last of my coffee, the one and only cup we were allowed per day, and followed Olive out of the dining hall.

"We're still doing our Slasher Saturday tonight, right? If so, I was thinking of something more upbeat, in light of everything. What do you think about a comedy? Like *Shaun of the Dead* or *Zombieland*?"

"Sure," I muttered, glancing behind me to see if the ghosts were following.

"I'm so jealous, I should have seen Nurse Clare yesterday too to get a day off," she continued. "What did you watch?"

"Um." I looked back again, this time to see Hannah's

skinny hand appearing around the wall, scratching at the paint, reaching for me.

"Charley?"

"Oh, I watched *Insidious*."

"I'm even more jealous!"

While Olive droned on about memory inhibition and demon possession, I changed quickly for the day, sliding out of my slippers into a pair of high-tops. Saturdays at Harrogate were fairly busy, considering the weekends were supposed to be our free time. Most students were encouraged to join a school club of some kind, whether it was gardening, archery, dance, art, science and technology, creative writing, or cooking. I tried the Creative Writing Club when I first transferred, but after I wrote a short story about a serial killer in a white hockey mask who ate his victims' hearts, I was discouraged from coming back. Then I accidentally set fire to someone's apron in Cooking Club while attempting soufflés, twisted my ankle on a wheelbarrow in Gardening Club, and, unsurprisingly, wasn't even allowed to audition for archery. So now, Olive and I chose to spend our Saturdays painting stage props for the Theater Club. Olive had auditioned three times but was yet to be selected for any role. Personally, I found her rendition of Hannibal Lecter's monologue from *The Silence of the Lambs* quite impressive. Her Southern accent still needed a little work, though. Hopefully she would perfect it in time for the next audition.

SCARLETT DUNMORE

While Olive finished up the leaves on what I thought was meant to be a tree but looked more like Slimer from *Ghostbusters,* I dotted sequins onto a curtain using a kids' glue stick, trying not to look up at Dead Sarah and Dead Hannah, who were hovering beside a Styrofoam dog, looking like they wanted to pet it.

"Mine's not sticking," I complained, picking another fallen sequin off my sneaker as sweat dripped down my hairline.

"Why is it so humid in here?" Olive panted. "My paint's not drying, and I think they need the tree for tonight."

"Let's bring them outside, the fresh air should dry your paint and harden my glue."

We dragged a three-meter-long velvet curtain and a cardboard tree out of the back door of the gym, where the Gardening Club had just finished replanting Blyth's herbs. She'd built a fence around them. With a gate that locked.

"How long should we wait?" asked Olive, blowing on her paint. Up above, the sky crackled and thundered.

"Oh no, I think it's going to rain." We grabbed the props and started carrying them back inside, just as the skies opened up.

"No, my paint is running!" cried Olive, water dripping off her face.

A tug pulled me back, and I stumbled a few steps. "Wait, I think my curtain is caught on a bush!"

HOW TO SURVIVE A HORROR MOVIE

The rain continued pouring, running down Olive's tree, spilling green paint all over the grass and path. Behind me somewhere, the sound of popping and snapping bones swirled around in the wind and the rain. We fumbled with the curtain, pulling it harder and harder.

"It's going to rip," I warned.

But it was too late. A deep tearing sounded over the rain, and the curtain split in two. Then a bloodcurdling, toe-curling scream pierced the air, coming closer and closer. A large thud startled us off our feet and down to the wet ground.

When we looked up, still clutching the torn curtain, we saw the body of a student, back arched the wrong way, impaled through the torso by Headmistress Blyth's new fence. A trickle of blood spilled from her mouth onto the lemon thyme.

Olive and I screamed in unison as we fled, beginning in a low alto and ending in a high soprano by the time we reached the gym.

"B-b-b . . ." Olive stuttered, grabbing Ms. Evans, the Theater Club leader.

"Body!" I howled. Paintbrushes and props clattered to the floor.

A heavy silence rolled out across the gym like a thick mist from a Stephen King novel, as students debated whether this was our idea of a twisted joke or if we were just that unlucky and had come across a third dead body in the last week.

We *were* just that unlucky.

A couple of students ran outside, leaving the door open so that the lashing rain came inside. Soon their screams were louder than the patter of raindrops and they barreled back into the gym yelling, "Dead body!"

The Theater Club erupted into chaos. Cardboard cutouts of Victorian houses were thrown across the room as people sprinted toward the safety of the main building. Glitter, sequins, paint, spray cans, all the borrowed supplies from the art room were now on the floor, oozing and spilling and seeping across the hardwood. Costume racks were knocked over, and top hats, corsets, parasols, and feathery things were trampled in the chaos, occasionally tangling around someone's ankles and tripping them up. And the screams. The Harrogate Theater Club had perfected the drama of panic. Olive and I stood in the middle of the gym, watching it all unfold, wondering whether they were running from the body outside or from us. It took about ten minutes to have Blyth and half the faculty in the gym with us, also storming around in a panic. Fifteen minutes later we were sitting in Blyth's office, still wet from the rain, shivering from our damp clothes.

"What happened *this time*?" asked Mr. Terry, his clothes soaked from his trip outside to drape a bedsheet over a girl's body. Headmistress Blyth stood behind him, on the phone to the police on the mainland, again.

"We went outside to try to dry our props—" I started.

"It was really muggy in the gym," interjected Olive, shaking beside me. "And it started to rain—"

"We got absolutely soaked."

"And when we went to go back inside, that's when we heard it—"

"This horrible scream!"

"And then we saw her on the fence—"

"She fell onto the fence! The herb fence!" screamed Olive, feverishly clutching Ms. Evans's hand.

"Calm yourself, Miss Montgomery," Blyth snapped, still cradling the phone.

"That's all we saw, Headmistress. We heard the scream and then we saw the body fall onto the fence. She died immediately on impact, there was nothing we could have done," I added calmly.

"Ah, Martin, there you are," sighed Ms. Blyth, waving Mr. Gillies into the office.

He stood in the doorway, his hair and raincoat damp.

"Where have you been?" Blyth asked him, beckoning him closer.

"I've just heard," he muttered, shaking the rain from his collar. He gazed down at Olive and me, his eyes dark and empty, then joined Ms. Evans, whose cheeks were caked in mascara-tinted tears, beside the filing cabinet. Ms. Blyth whispered a few words into the phone receiver, said goodbye, then placed it down. "The police will get the next boat out here. In the meantime, I want all students indoors for the remainder of the day. There will be a curfew until tomorrow morning. Staff will do checks on all the dorms, touching base with the students—especially Meghan's friends."

"Meghan?" asked Olive.

"Meghan Fraser. She was in your physics class, Olive."

"Oh. I . . . didn't recognize her, not like that," she whimpered, wiping a tear.

"Meghan's parents will have a lot of questions, as I'm sure students will, which I'll endeavor to respond to as best I can once we know more about why Meghan jumped."

"Jumped?" I asked, that word not sitting right with me once again.

"Why else would she have been on that roof?" Mr. Gillies asked.

Another jump—*another* suicide? I stood slowly, all eyes on me. "Can we be excused, please? I think we need to lie down."

"Of course, back to your dorms. Let me or another staff member know if you need to talk," Blyth replied. "Or if there's something you want to share."

The way she said that turned my belly ice-cold, like she wanted us to say something, admit something. Did she think we were involved somehow? That we were a part of these deaths?

I nodded and gestured for Olive to follow. We walked down the halls, devoid now of voices and laughter, everyone back in their dorms, processing this as best they could. Our room seemed colder when we got back, everything in it suddenly foreign to me. The bed didn't look welcoming and the clothes on the floor didn't seem like mine, nor did the pile of horror DVDs and Stephen King books on the dresser. Everything seemed different, empty.

I shivered and reached for a towel. "I'm going to take a shower," I said loudly.

"Me too."

We ambled down to the shower room and flicked the lights on. They flickered and spluttered and roared to life, illuminating the sinks, mirrors, and hair dryers. The showers, which were completely vacant at this time of the afternoon, were nestled beside a large open changing cubicle. Each shower had a flimsy white curtain for privacy. I shimmied out of my damp clothes in the cubicle, wrapped a towel around my body, which was prickling with goose bumps, and went into the first shower. I turned the silver-knobbed handle. Steam rose and struck me in the face. Needing more, I stepped farther in and let the hot water wash over me, running down my hair, shoulders, torso. I breathed in deeply, closed my eyes, and felt the steam soothe my frantic heartbeat. I breathed out and let the hot water envelop me. When I finally opened my eyes, my vision was filled by a blurred mass in the corner right in front of me. I sucked in a breath.

Something was in the shower with me.

I rubbed the water from my face roughly and looked again, eyes wide and straining. There she was. Meghan Fraser. She stood in the corner of the cubicle, her back to me, the water slicing through her but not touching her. Then she turned slowly to face me. Blood was smeared around her mouth, her eyes were bloodshot, and her back was arched the wrong way. Protruding from her torso was a fence spike, a sprig of rosemary still attached.

I screamed and stumbled back, sliding on the floor, legs everywhere. Meghan's eyes widened in fear and confusion. She clutched her chest dramatically and screamed with me, her neck tipped back, her voice projecting upward. I covered my mouth with a hand, stifling my scream, but Impaled Meghan continued wailing, her voice reverberating off the shower walls. Several octaves later she finally stopped and gazed down at me, still sprawled on the floor. "Ugh, cover it up." She shielded her eyes and turned away.

"You're not real. You're not real," I repeated over and over again, pulling myself up the wall, back onto my feet, albeit a little less steady than before.

"Charley," called Olive from her shower cubicle. "Are you OK? Is that you?"

HOW TO SURVIVE A HORROR MOVIE

"Not real, not real, not real," I said over and over again, yanking open the shower-room door, the cold air from the hallway hitting my wet face. I threw on my robe and marched all the way back to my dorm, repeating it over and over and over.

Meghan followed close behind, stumbling. "Slow down! I'm still sore from Friday's workout! It was leg day!" she called to me.

"You're not real!" I yelled into the hallway, before slamming the dorm door closed and collapsing facedown onto my bed.

Rule #11

IF STILL IN DOUBT, SEEK RELIGIOUS ADVICE

Come Sunday morning, curfew was lifted but the hallways were thick with whispers of a suicide pact. One that involved Olive and me.

Apparently we were the pact supervisors, present for every suicide to ensure its success, maybe even finish the job if there was any chance of survival. A double tap. Harrogate's sixth-year girls had more imagination than I'd thought.

At breakfast, everyone stared at us, watching our every bite. Olive slurped her coffee clumsily, still in shock from the day before and also exhausted from another restless night listening to me repeat "You're not real" over and over again. My throat was killing me today, and it was all for nothing. Now I had *three* ghosts sitting with me. And one could talk. The table was starting to get a little full.

"Are you still planning to attend service today?" said Olive.

I nodded, needing it now more than ever.

"Want me to come with you?"

"No, it's fine. Unless you want to ogle Thomas?"

"No, I can't see him today."

"Why?"

"I have a pimple on my nose. Today's not my day." She pouted, her bottom lip out.

"OK, well, at least you can get some peace to do your French readings for next week."

Most people took one language at school, barely getting through it, but Olive took three, excelling in French, German, and Latin. Between those and her advanced physics, advanced chemistry, and advanced math, her workload was ten times mine, and she was still ahead, whereas all I had done this week was submit a shockingly bad English paper. It was a fail for sure, but Ms. Evans was kind, knowing what I'd been through over the last week, and gave me a borderline pass.

We slumped back to our dorms after thick, sludgy porridge, and while Olive snuggled down in bed with Voltaire and a bag of Monster Munch, I layered up and headed out for Sunday service. The air was dry and crisp, but the grass was still soggy from yesterday's rain, so I kept to the path. It snaked up to the left, past the back of the library, where the morning sun struck the stained-glass window and briefly spilled out onto the main coastal path. I gazed out beyond the rich-turquoise North Atlantic.

SCARLETT DUNMORE

Toward life beyond the island. I wondered if people knew what was happening here, if they'd heard on the news, or if everything was being hushed up so as not to harm Harrogate's enrollment and success rates. I'd bet anything on the latter.

The cold wind buffeted me, and I shivered. Behind, I heard the familiar snapping, popping, and wailing of Hannah, and the wheezing and gurgling of Sarah, as all three ghosts trailed behind me.

"You can't ignore us forever," Meghan called to me.

Why did this one have to talk? She could have at least fallen mouth-first onto the fence. I placed my hands over my ears and continued on to the friary. But she started yelling louder and louder. "I know you can hear me!"

"You're not real," I mouthed, my hands still pressed to my ears.

Soon she started dancing around, circling her arms up in the air, the iron spike sticking out of her chest. I ignored her and tried to focus on the path, on the crunching of gravel and sand beneath my shoes.

She opened her mouth and began projecting vocal noises into the ocean-thick air—lip trills, tongue-twisters, and something that involved flapping her tongue around. I pressed harder until my temples began to ache under the pressure. What if I saw these visions for the rest of my life, forever hearing their choking sounds and popping bones? What if Meghan practiced her vocal warm-ups at

HOW TO SURVIVE A HORROR MOVIE

2 a.m., trained to project from years of Theater Club? What then? I could stick a knitting needle in my ears, try to permanently deafen myself, although that seemed quite extreme. Maybe investing in a pair of high-end noise-canceling headphones would be more reasonable.

Meghan began waving her man-sized hands in front of my face, making it difficult for me to walk. I couldn't see past them, so I started stumbling over rocks, gradually veering farther and farther off the path. "Stop it," I grunted, tripping over myself. I couldn't see the path anymore; all I could see was Meghan, with Blyth's herb fence sticking out of her. "Go away!" I pitched forward.

Suddenly, hands gripped my shoulders. I screamed and slowly dropped my hands from my ears. I gazed down, wind whipping at my face. I was hundreds of meters from the friary path, standing far too close to the cliff edge. Another step and I would have fallen, hitting the rocks and breaking my neck like Hannah Manning. Maybe I'd have returned a ghost, too, and spooked Olive, maybe Nurse Clare, to show her how real it all was. And most definitely Rochelle. Just for fun.

Down below the ocean thrashed and threatened. Gentle hands pulled me back from the edge, and when I slowly turned around I saw strands of red hair floating in the wind. Then those deep-green eyes and that freckled nose.

"Walking a bit close to the edge, aren't you?" Saoirse finally said. Her voice had a lovely rhythm to it, going up slightly at the end, like a trill played on a piano. "Are you OK?"

"Um . . . um . . ." Was this really about to be our first conversation? I had to say something cool. "Um . . ." Why was I struggling to say something cool? "There was a bee," I blurted out.

She raised an eyebrow. "A bee?"

"Yeah, I was trying to swat it away and veered off the path."

"Because of the bee?" She looked around, searching for it.

"It was trying to get in my ears," I added.

"Is it gone now?"

"It's gone now."

"Good, now you won't plummet off the cliff."

"Death by bumblebee," I snorted, immediately wishing the ground would swallow me whole.

"Heading up for service, or just out for a walk?"

"I thought I'd pop into the service, you know, see what all the hype is about." I shrugged, not wanting to add that I was hoping to absolve myself of all my sins so I would stop being haunted by dead girls.

"I'll walk with you." She smiled, and I smiled back, wondering if I had any raspberry seeds in between my teeth from the breakfast jam. We walked slowly together, returning to the path. Soon it started to rise, taking us a little closer to the clouds. Strangely, I couldn't hear the ghosts anymore, just the thudding of my own heart.

"I'm Saoirse, by the way," she said as the friary came into sight.

"I know. I'm Charley."

"You're new, right? You transferred this year?"

"Just before the summer. May, actually."

"Ouch. Tough time to transfer."

"Yep." I smiled.

"Couldn't wait till August?"

"My mom was in a hurry to get me in here." She nodded and kicked at a rock on the path. "She got a new job," I quickly added.

"Well, I've been here since day one, very boring."

"As someone who's spent most of her academic life in mixed-gender city schools, I can say you're not missing much."

We walked up to the steps, and I slowed my pace, desperately wanting to prolong the conversation. "Did any of your family go to Harrogate too?"

"Nah, just me. My parents went to school in the city, and they turned out OK, so not sure why I was sent here."

We reached the friary doors and glanced around. Most of the pews were already occupied by students. I hoped for a spot where we could sit together, continue the conversation, maybe even arrange to hang out. I still needed a date for the Halloween formal. A *real* date. Olive didn't count.

"Where do you want to sit?" I asked her.

"Saoirse!"

I glanced up and saw a couple of fifth-year girls waving to her from the front pew. "Um." She looked at me, then looked at her friends.

"On you go," I said. "I'm not much of a front-pew kind of person. Besides, I don't know if I'll stay the whole time. I might sneak out early."

She nodded. "Well, it was nice to meet you, Charley. Stay away from bees and cliff edges."

I snorted again. She was *really* funny. "Will do."

As she joined the group at the front, I plopped down on the end of a back pew, the cold ocean draft from under the door poking at my back. Across the aisle, I saw the slim figure of Rochelle in a dress so tight it looked like it had been painted on by the Art Club. Beside her sat the other two Elles, along with a couple of guys from Eden. Gabrielle giggled loudly as one of them whispered in her ear. I could smell her perfume from back here and immediately began coughing. Ghost Meghan shushed me.

As seabirds flocked and squawked over the friary roof, the service began. The minister talked about the deaths of Hannah, Sarah, and Meghan before branching out into a much wider discussion about loss, life, and healing.

HOW TO SURVIVE A HORROR MOVIE

Hannah floated in the front, softly crying while trying to touch the minister, while Sarah drifted up and down the pews, likely looking for her Eden boyfriend. Meghan, on the other hand, hovered contentedly in the back, continuing her Theater Club vocal warm-ups. Quieter this time, thankfully.

I checked my watch several times during the service, wondering how sixty minutes felt like six hundred, and then finally it was over. When the students began filing out, excited for the main event of today, which was a conversation with the opposite sex on the friary grounds before they headed back to the dorms, I pretended to tie my shoelaces, stalling my exit. Saoirse smiled softly as she walked past, arm in arm with a friend. I waved weakly. After the last student left, I straightened up and slowly walked to the front. My footsteps were loud in the aisle and echoed off the stone walls and sculpted saints. I caught the eye of one statue, a bearded man hunched over a staff of some kind, like a character from *The Lord of the Rings*. His eyes followed me as I walked. Before I knew it, I'd walked right into the back of the minister.

He startled and turned to meet me. "New face," he said finally, moving back to give us space.

I contemplated saying that I always came, and sat in the back unnoticed, but then I realized he'd see through that lie, so I nodded instead. "Sorry to bother you, but can I talk to you for a moment? Maybe in the confessions box?

I could, like, declare my sins out loud so everyone, spirits and all, could hear?"

"We don't have a confessions box here. This is a non-denominational community," he said, gesturing to the chapel, to the empty pews and the marbled ledges.

My shoulders dropped. This was my last hope.

"However," he added, "we can grab a seat right here and you can tell me if anything is bothering you."

I nodded and tentatively sat down in the first pew beside him. "I, um, don't know how to say this . . . I think I'm being haunted by ghosts."

"OK," he said slowly. "Well, the last week or so at Harrogate has been very hard on you girls, and it's normal to experience thoughts and maybe visions at a time like this."

"I know, I saw the nurse and she said the same thing. But the ghosts aren't going away. In fact, they're getting louder and harder to ignore, and I was wondering if I did this somehow. If I'm being *punished*."

I thought about the life I used to have. The mistakes I made, the ones that haunted me at night like the ghosts were doing now. Maybe this was karma and I deserved it. Everything just changed after Dad died. I didn't know who I was anymore, and I didn't want to feel, so I started going to parties, drinking. And then came the drugs, the stealing, the lies. I was just numb, and whatever I was doing helped in some strange and toxic way. But then I was caught, and while I sat in the jail cell overnight, I saw *something*. Something I didn't tell anyone about.

I saw my dad.

I knew it was crazy because he was dead. But I saw him. He was as clear as the steel bars in the tiny juvenile jail cell where they held me. He stood in the corner of the cell, partially submerged in shadow. His eyes were fixed on me and his arms were still, his hands no longer trembling from pain. A sound crept into the room, dancing between the bars. It was a high-pitched beep followed by a clock ticking and something that sounded like decompressing air. Those were the last noises I'd heard in my dad's hospital room as he lay hooked up to all of the monitors and machines like some android from a science-fiction movie. I said his name loudly, then he disappeared. Vanished. And I never saw him again. I occasionally heard the sounds—the beeping and whizzing of air, the tick-tick-ticking of a clock—but I never saw my dad again.

After that, I sat in the cell for hours, the shadows of night pressing on the space around me. And I thought about Mom all alone, and about the future I was throwing away, one Dad had worked two jobs for. So, the next morning when the police and the social worker offered me a deal, I took it. I answered their questions, and I talked and talked. I said things, anything, to get myself off. But I didn't fully comprehend what the consequences would be, and people turned on me, called me a snitch. School became unbearable after that, and suddenly life on an isolated island, far away from the people who hated me, was remarkably appealing.

"If ignoring the ghosts hasn't helped," he continued, "then I'd suggest *not* ignoring them. Look them straight in the eye and acknowledge them, and maybe ask them what they want. Maybe they need help, just like us."

I thought about my dad again, about seeing him in that cell corner. Maybe I wasn't hallucinating. Maybe I had some kind of a gift. Maybe I really was that little boy from *The Sixth Sense*.

"You want me to talk to the ghosts I'm seeing?"

"Finally," Meghan exclaimed from the back pews.

"Yes, why not?" he said.

I nodded, my belly churning at the thought of facing them, looking at them directly without screaming the dorms down. But if there was a chance that they would go *poof!* and disappear or walk away toward a lovely warm light, then I'd do it.

"Thank you," I said. "That actually helped a lot."

"Good. See you next Sunday?"

I nodded awkwardly and squeezed past him out of the pew. Then I jogged all the way back to Harrogate, the wind hitting my face. My legs throbbed from the unwanted exercise on a Sunday morning, but didn't buckle. When I got back, I was relieved to find my dorm empty. Olive was likely hiding in a stack of books in a corner of the library. I shut the door, pulled the curtains closed, and stood in the middle of the room, then took a deep breath, clenched my belly, and readied myself.

The wind howled at the window, scratching to get inside. A dull buzzing from my laptop filled the room. "Hello . . . Ghosts? Are you there?"

A clatter from the hallway twirled me around to the door, where I heard the muffled voices of students walking back to their dorm rooms. When I turned back, the face of dead Sarah Keenan stared at me, eyes wide and empty, neck broken and hanging down, a red rope around her throat with a small trickle of blood oozing down and dripping onto her chest.

Drip. Drip. Drip.

I inhaled sharply, my stomach churning.

Meghan appeared beside her, the iron spike protruding from her ribs, blood spattered across her tight white T-shirt that had the words "Dream Big" displayed across it in happy yellow lettering. "Well, well, look who decided to speak to us," she scoffed.

I swallowed the lump in my throat. "I've been thinking. For some unknown reason only I can see you, and unless I am actually going insane or have a brain tumor like I initially suspected, that means that maybe only I can help you."

"What are you saying?"

"I'm saying—and please don't make me regret this—I'm saying, I'll help you. I'll help you get on your way to the light, or whatever."

Her eyes glinted, and suddenly the corpse of Hannah Manning stood beside her, her neck still twisted from the fall, her mouth full of what I hoped wasn't a crab. Again, my belly flipped and curdled, my organs and partially digested beef tacos from the night before turning to mush. I swallowed down the bile and took a deep breath.

"Does that mean you'll stop ignoring us now?" Meghan asked.

"Yeah, I guess."

"Cool."

"Cool," I repeated.

Rule #12

AVOID EMPTY STAIRWELLS

I remembered the boat ride across to the island on my first day here, how I felt with the mainland at my back and this in front of me—a dark foreboding piece of land jutting out of the North Atlantic. Harrogate School for Girls towered over the ocean, sitting high on the rock looking down menacingly like a gargoyle perched on a cathedral. Turrets and stained-glass windows, wrought-iron gates and old masonry. It sat so close to the cliff edge that I worried it would tip and fall with me inside, along with my cherished Stephen King hardcover editions.

As the boat drew nearer, everything got bigger—the school, the friary, the rock it sat on, the pressure on me to succeed here. And I remembered suddenly feeling so insignificant and small, sitting on the boat with my feet crossed and my hands in my lap, with my little raincoat zipped up to my chin. I was starting a new life here and had told myself things would be different, that I'd participate in everything, and be present and smile all the time so people thought I was happy. But the darkness still sat inside me, like a little balloon in my belly, slowly swelling, threatening to burst at any moment. I'd be a good girl here. A better student, a better daughter, a better friend, and a better girlfriend.

We sailed for about thirty minutes, slicing through dark waters and rough winds, my yellow roller suitcase sitting beside me on the bench, sliding back and forth on the rocky seas. Then the ocean started turning a deep turquoise, shimmering in the May sun. My hair tangled in the moist salty air and soon crusted to my cheeks and forehead. I wondered whether my mother's lipstick was still visible on my forehead from where she'd kissed me goodbye at the docks. She'd wanted to come across with me in the boat, but I thought that would make it harder to watch her leave. This way I was leaving her, which reminded me that I *wanted* to be here, that my old school had become so unbearable that this was the best option for me if I was to have any chance of getting into a university and forgetting my past. Yet a small part of me, deep down inside, had begged me not to get on the boat.

I never knew why that was, until today.

"Tell me again what happened, slower this time?" I gasped, needing to hear the words again as I sat cross-legged on my bedroom floor, in front of the wall with my

Stephen King posters tacked onto it. Olive would be gone for at least another hour.

Impaled Meghan sat opposite me, the metal fence spike sticking out of her torso and resting on her knees. Thankfully, after about ten minutes I stopped staring at it. I'd asked Hannah and Sarah to go to another room as I'd found Sarah's broken neck and the crab leg sticking out of Hannah's mouth just too damn distracting.

"We've been through this," moaned Meghan.

"Please, one more time. I just can't get my head around it. It doesn't make any sense."

"Fine. I was downstairs in the gym with the Theater Club preparing for our November performance of—"

"*The Crucible*, yeah, yeah, I know. I'm in the Theater Club with you."

"You are?" she exclaimed, her eyes wide.

"Yes, I'm glad my presence has been noticed," I muttered. "Did you play Toto in *The Wizard of Oz* last spring?"

"No, I—"

"No, don't tell me, you were one of the munchkin villagers?"

"No, I'm—"

"Were you the winged monkey?"

"No, I'm on props. I'm currently decorating a sequin curtain, although I'm not entirely sure where velvet and sequins fit into the Salem witch trials."

"Oh, props!" she said, nodding. She remembered me, I think. "Well, that's not exactly Theater Club."

"Yes, it is," I corrected her.

"No, not really."

"I'm *in* the Theater Club."

She scrunched up her nose. "Have you ever *performed*?"

"Well, no, but—"

"See?"

"But I'm decorating a curtain."

"Yeah, not the same thing."

"I'm in the Theater Club!" I yelled.

"You're in the Theater *Prop* Club."

"No, I'm in the real Theater Club, the one and only, the same one as you . . . Wait, why are we debating this?! OK, back to your story."

"So, I was in the gym practicing lines as us *performers* of the Theater Club do—"

I groaned.

"But I couldn't hear myself because it was so loud in there, and someone had bumped up the heat. Heat gives me this really ugly rash on my neck."

"Yeah, it was unusually warm in the gym that day."

"Anyway, like I said I don't deal with heat that well, everyone knows that, so I went out into the hall to get some air, but I could still hear the noise and clatter from inside, so I went into the stairwell. I started going over my lines—did you know I got the part of John Proctor?

HOW TO SURVIVE A HORROR MOVIE

At first, I was raging: Asking me to play a man? Do I look like a man? But then I saw that Proctor is the lead character and he has more lines than anyone, so I was fine after that . . . Oh no, I'm not the lead anymore! It'll go to Rochelle!" She buried her face in her hands and wailed.

"Rochelle's in the Theater Club? I didn't see her that day."

"She's in all the clubs but doesn't actually attend them. She just wants to list them on her CV. She's in the French Club but she can't even say *Je m'appelle Rochelle*!"

"OK, anyway, back to the story, you're outside the hall—"

"No, I'm in the stairwell now."

"Fine! You're in the stairwell, then . . . ?"

"Then I hear a noise, like a clatter of something dropping on the stairs. I look up the staircase but don't see anything. I shout to see if anyone's there, but nothing. So, I carry on; at this point I'm about halfway through John Proctor's big monologue, you know the one?"

"No, but back to the—"

She stands up. *"A man may think God sleeps, but God sees everything. I know it now. I beg you, sir, I beg you—see her what she is!"*

"Meghan!" I exclaimed. I had been forced to watch two performances of *The Crucible* at my last school, I didn't need to sit through another.

"Anyway," she continued, much to my relief, "I heard more strange noises, and went upstairs to investigate—"

"Sorry, now I have to interrupt. You were in an empty stairwell alone and you heard strange noises and you went to *investigate?*"

"Yes," she said slowly, dragging out the *s* annoyingly.

"Haven't you ever seen a horror movie? Avoid isolated stairwells and never ever investigate strange noises; in fact, run from them!"

"Now who's getting worked up? And, no, I've never seen a horror movie. We live on an island in the middle of nowhere. I don't need anything scarier than that."

"True," I mumbled.

"So, I went up the stairs to the roof access door and it was open. It's always locked, ever since the Eden boys snuck up there one night and smoked weed. I saw something on the ledge of the roof, like a black hoodie, so I walked up to it to bring it down to lost and found, and that's when I felt a push from behind. Like a hard push."

"Someone *pushed* you?"

"Someone pushed me off the roof. I didn't jump! I'm so sick of people saying that I jumped. Why would I? I'm going to the Gaiety School of Acting next summer! I'm practically on my way to the BAFTAs," she cried, flicking her hair back. "I'm like the next Margot Robbie!"

A quip danced on my tongue but I swallowed it down. "So, you didn't jump?"

"No!" She flung her arms up in the air.

"And Hannah and Sarah?"

"They didn't take their own lives either."

I shuddered. "How do you know that? Can they talk to you?"

"No, but they nod and grunt and moan if I ask questions. Hannah mostly cries." Meghan leaned in and whispered, "I don't think she's taking the whole ghost thing too well."

"Are they here now?"

"No, because you told them to leave."

"They were grossing me out. I have a very weak stomach."

She rolled her eyes. "Yet you watch horror movies?"

"That's just red food coloring and corn syrup."

"Yuck."

"Where do you all go when you're not floating about here, making me gag?" I asked.

"We can't go far. We're stuck to you for some reason. But we can go to the next room sometimes." She floated to the door, then launched herself forward, leaving only her denim-clad bottom behind. I scrunched up my nose and glanced away, out of politeness. "They're just out in the hallway," she called back to me. She pulled her head through the wall, her blond hair bouncing off her shoulders. She clutched her temples. "Head rush."

I tilted my head and squinted at her. "Do you guys have to do what I tell you? Like, can I command you to do things?"

She snorted. "You wish."

I straightened up. "Stand on one leg."

Meghan stared at me, her eyebrows furrowed. "That's the best you got? If you could command us to do anything, you'd just tell us to stand on one leg? First, I did a lot of one-legged squats on Friday at the gym, and I don't fancy doing more, and second, like I said, you wish. *You* stand on one leg."

"I don't want to stand on one leg."

"Well, why would I want to stand on one leg?"

"I know you don't *want* to stand on one leg, I was just testing—" I shook my head and put my hands up in defeat. "Never mind, we're getting sidetracked here. There are more important things to focus on." I took a deep breath and turned slowly to the hallway, to the students beyond. "For starters, there's a serial killer here at Harrogate."

Hannah and Sarah floated in, stopping by Meghan's side. They looked fierce, their eyes wide and ablaze. The anger shimmered and radiated off Hannah's skin. Either that or the salt water.

"So, what do we do?" Meghan asked, her hands on her hips.

"We take it all the way to the top." I pointed up to the ceiling.

Meghan looked up. "You do know Blyth is across the courtyard, not upstairs, yeah?"

Rule #13
LIMIT THE POSSIBILITY OF MASS CHAOS

"Murdered?" repeated Headmistress Blyth for the fourth time. She exchanged glances with Mr. Gillies, who stood beside her, his hands in his trouser pockets, his tie slightly crooked.

"Yes, murdered." I nodded slowly, suddenly very aware of the buzzing of her computer screen and the tapping of a keyboard outside her office. The secretary probably had a lot of emails from anxious parents to respond to.

"Miss Sullivan, I have heard that you and your roommate have an overactive imagination, possibly fueled by your interest in scary movies. However, this is real life."

"Three people have been murdered!"

"Three people have taken their own lives. Tragic, yes, but very different from murder," Mr. Gillies interjected, his voice firm.

"But that's what I'm saying. These deaths weren't suicides. There's a serial killer here in the school!"

"A serial killer?" Blyth protested. "Miss Sullivan, have you heard yourself?"

"I think we need to call the police, get them involved, close the school to prevent more killings, send everyone home—"

"Ah." She nodded, sitting back in her chair. "I see what this is about." She glanced over to Mr. Gillies. "Martin, will you give us a moment, please?"

Mr. Gillies looked furious, either at being called Martin again in front of a student or at being kicked out of the conversation. His eyes grew dark and he tightened his jaw, his mouth thinning into a line, but then his face softened and he nodded before quickly leaving.

Blyth leaned forward, her coffee breath striking me. "You know, you may be surprised but you're not the only student to sit in my office and fabricate some ridiculous story for the purpose of getting back home. Island life isn't for everyone. It's a different kind of living out here. It's not like the city at all."

"That's not what's happening here, Headmistress."

"This is not a prison, Miss Sullivan. You are free to leave whenever you choose. This is a boarding school where serious students come to focus on their academic work, their extracurricular interests, and their futures. However, if you'd rather return to the juvenile detention center, then I can certainly make a call and arrange for Mr. Terry to take you over to the mainland tomorrow."

HOW TO SURVIVE A HORROR MOVIE

I gasped, my face draining of color, my blood chilling.

"Yes, I know, Charlotte—or is it Lottie you were called back home? I knew even before you came here. Do you really think we don't do background checks on our students and their families? I knew your history, and I also knew you were out of options. You're not here because of money or grades. You're here because I happen to know your aunt Rhoda. In fact, she and I were former schoolmates here, and are still friends."

"I didn't know that."

"I asked her not to mention it. I wanted this truly to be a fresh start for you, and if you needed to change your name to hide your past, then fine; whatever it took for you to really buckle down and concentrate on your studies for your final year. But then I hear you're showing up late to your classes, you're almost failing PE and English, you're not making friends, and now this?" She sighed. "Contrary to what your peers may say, I'm not a battle-axe, Miss Sullivan. I'm strict because I have to be. I'm responsible for the well-being of five hundred young girls on an isolated rock in the middle of the North Atlantic." She clasped her hands tightly. "Do you know what the students from Eden School call my girls now? The Suicide Squad."

"That's actually not bad," I muttered. Eden boys were more imaginative than I gave them credit for.

"It *is* bad, it is very bad, especially if this reaches the media. Harrogate will be closed indefinitely, and I have fought hard to keep this place afloat, and sacrificed more than you will ever comprehend," she said, her eyes glistening. "And for many of these girls, they will be returned to homes and lives they came here to get away from. Not everyone is from a loving family like yours. There's a reason Harrogate runs a summer program for some students. It's for those who can't return home for their own safety, and for those whose families don't want them back. They have nowhere else to go. Harrogate is their home. Let's keep it that way."

I gazed out the window at the students clustered in the courtyard, some perched on the water fountain, animatedly talking with their friends, sharing stories, others sitting on blankets on the grass with heavy hardbacks on their laps. It was a milder day today, one more reminiscent of autumns spent back home on the mainland, surrounded by trees bearing leaves of copper, amber, and speckled gold. I missed the walks into the hills with my dad on weekends, the sound of his voice when he found acorns that hadn't been crushed under boots, and how he always picked a single leaf to bring back home to Mom. The perfect leaf. One that still held the shimmers of perfect foliage. And how he rested it on the dashboard of the car as he drove us home, back into the city, to the bustling traffic and glass buildings. I never understood why my parents chose to live in the city when they loved the outdoors so much. My dad would have loved it here, all rugged and rural.

HOW TO SURVIVE A HORROR MOVIE

Outside in the hallway, the first bell rang out, shattering the heavy silence in the room. "When was the last time you called your mom?" she asked.

"Maybe two weeks ago."

"What class do you have now?"

"Wood shop. I'm making a DVD tower for my room."

"I'll tell Mr. Gillies you're going to be a bit late this morning," she said, standing up. She pushed her phone toward me. "I want you to call your mother."

I waited until the door clicked closed, took a deep breath, and dialed my mom's cell phone, slowly punching in each number. The line crackled, typical island reception, then went straight to voicemail. I tried the landline, hoping she'd be home. A low ringing vibrated in my ear. After about five rings, our old answering machine clicked in.

"*This is Fiona Ryan. Sorry I'm not in to take your call*— Hello? I'm here! Hello?"

"Mom?"

"Lottie? . . . *just leave your name and number and . . .* Hold on, I'm trying to switch off this damn machine . . . *I'll get back to you when I can . . .* Stop!"

Silence set in as the machine clicked off. "Lottie?"

"Mom?"

"Oh, good, I thought I'd hung up on you there! Finally, I get to talk to my daughter!"

"Sorry, it's been crazy here."

"Why, what's going on?"

"You haven't heard anything?"

"Heard about what?"

Well, Headmistress Blyth had succeeded in keeping the deaths out of the media, then. I wondered how she'd managed to convince the families of Hannah, Sarah, and Meghan to keep quiet.

"Nothing," I lied. "It's just a busy time for all of us. There's this stupid academic debate thing, plus preliminary exams are coming up and all that."

"Well, don't get too stressed about it. And make use of the after-school tutoring program if you need to. I heard it's very good."

"I will."

"How's Olive?"

"She's good."

"Say hi from me."

"Will do."

"Are you eating well? Sleeping OK? Getting enough hydration?" Typical nurse, always asking me about my health.

"Yes, yes, and yes."

"I'm just popping to the post office with a care package for you—some of your favorites from home, plus the new Stephen King book you've been asking the library for."

"Aw, thanks, although I should receive that by Christmas." I laughed.

"You really are living on an island, eh?"

"Yep, they love to talk about 'island life' and 'island time' here."

"I miss you."

"I miss you too, Mom."

"Only nine weeks until Christmas break, not that I'm counting or anything."

I laughed. I'd missed my mom's voice more than I'd realized. I really wanted to tell her everything—the deaths, the ghosts. But I knew as soon as I did, she'd be on the first boat out here to get me. And I couldn't leave, not yet. I had to do something. No one believed me, which meant there'd be more deaths, more killings, more students not returning home for Christmas break. And since I was the only one who could see the ghosts, I was the only one who could stop this. If we were the Suicide Squad here at Harrogate, then I was Harley Quinn: cunning, smart, passionate, headstrong . . . hopefully a little more even tempered, though.

Rule #14

INTERVIEW WITNESSES— EVEN IF THEY'RE DEAD

School was in session.

Technically school had always been in session, but this was a very different kind of lesson, because today I was learning from *ghosts*.

Yes, that sounds crazy.

While Olive frantically took notes on Voltaire in the library, I stood in the center of our bedroom. A large white sheet of poster paper was taped onto the back of the door. In my hand was one black marker and one orange one, fitting for Halloween, I thought, although perhaps a touch overdramatic. Hannah, Sarah, and Meghan sat cross-legged in front of me. Hannah was a bit too close. Her rock-smashed face made the eggs in my stomach churn and curdle.

"So, Meghan, you first—what do you remember about the person who pushed you?"

"Not much."

HOW TO SURVIVE A HORROR MOVIE

I sighed and crossed the floor to my bed to slide out my emergency stash of sodas. I was going to need the sugar and caffeine hit. I offered one to Hannah and Sarah, who shook their heads, painfully and awkwardly, then mindlessly tossed one to Meghan. She held her hands out to catch it, a smile spreading across her face. It sailed through her ghost fingers, then her torso and hit Olive's bed behind her.

She glared at me. "Seriously?"

"Sorry." I winced. My fingers caught the edge of the ring and pulled it back, the fizz releasing with a pop, much like the sound of Hannah's bones. I put the can to my lips and gulped thirstily, then wiped my mouth. "That's good." The ghosts scowled at me. "Sorry," I muttered again, putting the can down and getting back to the poster. "So was the person my height? Smaller? Taller?"

"Um, maybe a little taller?" said Meghan. "But it's hard to tell. I didn't get a good look at them."

"What were they wearing?"

"I remember dark clothes, and when I fell, I remember looking up and seeing a gold face staring down at me. It was strange, like I was suspended in the air, just floating for a moment. Then . . . ouch," she said, touching the spike through her torso.

"A *gold* face?"

"Yeah, I think so."

"Creepy," I murmured, feeling a shiver building at the base of my spine.

"Yeah, creepy."

"So, what do you remember, Sarah?"

She opened her mouth to talk, but all that came out was gurgling and wheezing. The noose round her neck was still tight.

"She can't talk, remember?"

"I know," I said to Meghan. "Sarah, can you shake your head or nod *yes*?"

She tried to wiggle, the small bones in her neck crackling as she did so. My breakfast immediately curdled in my stomach. I should never have opted for the creamy scrambled eggs. Dry toast and water tomorrow. I swallowed hard. "Does this sound like the person you saw too?"

She cracked her head up to the sky, then a sharp bone popped out as she dropped it back down. I clutched my stomach.

"I think she's nodding," Meghan suggested. "I've done a lot of theater training on nonverbal cues."

I ignored her and carried on addressing Sarah. "You remember a gold face too? And black clothing?"

Again, her bent crooked neck shot up and then down, awkwardly and painfully. "Great, we're communicating!" I exclaimed. "OK, how about you, Hannah?"

She leaned forward, the popping and crushing of her bones loudly filling the room. I took a deep breath and looked at her. Was that part of her jaw hanging off? "Excuse me," I muttered, rushing to the sink. Yep, up came the creamy scrambled eggs. And a mushroom. I wiped my mouth and tried my best to wash away the remnants of my breakfast from the sink, then gazed at the poster on the door. All I had written down was:

Black Hoodie
Over 5′5″
Gold Face (Mask?)

"Hannah, does that sound like the person who pushed you?"

She rose to her feet, popping, cracking, and snapping all the way to the door, then she raised a creaky arm—the other one was crushed like her jaw—and pointed to *Gold Face*.

"You remember a gold face too?" She nodded, her expression heavy, her cheeks wet with tears. "Why were you out during the storm?"

She desperately tried to part her lips, to say something. Anything. But all that came out were muffled sounds and a deep wailing. I thought about the photos I'd seen of her the days after her death. The wavy hair, the almond-shaped green eyes that were often hidden behind black-rimmed glasses. The smile, and how it pinched her cheeks. "I'm sorry this happened to you," I whispered to her. "But I'll help if I can."

Her eyes glistened, and for a moment I thought she

was going to cry again, but then she reached a hand out through the air, hovering above my palm.

I nodded and returned to the poster, the marker tight in my grip. "Were you out walking?" The bones in her neck popped and snapped as she tried to shake her head. "Were you meeting someone?"

Pop. Snap. Crack.

"Were you running from someone?" Silence. Then she slowly tried to lift a hand again. "That's a yes! You were running from someone who was chasing you. Did you see who it was?" I waited for the cracking and snapping response. "No?"

I sighed deeply. We had nothing so far except a piece of clothing that could belong to anyone and the possibility of a gold mask or some well-crafted face paint.

"So, we're looking for someone with a black hoodie and a gold face."

"We're looking for a *Harrogate student*," Meghan said, rolling her eyes.

"How do you know it's a student?"

"Who else would know the building? Or where Mr. Terry keeps the keys to the roof? And that turning up the heat in the gym would make me break out in hives? Who else would be jealous of my budding acting career?"

"That's true. Well, not that last part. But you're right, only a student would know the sixth-year class schedule. And know where and when Theater Club meet, know you get hives, know that Sarah does laps alone after netball practice on Tuesdays, and maybe even know what dorm Hannah was in." I drummed my fingers on the marker. "But we don't know yet if these were random killings or if the victims were chosen. The killer perhaps got lucky and stumbled upon three people who weren't following the survival rules."

Strangled Sarah raised a shaky hand, glancing from side to side.

"The survival rules are the basic rules we learn from horror movies," I explained to her.

"Here we go again." Meghan rolled her eyes.

I ignored her and continued, "Don't investigate strange noises. Don't go into stairwells. Lock your doors at night. Avoid empty hallways, darkened rooms, or walking through woods at night. And never ever say 'I'll be right back' and—"

"So, what you're saying is this would never be you?" Meghan said, gesturing to herself and the others. "Because you'd avoid being killed off by following these stupid rules you learned from a Hollywood horror movie where a busty blonde is being chased by a serial killer in a mask?" She snorted.

I stared at Meghan—the busty blonde who was killed by a serial killer in a mask—waiting for her to also reflect on the irony of what she just said.

Nope, she didn't get it.

SCARLETT DUNMORE

I checked my watch. We had time. I yanked the curtains closed, blocking out the afternoon sun, then marched over to my DVD collection. I skimmed a finger over the titles, stopping at a nineties classic: *Scream*. "This should do it," I muttered. The ghosts circled around me, curiously watching me operate the aging DVD player.

"What is that?" Meghan asked, prodding a finger at the machine.

"It's a DVD player."

"Don't you have Netflix at home?"

I shooed her away from the black box. "Just pay attention to the movie."

They leaned in as the opening credits flashed on-screen: a bloodred title pitched against the persistent ringing of a phone, followed by a woman's scream and the beating of a heart.

Hannah jumped and took a step back.

Opening scene: a family living room, whitewashed walls, leather hardbacks on the shelves. The lamp illuminates a phone. It rings once.

"Hello?" *answers the young blonde, home alone—*

"First rule," I announced, pausing the screen on the smiling and optimistic victim, "never answer the phone when you're home alone."

"Do you mean cell phones too? Or just those old landlines that my parents used to have?" Meghan asked.

"Cell phones too."

"What if someone's trying to reach me?"

"Someone *will* be trying to reach you." I nodded. *"The killer."*

Meghan pulled a face. "No, I mean what if someone important is trying to reach me, like my agent?"

"Next," I stated, ignoring her. I pressed Play and watched the scene unfold. "See how he's engaging her in a dangerous game? Don't play, and if you have no choice, then don't play using their rules. Make your own."

Sarah grunted and wheezed.

"Yeah, I don't get it either," Meghan grumbled. "What is she making anyway?"

"Popcorn."

"On a stove? That looks like a safety hazard."

Hannah tried to nod, her eyes wide.

"OK, let's fast-forward a little," I muttered. I stopped at the breaking of the golden rule. "Here, she's only *just* locking the doors. They should have been locked as soon as she entered the house. And here, asking 'Who's there?' when the killer knocks on her door? And here—"

"Whoa, you're getting way into this," Meghan scoffed, shaking her head.

"Going outside in the dark to try to run from a killer, when you live in the middle of nowhere? Such a bad decision," I said, waving the remote control around. Sarah ducked. She must have seen my skills in PE at some point in the school year.

SCARLETT DUNMORE

"Are you learning anything?" I asked them.

"Yeah, how not to act in a horror movie," scoffed Meghan. She turned away from me, exhaling loudly.

"What are you doing?"

She spun round, her eyes wide, her lips parted into an *O* shape. She clutched her hair and screamed, "No, Steve! Don't die!"

"Um, Meghan?" I waved my hands to stop her before she got any further into her reenactment of the scene.

She took a deep breath in and smiled. "And that's how it's done. Understated and—"

"That was understated?"

She scowled and crossed her arms while I continued fast-forwarding, pointing out all the rules of the movie, explaining when and how each character had ignored them. And ultimately lost their life because of it. Occasionally I glanced at a terrified Hannah, who was huddled in the corner, and Sarah, who was too busy looking at the items on my bookshelf. At the end, I paused on the closing credits and threw the remote down on the bed. "And that was your first lesson in movie survival." I put my hands on my hips, satisfied with the opportunity to pass on my movie wisdom.

"Do you really think anyone in real life would try to escape through a doggy door?" Meghan sniffed. "I'm no horror expert, but even I knew that was a bad decision."

HOW TO SURVIVE A HORROR MOVIE

"So, what did you think of the movie?"

"Terrible acting. Do you really not get scared watching horror movies all the time?"

Hannah stood in the corner with her hands still over her eyes.

I shook my head. "To me, that's not scary. In fact, I'm very rarely spooked—" Suddenly the door flew open, slamming against the wall. I screamed and all three ghosts quickly vanished. "Olive! It's just you!" I gasped, clutching my chest.

Behind me, the cupboard rustled with moans and groans. Meghan's pitchy voice spilled out from under the door, "Hannah, you need to move over more. Ouch, Sarah, that's my foot!"

I shushed them, then quickly remembered Olive couldn't hear them anyway.

"Sorry. I had to kick it open," she said. She was balancing a large stack of textbooks in her arms plus a coffee cup and her backpack.

I jumped up and saved the coffee cup, not wanting her to spill an entire caramel latte onto our dorm carpet. Again.

"Thanks." She glanced at the TV screen, which was paused on the final scene. "What's this? Are you watching *Scream* without me?" She turned to kick the door shut, then stared at my very pathetic summary of today's findings written on the poster paper. "Charley, what is going on?"

"I'm trying to find out who the Harrogate serial killer is."

"What?" she said slowly. "How did we go from three tragic suicides to a *Scream* plot?"

"Hannah didn't jump, she was running from someone, someone who had entered her dorm at night—which was unlocked, I should add. Sarah was hung up like it was a suicide but she was murdered. And Meghan was pushed from the roof. She was practicing her lines and heard a noise, then saw someone."

"OK . . . and how do you know all this?"

"Um . . ."

"Please don't say the ghosts told you. I thought that was all over, Charley," she said, shaking her head.

Olive was my friend, but she also cared about me, so if she didn't believe me then she might worry about my mental health and report it. Then I'd be sent back to the mainland, back to therapy, and maybe back home. I couldn't go home. I needed to be here. I needed to solve this. I was the only one these ghost girls were talking to.

"Don't ask me how I know. I just know."

Olive slumped back, a frown forming on her pale, freckled face.

"Please," I begged, reaching for her hand. "As a friend, my best friend, please just believe me."

"OK, let's table that one for now," she said. "So, what do you have so far?" She jumped up and started reading the list.

"Not much, I know."

"You think the killer wears a gold mask?"

"I think so, but I'm not sure yet."

"Why a mask?" she asked. "Seems a little overkill, excuse the pun."

"Because this is clearly someone who wants the drama, the notoriety, the attention. And if we use our horror movie knowledge, we know better than anyone that a costume can really make or break a killer."

She gestured to the TV screen. "*Scream*—such an epic costume."

I nodded. "Ghostface was *the* costume for a Halloween party, especially at house parties."

"*Halloween.*"

"The Captain Kirk mask—another wardrobe essential. A hockey mask in *Friday the 13th.*"

"*The Prowler.* Early eighties—"

"Yes, the Second World War gear. Also, do you remember *Girls Nite Out?*"

"I forgot about that bear costume! Creepy. Don't forget *Texas Chainsaw Massacre*. I mean, his mask was made from his victims' skin."

Olive shuddered. "I know *Carrie* technically doesn't count, but Sissy Spacek wore that blood like a mask." She plopped down on the bed and looked at me. "Charley, I know you don't want to hear this, but I think we should go to Blyth."

"No—"

"If this is true, this is information she needs to have! And the police!"

"Olive, we can't! Remember in *A Nightmare on Elm Street* when Nancy tried to tell her parents the truth and they didn't believe her? They referred her to a sleep therapist! Listen to our story. It sounds as far-fetched as a disfigured man in a fedora stalking and killing teens in their sleep! No one will believe us—certainly not Blyth."

"We should at least try to convince her," Olive pleaded.

"I've already tried and it didn't go well."

"Did you mention the ghost thing to her?"

"No, of course not."

"Good. I kinda like having you as a roommate. I don't want a new one. OK, fine, so let's call the police."

"If Blyth didn't believe me, the police on the mainland certainly won't. We need something, like proof or a reliable witness that's not, um . . ."

"Don't say 'dead.'"

"I just need more time. But I don't think these were three isolated incidents. I think whoever this is will kill again."

"It's bad enough Eden boys calling us the Suicide Squad, but this?"

"I know this sounds crazy, but it makes a strange kind of sense. Something felt wrong about the deaths at the time."

Olive sighed and rubbed her forehead.

"Olive, please. I need you. I can't figure this out myself. And if I turn out to be wrong, then great. But what if I'm right, and someone else is killed?"

She stared woefully at the stack of library books on the dresser beside her, then turned back to me. "OK. Let's do this, then. Let's find the Harrogate serial killer like in the movies. Just one condition."

"Anything."

"Don't let me die, OK?"

"Deal. We'll be the final girl, well, *girls*."

"Ugh," she groaned. "Everyone hates the smug final girl. It's just too damn predictable. And also, implausible. Like, why does everyone else die except for her?"

Rule #15

KNOW YOUR ENEMY—
AND YOUR RIVALS

After Meghan's body was collected and shipped back to the mainland in a box like an Amazon package, the gossip and whisperings of a suicide pact died down (no pun intended). Things returned to normal at Harrogate School for Girls. Extracurricular activities such as Theater Club resumed as scheduled, and decorating recommenced in the gym for the Halloween formal. Orange-and-black streamers filled the hallways, balloons were taped into corners—non-latex, because Olive had a latex allergy and had apparently "ballooned up" in her first year here when she joined the decorations team (pun intended).

Halloween was nine days away, and any concerns over whether the formal was still going ahead petered out. Snippets of conversations about costumes, makeup, and footwear blew down the hallways like a crisp October breeze. Those not obsessed with Halloween and all things spooky and chilling talked fervently about the prospect of having Eden boys in our school and assembled a "lookout" committee for the night, which involved low-pitched whistles, flashlights, and hourly shifts. Some even discussed the possibility of spiking the Halloween punch, which upset Olive greatly. As the self-proclaimed head of the Halloween formal, she'd spent weeks perfecting her recipe to make it more of a "bloodred" and less of a murky brown. We named it the Carrie. But much to our dismay, these decorations we'd worked so hard on were merely pushed back against the wall for today's big academic challenge, where we were pitted against Eden. No reason, in my opinion, to pull down the streamers that had taken months to reach the island.

While Blyth frantically barked orders, shifted Halloween decor, and rearranged seating, I called my mom again, painting the picture of a perfectly normal semester at school and not one of dead bodies, ghosts, and masked maniacal killers. So far, I had no idea if she was buying it or not.

"What's all that noise?" my mom asked as I pressed the receiver into my ear to block out the cacophony bellowing through the hallway and under the door to the common room.

"It's just students getting themselves psyched up for the big academic challenge."

"What is that?"

"It's just a silly quiz between Harrogate and Eden, but Olive tells me it's the annual battle of the schools."

"Sounds like it could be fun."

Or a total waste of my time. My priorities lay elsewhere—I had a gold-faced killer to find. "I just don't have time for this at the moment." I rubbed my temples.

"Why? What's going on?"

"Um . . ."

Silence bled down the line, heavy and thick. I thought about telling my mom everything, being honest for once. But what if she didn't believe me? What if I had lied one too many times? What would happen to me if Harrogate was shut down? Where would I go then? Back to juvenile detention with my old friends who I snitched on? Back to Sadie?

"Lottie . . . I mean, Charley, are you OK? You seem off."

"I'm just tired," I muttered, instinctively touching the gold "S" necklace around my neck, trying not to think of who I left behind back home, of who I abandoned in my desperation for freedom and absolution.

"Tired? Why?"

"It's uh . . . loud in my room." Strangled Sarah and Impaled Meghan squeezed into the phone box, pressing me against the glass.

"Sorry, thought I heard my name," muttered Meghan, elbowing Sarah off her. Beyond the glass, Half-Broken Hannah stood outside, wistfully gazing at the students who passed through her. Then she joined us inside the box.

"Is Olive a loud sleeper?" asked my mom.

Olive's snores actually seemed to blend rather harmonically

with the popping of bone and the squelching of hanging flesh. All of which was keeping me up at night, every night. My eyes were merely black holes on a face of ash and gray. I was wandering through a sleep fog most days, not entirely sure whether I was dreaming or awake.

"I can hear other students," I finally answered, glaring at the three ghosts who pushed and shoved each other for space. Beyond the confines of the cubicle, a flurry of excited students dressed in Harrogate green hurried past. I elbowed Impaled Meghan, feeling a gust of ice on my arm, while trying to loop a scarf around my neck adorned with Harrogate's school crest, crushed that it was ruining my sleuth vibe, and readied myself. "Mom, I've got to go. It's starting soon."

"Lottie?"

"Yeah, Mom?"

"I love you. And I miss you, every day."

Warmth pricked the corners of my eyes and I took a deep breath in, trying to calm my pounding heart. "I love you too. I'll be home soon." I quickly hung up the phone, stopping her from saying anything else that might cut deep, and walked out into the common room, into the hallway, joining a trickle of girls heading toward the gym. I searched for Olive's curly mop in the sea of students but couldn't see her.

Suddenly, a red mane was bouncing up and down in front of me. Saoirse.

SCARLETT DUNMORE

I smoothed down my hair, tucking any rogue strands behind my ear, and started moving faster, ducking around people, squeezing past arms and under swinging textbooks. She was walking less than a meter ahead of me now, the lemon and oak scent of her shampoo filling my nostrils. We could finally continue our conversation from before, and it would be a perfect opportunity to ask her to the Halloween formal and make my feelings crystal clear. She would either say yes, and I'd know she felt the same way, or she'd say no, and I could spend the rest of the school year crying in my dorm room while being haunted by ghosts. How would I start the conversation? A simple "Hello"? No, I'd casually say "Oh, hey, you again," like I hadn't noticed her, then ask her about her category while avoiding spilling the fact that I'd had a crush on her for four whole months and that I dreamed about her most nights. Her and mangled corpses.

I cleared my throat. She turned her head to the right like she'd heard me, and so I opened my mouth to speak—

"Ugh!" A hard blow to my stomach doubled me over. My arms draped over a big black smelly bag. Moldy food, dorm-room trash, and sickly sweet crushed juice cans stared up at me. I had walked into a trash bin. Of course.

My toes throbbed from where I'd stubbed them, and my belly ached from catching the edge of the bin. Had I hit it any harder I might have tipped into it headfirst.

"Are you OK?"

HOW TO SURVIVE A HORROR MOVIE

I looked up and saw Saoirse standing over me, her long red hair slightly curling at the ends.

It was then I realized it looked like I was *hugging* the bin.

"What are you doing?" she asked, a glimmer of a smile creeping onto her face.

I stared, momentarily transfixed by the deep pools of sea green that swirled in her irises. She stood, waiting.

"Oh . . . um . . . I'm just looking for recycling," I replied slowly, feeling my cheeks flush. She frowned slightly. I'd already said it now, so I had to commit to my stupid answer. I braced myself and dug my hands into the bin, past the sticky sides of the black plastic and fingered my way through wrappers and half-eaten apple cores. I plucked a juice can out to show her, and smiled awkwardly.

She frowned more.

"I'm chairing a committee for recycling. Looking after the Earth and all that," I added.

Then she nodded and said, "That's great. Well, I'll see you in there. Good luck."

I dropped the can back into the bin and opened my mouth to say "Good luck" back, but she was already moving fast down the hallway, away from me and away from the bin. My palms were covered in something brown and gooey. I wiped them numerous times down my blazer and grimaced.

Across the hall, leaning against the lockers, stood the three ghosts. Half-Broken Hannah weakly gave me two thumbs up, Strangled Sarah gazed at me blankly, while

Impaled Meghan nodded and clapped, a wide grin spreading across her face.

"Shut up," I muttered, marching past them.

Most of the students had filed into the gym by now, so I ambled behind the last group of girls, feeling embarrassed, sticky from whatever was in the bin, but also strangely excited. Yes, I fell over a bin and, yes, I then put my hands inside it, but this was our second conversation now and in such a short time. That meant something.

"Sullivan, better late than never," barked Mr. Gillies, startling me. He seemed to have aged overnight and was more hunched, his face slightly unshaven, strands of gray in his hair. "Take your seat."

I nodded and hurried in, gawking at the sight of the two schools pressed together. Harrogate green filled the right side, while Eden mustard was crammed into the left side, exuding overconfidence. A few boys stood in the aisle, teasing the girls like we were on a playground. Boys versus girls. I rolled my eyes and made my way down the aisle, through the cheers and chants that reverberated off the walls. We sat in our previously selected category groups, our brightly colored name tags on display for the Eden students to see and choose from. Five were selected from each group to compete, chosen by the opposing team after a coin toss.

When Mr. Gillies had posted the category sign-ups, I had been disappointed to not see the category "horror film trivia" on the board. I had spent most of the morning deciding which category would be least unsuitable for me, so that by the time I went back to add my name, most of the categories were already taken. Of course, Olive had nabbed the number one spots in science, foreign languages, and mathematics, even after I reminded her that we were asked to sign up for only *one* category. By the time the lunch bell screeched through the hallways and classrooms, all that remained on the notice board were spots in geography, geology, and grammar. Apparently, Harrogate students struggled with academic subjects beginning with the letter *G*. In the end, I chose geography, mostly because that was the first one that I came across, but as I sat in Harrogate's auditorium, watching the captain of Eden's geography group hand-selecting his opponents, I began to seriously regret my choice. Geography? What was I thinking? Hopefully I'd remain in my seat, never being chosen to actually participate.

"And for our last pick, we choose her." Her who? "The girl who just came in."

I glanced from side to side. Maybe there was someone else in the geography row who'd also had an embarrassing but yet glorious encounter with their crush and thus had arrived late. Mr. Gillies cleared his throat behind me, and when I stared back, his eyes widened. He gestured to the stage. It was definitely me, then. I groaned quietly and rose from my chair. Its legs shifted and made a very unflattering sound as they scuffed the floor, making the Eden boys giggle.

SCARLETT DUNMORE

Dr. Pruitt angrily quieted them as he stood beside the stage, partially hidden by a tall speaker. I edged down the line, occasionally stepping on the feet of a fellow quizzer, and staggered ungracefully into the aisle. Eden students sat on my left, row after row of glossy groomed hair, crisp white shirts under vests, and mustard blazers adorned with the school's coat of arms and signature motto, *Floreat Edena*. Latin for "May Eden Flourish." On my right were the girls of Harrogate, all made up like they were going to prom, with thick smears of fake tan, big eyelashes, and rosy red lips. And then there was Olive, bushy curly hair shoved into a bun and wrapped with a silver suede scrunchie. She waved animatedly at me, with both hands.

I slowed my steps and started looking for a way out. Maybe I could feign illness and suddenly pass out, being careful not to actually hurt myself, of course?

"Today would be good," quipped the Eden team captain from the stage. Everyone laughed.

I hurried faster down the aisle and up the stairs to our school table, which was lined with small microphones and buzzers like we were at a political board meeting. I chose the last seat at the table, closest to the edge of the stage for a fast exit if necessary and farthest from Rochelle, who had unfortunately picked geography too. Other than her, Rebecca from my English class, Kirsten from wood shop, and another girl from study period whose name I couldn't remember were seated at the table. Rochelle was, of course, our captain, likely having appointed herself, and she called upon the Eden students to take their seats at the opposing table.

"Jack, Connor, Kyle, Thomas . . ."

I rolled my eyes. Of course she knew the names of all Eden's sixth-year students.

". . . and Broden." She grinned when she said his name and immediately started batting her eyelashes like a cartoon character.

The last boy shuffled onstage, sighing loudly so everyone knew his level of participation would likely disappoint. He and I would be equal matches.

Pop. Crack. Snap.

Half-Broken Hannah perched in the front row, sitting in a girl from my modern studies class, hanging bone and cartilage swinging down in front of the poor girl's oblivious face while she shivered. I looked around for Meghan and Sarah, and someone elbowed me in the ribs. I turned my head and saw Kirsten beside me giving me the stink-eye. Had we started already? What question were we on?

Oh, question three. Oops.

Headmistress Blyth cleared her throat for the question. She was looking smart today, in a dark green dress, black tights, and pumps. Her hair was wound up in a bun, and she wore a badge with the school crest. She clutched a silver stopwatch in her fist, her hand trembling slightly. "Kinshasa is the capital of what country?"

Eden buzzed. "DR Congo."

"What European country has the largest population?"

Eden buzzed again.

"What country has the longest coastline?"

"What is the biggest landlocked country?"

"What country is less than 1.5 meters above sea level, making it the flattest country?"

Question after question, Eden buzzed and got it. While my buzzer sat completely untouched, the other students in my team at least tried.

"Wow, you're doing terrible." Impaled Meghan snorted over my shoulder. A drop of her blood oozed onto the wooden table.

"I'm trying," I replied between clenched teeth.

"Are you? Really? Or are you still thinking of that redhead?"

I raised my hand above the buzzer.

"What country was formerly known as Siam?" I didn't know the answer to that one.

"What was the last country to abolish slavery?"

Or that one.

"Toubkal is the highest mountain peak of what country?" And I definitely didn't know that one.

Rochelle scowled at me, her glossy lips twisting in a sneer.

"Charley, join in," Kirsten whispered.

"Yes, Charley, join in," repeated Impaled Meghan with a grin.

"You could at least help me," I muttered to her.

"How many countries are in central Africa?" quizzed Blyth.

"Three," Meghan added confidently.

My hand struck the buzzer. "Three!"

"Incorrect. Eden's question."

I glared at Meghan, who simply scrunched up her nose and muttered, "Sorry, it's not like actresses need to know subjects other than drama."

Olive's crush, Thomas, cleared his throat. "Nine."

"Correct!" said Blyth as she shook her head in disappointment.

Cheers erupted among the Eden students while the Harrogate girls booed me. So much for camaraderie. Blyth scribbled on the scoreboard: *Eden: 11—Harrogate: 2.*

Ouch. Now that was quite a loss.

The spotlight turned out to the audience, to the front row of Eden boys with their smug smiles, overstyled hair, and gleaming white teeth. I gazed out over Harrogate, looking for that mane of red, that freckled nose, and those deep-green eyes. Suddenly, a flicker of gold struck me, and I closed my eyes. When I slowly peeled them open I saw a figure in the back, standing still in the darkness, crouching beneath the shadows of half-removed Halloween streamers, pumpkin banners, and black balloons. Perhaps it was a teacher or a staff member. But they weren't moving. They just stood there, like a statue, cold and hard. And then I saw it. The same flicker struck my eye as the statue moved. A flicker of *gold*. Gold like the face that hunted and killed those girls. Gold like a mask.

I inhaled sharply and tried to reach for Meghan. All I felt was ice and emptiness. "Do you see that?" I whispered to her. Was I hallucinating?

I turned slowly to see the ghosts' faces. Meghan stood protectively in front of Hannah, who trembled and huddled behind her. Sarah choked and wheezed, waving her arms up and down. No, I was definitely not hallucinating.

"Time to leave, Charley," Meghan warned, taking a step back.

I pushed my chair and heard it fall to the ground, echoing around the hall. Students jumped, a few stifled giggles with their hands. Blyth scowled at me. I pointed. "There's . . . there's . . ." I stuttered. I couldn't get the words out. Blyth just stared at me, her eyebrows furrowing, her jaw clenching. I desperately looked to the aisles, but Mr. Gillies was gone, and when I turned, Dr. Pruitt had vanished from his spot too.

At the back, the gold face stared at me. "I . . . I . . ." Someone shushed me from somewhere on my right. Around me the sounds faded, drowned out by the rapid beating of my heart. I couldn't speak, couldn't breathe.

"Charley, sit down. It's the last question," Rochelle hissed down the table. "This could be our moment."

"Take a seat, Miss Sullivan," snapped Blyth. She turned to the audience and continued, "On what continent would you find—"

The dark figure moved slowly. Their gold face still turned toward me, watching me like I was watching them. They were here to kill again.

"—the world's largest landmass?"

I had to do something. I slammed my hand down hard on the buzzer, the siren ripping through the air. Beside me my table jumped and Rochelle let out a startled squeak. Eden's geography panel glared at me, hands hovering above their own buzzers.

"They're here!" I screamed, slicing through the silence.

"Pardon?" stammered Blyth. "The continent, Charley. I need the name of the continent."

"The killer!" I howled, pointing fervently. I suddenly felt like Sarah Michelle Gellar in *I Know What You Did Last Summer*, screaming hysterically to a bewildered and completely ignorant audience as her boyfriend got stabbed in the stomach with a rusty fishing hook.

All around me chairs screeched and whispers turned to yells and occasional screams. Blyth dropped her question book, the spine of the hardcover thudding on the wooden floor and echoing through the gym. She glared at me, her face flushed crimson, her eyes bulging. I pointed to the back of the room, where the killer had stood, shrouded in gold and black. Blyth turned to where I pointed. But there was nothing except for orange streamers, plastic banners, and black balloons. They were gone.

Rule #16
CAST THE MOVIE

The next morning was a fog of office visits, sticky breakfast plates, and weighty textbooks. I had spent the first hour before breakfast trying to convince Headmistress Blyth that I didn't need to be committed to Wexford General Hospital, and the last hour begging her not to call my mom. Finally, I relented and apologized for disrupting the academic challenge, thus forfeiting the game to Eden. I think that was what hurt her more—losing to them, not the possibility of a serial killer in her school. I had tried to tell her it wasn't exactly a forfeit as they were winning anyway and a comeback for Harrogate was out of the question (no pun intended), but that just seemed to anger Blyth more. She had somehow convinced herself that her girls would pull it together and beat Eden.

And they called me delusional?

Olive had been in a sulk all morning. She'd put up a good fight during the foreign languages round, even getting into a heated disagreement about the origins of Malayalam, but in the end, Eden won. Just like they'd won all the rounds.

No one believed me about what I saw. And, of course, only I had seen the killer with the gold face standing in the darkness at the back of the room, and I wasn't exactly a credible witness. I took the punishment, which was a ban on participating in the next academic challenge. To me that was more like a reward, so all in all, both Blyth and I left her office equally satisfied with the outcome.

After another stab at my English essay (pun intended), I finally turned back to the next chapter of Stephen King's *The Outsider* and waited for Olive to come back from the library. Today was a Saturday like no other for us. We hadn't preselected a genre to choose from, we hadn't bargained for use of the microwave down in the common room for our preferred popping time of 7 p.m., we hadn't yanked on our joggers or pajama bottoms and thick socks, or even arranged our bedding and beanbags on the floor to watch a movie. No, today was not Slasher Saturday for us. Today was party at Eden night. Yes, Olive and I were going to a real party—with real people.

We looked longingly at our PJs folded neatly on our pillows and opted for a complete wardrobe examination that included trying on every item, opening suitcases, searching the back of drawers, and finally ripping open a black bag of unworn clothing that was labeled for the charity shop upon return to the mainland. It seemed we had arrived on this island lacking suitable party attire, but we managed to fashion something that conveyed revelry and teen mistake, of course with a large dose of movie style in the form of retro graphic tees and black beaded bracelets with tiny silver skulls that dangled and swayed when we walked. Half-Broken Hannah very kindly tried to help me with some face powder but, after several attempts, couldn't physically pick up the powder box to hand to me. I thanked her for her efforts anyway; ignored Impaled Meghan, who grimaced at my wardrobe choice; and continued piling on the thick gloopy black mascara that threatened to clamp my eyes shut forever.

Finally, we were ready for our evening of debauchery, which for us meant covert student interviews. We touched up our makeup, secured our hairstyles with an alarming amount of hairspray—we would have to avoid open flames—and climbed out of our window, which we soon realized had been completely unnecessary as the back door was right beside our room.

The sea wind whipped heavily at our faces, making us immediately regret our decision to forgo our weekly movie night to do this. But we zipped our coats up higher, tucked our scarves in a little tighter, and persevered, knowing that while everyone else was occupied with the Halloween formal being only a week away, there was a killer out there, plotting their next murder.

HOW TO SURVIVE A HORROR MOVIE

The path to Eden picked up at the coastal trail where Olive and I regularly walked and headed northwest along the island, up past the friary. There were no other paths south from Harrogate. It was filled tonight with the sounds of excited girls and hurried footsteps. Most knew to pack their heels and wear sneakers for the hour-long walk to Eden to avoid rolling an ankle, but we passed the occasional inexperienced student trembling and wobbling on stilettos, desperately clutching the wooden safety rail with both hands.

The ghosts floated behind us, Meghan in the lead, practicing her lip trills and vocal warm-ups while she periodically looked at her still intact manicure, Sarah wheezing animatedly in the middle, and Hannah at the back, sobbing as she stared out at the cliffs where she'd lost her life.

The stones crunched under our boots, the ground thick with salt and limestone. A moist light fog surrounded us, and we pulled our hoods up to avoid the dreaded island-mist hair.

"You sure about this?" asked Olive.

"Absolutely not. But right now, most of our year is at Eden except us, so if the killer is among us, then he or she will be there."

"Exactly the reason we should probably stay home tonight." Olive gestured to the dark foreboding building sitting behind us on the edge of the rock, twisted vines coiling up the stone walls of the Elizabeth Wing.

Harrogate wasn't home to me, but after six years it

probably was to Olive and to many other girls who'd spent their whole academic lives here. And Blyth said that for some girls, this was the only home they had, their old ones back on the mainland having long forgotten them. Life had been tough after my dad had died, especially for my mom, who had to pick up extra shifts to cover the mortgage, but I'd always had a safe place to go back to. Some of these girls didn't, so this was home. And now someone was trying to take it from them.

"Right now, we're the only ones who know there's a killer, so it's up to us to do something, otherwise our graduating class is going to be very small next summer."

"Silver lining: less competition for college," Olive quipped.

Hannah glared at her, eyes ablaze. I swallowed a laugh and turned away to the sounds of the ocean below us smacking against the rocks, exploding into bursts of salt and spray.

"I have a bad feeling about this," Olive said.

"We have the upper hand—the killer won't expect us to be there tonight. That buys us time to do our research."

"Like Charley in *Fright Night*."

I cringed, knowing I'd named myself after him before I moved here, the teen hero obsessed with horror movies and hell-bent on exposing the monster who lived next door. Unlike Meghan, I was sensitive to irony.

"What's the agenda for tonight?"

"I thought we could circulate—" I suggested.

"Because we're such good circulators."

"Let's definitely talk to Sarah's boyfriend, Archie, to ask if he knew anything."

Sarah spluttered excitedly at this.

"Whoever saw them last—friends, and more importantly, enemies."

Meghan scrunched up her nose. *"Enemies?"*

"Yep," I said, kicking a stone off my path.

"Ugh," groaned Olive. "Does that mean we have to talk to the Bitches of Eastwick?"

"Yep, the Elles are our best friends tonight."

"Charley, who are we kidding? We're hormone-crazed students at an all-girls boarding school, not detectives. This is what the police are for."

"The police won't believe us, just like Headmistress Blyth. And if this turns out to be nothing, and I'm just seeing and hearing things, then we won't have put Harrogate in the media spotlight for no reason, and we won't have jeopardized people's academic careers. At this point we're just . . . *checking*."

"Checking? *Checking* if there's a serial killer at school?"

"Yeah." I nodded, realizing how bizarre that sounded spoken out loud. "Besides, we're practically experts!"

"We are?"

"Here we go," muttered Meghan, marching in front of us.

SCARLETT DUNMORE

"Look at all the high school slasher films we've watched—there's a pattern, a trend they follow. The killer is always part of the main cast: the prom queen–slash–cheerleader, the jock, the shy best friend, the love interest . . ."

"The transfer."

"Yes, the transfer, who is sometimes also the school loner. Occasionally there's the wronged relative."

"Like *Prom Night*," Olive said excitedly, tripping on the edge of the coastal path.

"Yes, most slashers follow a predictable pattern: *The Babysitter*—obviously it was going to be the prom queen; *Sorority Girls*—of course, the boyfriend; *I Know What You Did Last Summer*—the father; *There's Someone Inside Your House*—the shy friend; *Heathers*—the school loner; *Halloween*, parts one to, I don't know, a hundred—the brother; *Jennifer's Body*—the cheerleader."

"Technically that was the devil," corrected Olive. "And the casting for that was all wrong." She shuddered. "So, what you're saying is that we fill those roles to find our killer?"

"It's a start, and it's what we know. We *know* horror movies, Olive."

The chill picked up, and we huddled deeper into our scarves as the wind pierced the weave. The walk to Eden was considerably longer than I'd thought, and the warmth and safety of our dorm room was calling to me more than ever. As was the movie and popcorn that we'd left behind.

"OK, so prom queen: Rochelle?" Olive continued.

"Don't forget about the other Elle dolls," added Meghan.

I nodded. "Yes, let's also add Annabelle and Gabrielle to that list too."

"New transfer–slash–school loner: you. Sorry." Olive winced.

"Shy best friend: you. Sorry," I countered.

"We don't have any boyfriends . . . or girlfriends. So that's out for now."

"Assuming we're the protagonists of the movie," I quickly added.

"We must be. We're the only ones finding the bodies."

"You're right, Olive. Why didn't I think of that? We're the main stars! The killer has cast us as their protagonists. We're being led to the bodies. They want us to find them!"

"So, if we're the protagonists and not the suspects, then who are we now casting as the transfer and the shy best friend?"

"You know the roster better than me."

"Well, Kirsten from wood shop doesn't exactly fit the bill for school loner, but other than you, she is the newest transfer. She came the January before you."

"OK, so we talk to her tonight too. And the role of best friend?"

She shrugged. "We don't have any other friends."

"True." I nodded, though I glanced at the three ghosts who fumbled, limped, and dragged their limbs behind me on the path, desperately trying to keep up. Other than

Olive and my ex, Sadie, these three girls were the only people I'd spent much time with. Were they my friends?

"So, who's the jock?" Olive asked, nudging me.

"You know the Eden boys better than I do."

"Actually, not really."

"What? You've been to parties over there, that's what you said."

"Because I wanted you to think I was cool when you first moved here."

"Olive, look at me—I'm wearing a *Stranger Things* T-shirt that says 'Hellfire Club'! Did you really think cool was on my radar?"

"I'm so in love with Steve," she murmured.

Meghan leaned in. "Who's Steve?"

I grinned and shook my head as we descended deeper, going farther south on the island than I ever had before. The wind had died down slightly, with this side of the island seeming much calmer. Even the waves were softer, the ocean less menacing. Soon we saw the rooftops of Eden School for Boys silhouetted against the moonlit sky.

It was a garish glass building, illuminating every corner of the rock it sat on, like a lighthouse beacon. Certainly an incredible piece of architecture, but perhaps a better fit for a cityscape than a rugged island buffeted by storms.

Olive inhaled loudly, her breath hitching as she came to a nervous stop. I looped my arm through hers. "Come on, let's cast our characters and find our killer."

Rule #17

INFILTRATE THE HIGH SCHOOL PARTY

Eden School for Boys had been built only fifty years ago, and while few remembered Harrogate as a monastery, everyone old enough remembered the monstrous erection of Eden (pun intended). It took a slow and exasperating eight years to construct. Tall sheets of glass, panels of Scandinavian wood, and blocks of reinforced concrete were shipped in from the mainland and beyond, dragging city workmen and the noise of modernity to what was once a peaceful island of untouched natural beauty.

According to Olive, it was modeled after the German-influenced Centennial building in Poland but more closely resembled a planetarium with its domed roof and quatrefoil shape. Inside was not much warmer or cozier—white walls, exposed steel, spiral glass staircases, and modern art by brash American painters such as Joseph Stella and Charles Demuth where geometric fragments of color were arranged into an origami design and subsequently sold for shocking prices.

SCARLETT DUNMORE

In short, it was one ugly building.

"Welcome to Eden School for Boys," announced Olive, gazing up at the glass dome, which was a blemish on an otherwise flawless island view. It was so gigantic it hid the ocean behind it, and the moonlight striking the glass panels dazzled us.

"Where's the party?" I asked.

"I heard some girls in class yesterday talking about the pool house?"

"There's a *pool house*?"

"While our pool is for 'recreational use to improve female body confidence' and all that crap, the Eden pool is fifty meters and built to train future Olympic medalists."

"Well, I'm sure the dean will love that it's being used for parties and drinking."

Olive scoffed and gestured to the back of the building.

We avoided the garish spotlights that poked out of the soggy earth and found our way onto an immaculately clean stone path that led us through groomed rose gardens and herb patches that had fared better than Blyth's. While Impaled Meghan stuck close behind us on the path, Half-Broken Hannah and Strangled Sarah floated through the rosebushes, unable to find the way due to the unfortunate angle of their broken necks.

The dome branched off into long tubular wings that resembled an underwater research lab, each with its own steel entry door with a keypad. We passed marble fountains and a set of tennis courts enclosed from the island weather, and probably heated too. I could only imagine how much a building like this cost to construct and what kind of parents it appealed to. Once past the courts, we followed the path that snaked around the gardens to the back of the building, where in front of us stood a large white brick building with glass doors. Outside the air was still and calm, and the darkness of the night was heavy upon us.

Pop. Snap. Crack.

I turned to find the three ghosts standing beside me. Meghan held Sarah and Hannah firmly by the wrists, having had to redirect them back to the path far too many times.

"What is it?" asked Olive, gazing around at the empty gardens behind us.

"Nothing," I muttered. "Is this it?"

"It doesn't sound like there's a bunch of hormone-crazed teens inside, does it?" asked Olive. "Where's the music?" She tried the handle on the main door, yanking on it hard. "It's locked."

I looked to Meghan for answers, finding her standing so near that the fence spike protruding from her torso was almost touching me. "The door by the bathrooms will be unlocked," she said.

"Try the door by the bathrooms," I called out to Olive.

Our boots crunched and crackled on the crushed stone. Olive put her hands on the handle and it popped open.

"How did you know that?" Olive asked me, squinting suspiciously.

"Um . . . lucky guess."

Once we were inside, the door silently clicking closed behind us, we heard the slow thumping bass of music and the sounds of chatter and laughter.

"Soundproof walls. No wonder parties are held here," I said.

"Blyth would be camped out in front of the pool house if we had one of these." Olive stood at the second door, rocking back and forth on her heels. She coughed, cleared her throat, and then smoothed her hair, tucking any loose bushy strands behind her ears. She tugged at the red blazer she'd bought over the summer, which partially covered her graphic T-shirt of Ghostface, and exhaled loudly.

"You going in?" I eventually asked.

"Oh . . . yeah . . . of course."

I tried to not notice her hands trembling as she reached for the handle.

We swung the door open and were immediately hit by the heat from the bodies packed tightly inside. We threaded through the crowds standing in the hall by the bathrooms, then pushed our way into the main pool area. It was huge, and *hot*. Very hot. I gasped for the air we'd left outside, tugging Olive over to a window. I thrust it open, desperately lapping at the breeze like a dog in a hot car.

"No wonder the girls are only half dressed," wheezed

Olive as she peeled off her blazer. "It's like a sauna in here!"

I patted my hairline, which was already slick with sweat, and glanced around for the ghosts. Hannah huddled in a corner, woefully staring at a group of girls who were chatting animatedly, occasionally stopping to hug or squeeze each other's hands. Sarah wheezed and choked her way through the crowd, presumably searching for her former boyfriend, while Meghan tried desperately to pick up the plastic cup of beer beside her on the table, swearing loudly as her fingers floated through it over and over again.

"OK," panted Olive, tying her blazer around her hips. "What's our plan?"

"We start checking people off the suspects list."

We scanned the crowds, searching for cast members. The prom queen was dancing in the middle, at the edge of the pool, in a painfully tight outfit, while boys surrounded her like a horde of zombies from Romero's *Day of the Dead*.

We hadn't been there for long, but people were already beginning to stare, likely recognizing my face from the academic challenge. "We need to blend in more!" Olive screamed over the music.

We looked at each other, then started bobbing and swaying to the thumping beat. Dancing wasn't really my strength—I was more of a "sit and watch" kind of girl—but Olive was right: we needed to blend in. My limbs felt oddly alien, moving in ways I never thought possible. I was working up more of a sweat in the process.

"There's Kirsten, our transfer," Olive said, grabbing my arm. "Well, our second transfer."

I nodded and started making my way toward her. She was huddling with her friends, shoulder-swaying to the music with a plastic cup in her hand. An Eden boy walked into the middle of the group, and the girls parted like the Red Sea as they ogled him. I spied my opportunity.

"Oh, hey, Kirsten," I cooed, dancing up to her as casually as I could. Olive did a version of the robot beside me.

"Um, hi," she said, frowning, glancing around for her friends, who were still eyeing the Eden student near them.

"It's Charley," I said, extending a hand.

She hesitated, then tentatively took it. I shook as hard as I could, hoping to intimidate her, let her know that the protagonists of the movie weren't the least bit shaken by the recent killings. Assuming she was the killer. If she wasn't, then I definitely wasn't doing anything to refute people's latest concerns about me.

"I know who you both are," she shouted over the music, desperately trying to yank her hand back from my grasp. "We take wood shop together."

"I wasn't sure if you'd remember our names, being that you're a *new transfer*." I winked.

"I think *you're* the new transfer," she corrected. "And the two of you tend to . . . stand out."

HOW TO SURVIVE A HORROR MOVIE

"Aw, thanks." Olive beamed, proudly smoothing down her T-shirt.

"So, Kirsten," I started, "what do you think of Harrogate so far? Happy here? Not happy? Lonely? Angry? Resentful? Wouldn't you just *kill* to go home?" I winked at Olive.

"It's going fine," she said, laughing nervously. She started edging toward her friends.

"Surely you must miss home?" asked Olive, cutting her off from her group.

"Of course, but I actually really like it here." She shrugged.

"You do?"

"Yeah," she continued. "I've met some great people who I'll be friends with forever. In fact, Chloe and I are taking a gap year together after we graduate."

"You are?"

"Yeah, we're going traveling around South America." She took a long swig of her drink.

"Oh, that'll be nice," I muttered. She didn't sound like our killer. In fact, if anything she sounded happy, content, like she was enjoying her time at Harrogate. Killing off the entire sixth year, one at a time, probably wasn't on her to-do list before her travels.

"Are you in Theater Club?" Olive asked her.

"No," she said at the same time as Impaled Meghan, who popped up behind her, hungrily eyeing her drink.

Olive continued her interview: "Where were you on Saturday morning, then?"

SCARLETT DUNMORE

"I'm in the Creative Writing Club. We meet every Saturday," she replied. "We're putting an anthology together. I'm the editor."

My shoulders slumped. Friends, plans to go traveling, a valued member of the school Creative Writing Club, the one I was asked to leave because of my dark and twisted imagination. I was beginning to envy Kirsten from wood shop, not cast her as our killer.

She edged closer to the wall, trying to get away from us. "I'm just going to find my friends." She took another step back.

I nodded at Olive, who stepped out of her way, allowing her a path back to her group. Kirsten was not our gold-faced slayer. Before we could move on to the next cast member, a boy with short, spiky blond hair shimmied up with a big grin on his shiny face. "New girls. Welcome. Can I get you ladies a beverage, perhaps? Something to *cool you down?*"

I rolled my eyes and caught a flushed smile on Olive's face. I hoped she was just flushing from the heat. Did she really find this kind of banter appealing?

"No," I snapped at the same time as Olive said, "Sure."

I glared at her. This wasn't the plan. We were here to interrogate, not flirt. "I'll just be a minute. I'll get us drinks to *circulate*." She winked.

"Fine, but be quick."

She nodded, then flashed a large grin that made me

think she wouldn't be quick. Not in the slightest. I wound my hair up into a thick, messy bun and stood by the window, savoring what little breeze trickled in and aired out the back of my neck.

"Hot, right?"

I looked up and saw a guy with long floppy hair and a drink in each hand.

"Stifling," I said, looking away. I couldn't possibly have been giving off a "Come talk to me" vibe to make him think it was OK to approach me.

"What's your name?" he asked.

"Charley," I replied abruptly. He really wasn't getting the hint.

"Hi, Charley, I'm Archie."

I sighed. It was time to be clearer. "Look, Archie..." Suddenly Strangled Sarah appeared beside him, her face trying to press into his, her hands clawing at him.

"You're *Archie*?" I repeated slowly.

"Yes," he said, looking around. "Have we met? Did we hook up last year?"

"No, we definitely did not. It's just I recognize your name. Are you the Archie that was dating... um, dating..." I tried hard not to say *Strangled Sarah*. "Sarah Keenan?" I eventually got out.

He immediately went into grieving boyfriend mode, even mustering a slight glisten in the corners of his eyes. He must have been in Eden's Theater Club. If drama wasn't beneath them. They were probably more about the sciences than the liberal arts.

"Yeah," he said, gazing down.

"I am so sorry for your loss." I forced a sympathetic smile, then placed a gentle hand on his arm. Strangled Sarah glared at me, her bulging eyes and bent neck suddenly far too close to me. I stopped touching him.

"Yeah, it's been really hard."

"I'm sure it has." I nodded. "But you're really putting on a brave face for everyone, coming to the party and all. Good for you."

"I know, right," he agreed.

It was so difficult not to roll my eyes. "So," I continued, "is it always this hot here?"

"Kind of, yeah. Drink?" He held up the two cups to me.

"Sure." I smiled. I didn't really drink anymore, but I had to be polite if I wanted to ask him questions. The beer was surprisingly chilled and wonderfully refreshing. I ended up downing almost the entire cup before I could stop myself. "Thank you," I gasped.

"Would you like to go outside, get some air?"

"No, but maybe later." I batted my eyelashes and smiled sweetly.

"You know, you're really familiar. Sure we didn't hook up already?"

Strangled Sarah made a gagging, wheezing sound as

she desperately tried to talk. "Very, very sure," I insisted, eyeballing her.

"Oh, now I remember!" he said, smacking his forehead with a sweaty hand. "You're the girl who lost it on the stage!"

I laughed awkwardly. "Yeah, I love to shake up an academic challenge."

"Did someone dare you?"

"Yes," I answered far too quickly. "I was dared."

"Harrogate students have a weird sense of humor," he said, shaking his head.

"You have no idea," I muttered, looking over at Half-Broken Hannah standing awkwardly in the corner and Impaled Meghan trying to say hi to one of her friends by the pool. Sarah still stood very close beside me.

"I've never seen you at one of these parties before?"

I shrugged. "First time at Eden."

"First impressions?"

"It's a very *original*-looking building."

"It's incredible, isn't it? So naturally beautiful."

I nodded, unable to utter words. I had to get him back on the subject, discreetly, of course. "So, did Sarah say anything to you right before she died? Like, anyone she might have been afraid of, or having an argument with, or maybe being stalked by?"

"Stalked?"

"I mean, did she say anything weird, before, you know."

"No, I don't think so. Why?"

"Just making small talk. When was the last time you saw Sarah?"

"At a party here the previous weekend."

"Did anything happen that weekend?"

"You ask a lot of questions," he said, running a hand through his hair.

"Just curious."

"If you're talking about the fight, then it wasn't as bad as people made it out to be; I was there. There was some arguing and then a couple of shoves, but it didn't escalate into the epic fistfight people said it was on Monday morning."

"There was a fight?" I asked, glancing at Sarah. She wheezed and nodded enthusiastically, then pointed at someone behind me. I tried to turn but bodies shoved and danced and grinded into me, knocking me off balance.

"With my ex," Archie snorted, taking another swig of beer.

"What happened?"

"She's still so bitter about how it ended. Accused me of cheating on her with Sarah."

"Did you?" I asked bluntly, glaring at Sarah. She coughed and looked away, avoiding my stare.

"It's not cheating if you're in love!" he argued, dramatically clutching his chest. Sarah floated beside him, her eyes welling up, her gaunt and pained face trying to smile. She desperately tried to hug him.

"So, then what happened?"

"My ex went crazy—broke into my room, took a pair of scissors to my clothes! Her friend was the worst. She took a rock to my laptop. Dr. Pruitt invoiced Harrogate for it. They better pay up."

"Wow." A rock to a laptop was hardcore, even for me.

"Yeah, people think Anna's just a sheep, following her friends around everywhere, but there's something not right about that girl. She went mental." He drained the last of his beer and let out a loud belch. I grimaced and turned to Sarah, whose infatuation seemed unshaken.

I swirled the remnants of my drink, watching it slosh up the sides of the cup. "How did they get into Eden? It's like a fortress in here."

"Rochelle probably has master keys to both schools. I wouldn't put it past her."

"Wait, did you say *Rochelle*?" I shook my head in disbelief. "And the crazy friend you were talking about was Annabelle?"

"Yeah."

"*Rochelle Smyth* is your ex?!" I yelled.

"Are you seriously talking about me?" said an icy voice from behind.

And just like that, the crowd behind me parted. Rochelle and Annabelle stood front and center.

Rochelle glared at me, her eyes cold and dark. Empty like a killer's.

Rule #18

SOMEONE ALWAYS DIES AT A HIGH SCHOOL PARTY

"I . . . um . . ." I stuttered, not quite sure how to lie and where to start.

"I . . . um . . . ?" mimicked Annabelle, widening her eyes with their mascara-thickened lashes.

"If you have something to say about me then say it to my face. Or would you rather announce it in an assembly in front of the entire school?" snapped Rochelle. She was clutching a red plastic cup filled with a questionable neon-blue liquid.

My blood boiled. I scolded myself for being temporarily thrown. This wasn't me. I'd dealt with girls like Rochelle at my last school every day. In fact, I probably *was* one, not that I'd ever admit it to anyone, especially not Olive.

"If I have something to say, don't worry, I'll tell you," I said loudly, looking her straight in the eyes, which were surrounded with heavy black eyeliner and what appeared to be glued-on fake eyelashes that curled out and up, almost touching her eyebrows in the most unnatural way.

She blinked hard, her eyes wide, then quickly regained her composure. She scanned me from head to toe with a flicker of a smile. "Interesting outfit choice. You know Halloween isn't for another two weeks, right?"

"Funny, I was going to say the same thing to you," I replied, gazing at her body, which she'd squeezed into a scanty, frayed black-and-white leather ensemble that looked like something out of *Mad Max*.

Olive rushed up behind me and dug her fingers into my back.

"You know, it's a shame," Rochelle said loudly to the audience around her, "they seem to let just *anyone* into Harrogate now." She eyed me up and down again.

I took a step forward, then Olive pulled me away, tugging hard on my arm. We banged into bodies swaying to the music and inched around the pool, where students floated on their backs tossing a giant inflatable ball around.

"What are you doing?" I asked her, glancing back at Rochelle and her friends, who watched us walk away in what appeared to be defeat, much to my annoyance.

"No, what are *you* doing, Charley?" gasped Olive. "You're poking the bear—in her own habitat."

"I'm standing up to her. That's what you should do. Every time she fires a shot at you, fire one right back.

She'll back down from the challenge and choose another victim."

"Or she'll get even more pissed off and take an axe to me. It's Rochelle Smyth. This girl made my life a complete misery for five years. She ran my first roommate off the island. Bullied her until she couldn't take it anymore. After that I ate my meals in Nurse Clare's office for two years because I was scared of seeing her in the dining hall. She's pure evil."

I grabbed Olive's arm as she spun around to face me. "Maybe she *is* our killer?"

"That's too obvious, isn't it?"

"We cast her as the prom queen for a reason."

Olive shrugged. "She's certainly capable of it. She's that angry with life. And she also had a history with all the victims: Sarah stole her boyfriend." Sarah gagged and choked and gurgled behind Olive as she continued, "Meghan took the lead from her in the school play."

"Hey!" argued Meghan. "I earned that role!"

"What about Hannah, though?" I tutted, glancing at her sad eyes, twisted limbs, and sand-clotted hair.

"There was something between them," Olive said, gesturing with her hand. "Hannah went to Headmistress Blyth in third year claiming that the Elles had cheated on finals. It was dismissed, but their parents found out about it, and she made Hannah's life a misery after that."

Hannah nodded, her eyes glazed and mournful.

"I don't know, something doesn't feel right," I muttered, looking back at Rochelle. She stood facing Annabelle, her cheeks red and her face contorted like she was yelling, occasionally glancing at Archie to see if he was looking at her. He wasn't. He was looking right at me, and *smiling*. I had perhaps played my part a little too well. I shuddered and pulled Olive deeper into the crowd, trying to avoid his stare.

Suddenly, amid the sweat and hormones, I smelled the familiar scent of oak and lemon. I turned quickly and saw her swaying gently to the music. Saoirse had her back to me, and was chatting and dancing with an Eden boy and a girl I recognized from our dorm wing. I swallowed hard.

"Ugh, just ask her out!" exclaimed Olive.

"What? Who?" I shrugged, fake-casually.

"Who you've been staring at since you got to this island. Please. Do it for me. I can't take your drooling anymore. It's distracting me from lusting after Thomas."

I flushed an even warmer shade of crimson. Was I really that obvious?

"No, I can't. Besides, that's not what we're here for," I said, shaking my head.

"No, but she's right there. And who knows, she might be killed next and then you'll never get to talk to her."

"Olive!"

"Sorry."

"Fine, but only if you talk to Thomas tonight."

She pouted for a moment and looked up, then sighed. "OK. Deal." She spat into her palm and held it out.

I grimaced, pulling my hand away. "We don't need to do that."

She waved me off and suddenly I was standing by myself. Was I really going to do this?

I shimmied over to the beat of the music, stepping as the rhythm thudded and moving my shoulders to the electric sways. When I finally reached her I said "Hey!" a bit too loudly.

Saoirse and her friends turned and stared at me. I'd obviously interrupted the conversation at a bad time. But Saoirse eventually smiled. "Hey, Charley."

My whole insides exploded like a firework display on Bonfire Night.

"Aren't you that girl who freaked out onstage yesterday?" asked the Eden boy.

"Oh, yeah, that's me." How could I turn this around? "I thought I saw something."

"Like what?" he quizzed.

"I don't know. I was just panicking about the academic challenge, I suppose. You Eden students really pummeled us."

The Eden boy softened and immediately began talking about himself and his academic talents, giving me an out. I didn't want to waste my time trying to convince people who would never believe me that we were all in danger of being thrown from rooftops, shoved off cliffs, and strung up in storage rooms. I actually had something more important to say: "I love parties." I didn't really, but I assumed she did if she was here.

"Really? I'm more of a homebody," said Saoirse. "I like staying in most nights."

"Yeah, me too," I quickly countered, tugging at my sweaty collar. "It's hot, right? Are you hot?"

"I guess," she said with a smile.

She had a great smile. An epic smile. One definitely made for the movies. I grinned back. "Are you going to the Halloween formal?" I asked.

"Definitely. I love Halloween."

I stopped dancing, my eyes widening, my jaw agape. This just confirmed it—she was my dream girl. It was now or never. I smoothed my hair back and cleared my throat. "Would you, um . . . maybe want to go to the formal together?"

She looked at me, a moment too long, then started to speak . . .

Suddenly darkness flooded the hall, plunging us all into a black hole. Someone screamed in fright, then the music cut out, replaced by murmurs in the darkness. My hands searched for a wall or a chair to grip to steady myself, but all I felt was warm, moist air on my fingertips. Somewhere nearby I heard the gurgling and wheezing of Strangled Sarah, while Half-Broken Hannah's bones popped, snapped, and cracked. Well, at least I'd be kept company in the pitch-black by three murdered ghosts.

"Who turned off the lights?" a boy beside me shouted.

"Did we blow the fuse?" asked another Eden student. "Is the whole school out?"

A shuffle of bodies and feet followed, along with a couple of *ow*s and the occasional scraping of metal chairs on tiles.

"Doesn't look like it. The main building is still lit."

"Does anyone know where the fuse box is?"

"It's in the boiler room. Shine your phones."

All around us, screens illuminated, and the shimmer of the pool and the faces around it appeared once again. The Elles were gone from behind me, and in their place stood two girls from our year, swaying their phones like they were at a concert.

Sadly, Saoirse was also gone.

A couple of the Eden boys disappeared downstairs in search of the fuse box, while students got back to filling their cups with beer and neon-colored punch and chattering about trivial school gossip.

After a while, the light above flickered momentarily, then filled the room again. I squeezed my eyes shut, blinded by the yellow fluorescence. When I opened them, Impaled Meghan stood in front of me. I startled and turned away. Everyone cheered and clapped when the Eden students came back up, their hands raised, accepting the applause, like flicking a switch on a fuse box was a monumental accomplishment. I searched for Saoirse, but all I could see were bodies swaying and shuffling around, so I started looking for Olive instead, darting through the crowds, searching for that red blazer tied around her waist as a visual focal point. Beside me the Eden boys continued graciously accepting praise.

"Yeah, it was dark down there, then Joe's phone battery died and we couldn't see a thing!" one of them said and then laughed. "Totally wasn't the fuse box, someone had turned the mains off."

"That's not even funny," another said with a snort.

My skin prickled and tingled like I was cold. I wasn't—the opposite, actually—but still goose bumps rose on my arms.

Olive appeared from behind them, her curly hair bobbing up and down as she rushed toward me. "There you are! How did it go?"

"It was terrible. I asked her if she wanted to go to the Halloween formal, then it went pitch-black."

"The formal? I thought *we* were going together?" She pouted.

"Well, she didn't say yes. She didn't say anything because someone turned the lights off."

"I thought it was a blown fuse?"

"No, someone turned off the lights intentionally." The air pressed in around us, the sounds of bass and electronics creeping up the wall tiles and cocooning us as the music started back up. "Something feels *off*," I said.

Olive grabbed my arm. "Like horror movie off?"

I nodded. "Yes, like horror movie off."

We frantically stared around at the pool house filled with bodies, swaying to the music and edging closer to each other.

"It's a high school party—every teen horror movie has one, and each time someone dies. You know the drill," I instructed. "Check closets, rooms, and bathrooms."

She flicked her head back to me. "For what?"

"A body."

"A body?!" she yelled.

"Not another one," Meghan groaned.

"Shh! We need to be subtle, not draw attention just yet. The killer might still be here."

Olive nodded, her eyes wide and darting between faces. We strode out of the pool area, our arms swinging dramatically by our hips as we pretended to be casual, and ducked into the hallway beyond. It was dimly lit, the fluorescents above flickering. The clang of steel pipes echoed faintly as the pool vents worked overtime to circulate air with so many people squashed into the room. Three doors lined the hallway, all marked as bathrooms. Loud chatter spilled out from the first door, flooding the hall with shrill, ear-piercing voices that I recognized immediately. We edged the door open and found Rochelle and Annabelle standing at the sink with small makeup bags, wielding mascara wands like they were melee weapons.

"And did you see what she was wearing?" continued Rochelle, in that same grating voice I sometimes heard in my nightmares. "I told her I was wearing my new black-and-white dress tonight, and she shows up in almost exactly the same thing! That's why we discuss our outfits, so we don't all show up looking like triplets!"

"And did you see her talking to Archie earlier?" snarled Annabelle, adding fuel to an already flaming fire.

"Oh, don't worry, I saw that. What a snake—" Rochelle glanced into the mirror, saw our reflection, then spun around. "Can I help you?"

Annabelle turned too. "Excuse me, we're having a *private* conversation here."

"Yeah, in a *public* bathroom," I muttered, looking around the room.

"What are you doing?" Rochelle snapped, mascara wand still in hand.

I ignored her and slammed the door closed, edging back into the hallway. The next bathroom door was silent, a thick darkness spilling out from under it. Above us the lights flickered.

"Better check to see if it's empty first," Meghan warned.

I knocked loudly. "Hello? Anyone . . . peeing?"

Meghan smirked. "Peeing wasn't what I was thinking."

We waited a couple of moments, then barged in. The

smell that hit us was horrendous. "Gross," mumbled Olive through her fingers.

The last bathroom was empty too. In the hallway lining the far wall were tall thin lockers, some padlocked, some slightly ajar.

"You don't think a body could fit in there, do you?"

"I definitely couldn't fit in there," Olive scoffed, opening the first one.

Most were empty, bar a few smelly gym shoes and one pair of bundled-up Speedos that neither of us dared touch.

"OK, seriously, what are you doing?"

We spun around and saw the two Elles coming out of the bathroom, mascara wands still in hand.

"Um," I spluttered, not quite sure how to answer Rochelle.

"We're looking for a dead body," Olive said, perhaps slightly too casually.

"Excuse me?" asked Annabelle, blinking hard.

"A. Dead. Body," repeated Olive, overpronouncing every consonant.

I yanked her away and back toward the main pool area. I glanced around for the ghosts, but a sea of students closed in on us.

"Why are you looking for a dead body? Haven't you found enough?" Rochelle snorted, pushing through the crowd.

HOW TO SURVIVE A HORROR MOVIE

We dodged swaying dancers and stumbled over stray red plastic cups on the floor, all while trying to lose the two Elles, who annoyingly continued to follow us. The occasional handbag sat in a cloudy puddle of chlorinated pool water and neon punch. When I finally pushed through the crowds I found a large storage closet at the far end of the pool area—the perfect place to hide a corpse. I placed a shaky hand on the knob of the door and took a deep breath. Olive shimmied in behind me, peering over my shoulder. She poked a finger in my back, urging me forward.

I flung the door open with all my strength. Something heavy struck the top of my head and I shrieked. Olive started screaming behind me too. Whatever had hit me landed hard beside us, clattering on the tiles. Around us laughter broke out, masking the music. It wasn't a dead body at all. It was a bright green inflatable kayak. Now I felt stupid. I winced and looked at Olive, my cheeks burning a deeper shade of coral than her blazer. She opened her mouth to say something that I prayed was witty enough to distract from the kayak debacle when a piercing scream blasted through the pool house.

It was bloodcurdling. A scream so cold and sharp that it cut through the air and penetrated my skin and flesh. The only time I'd heard a scream like that was from Shelley Duvall in *The Shining*, which Olive and I had watched at least three times since I moved here. But this was no Kubrick movie; this was real life, and rather than running away from a scream like that, I instead rushed toward it, cutting through crowds, barging past dancers, weaving between swimmers coming and going from the pool. I turned back to make sure Olive was following close behind me, but all I saw were the cheerful faces of students I didn't know. In fact, no one was following me. And no one seemed fazed by the screaming, other than me. Had no one else heard it?

Confused, I pressed on, pushing through the café doors, and the small space beyond that contained metal tables and chairs and vending machines, filled with brightly colored toxic-looking sports drinks. At the back was a long silver serving station, with a hatch leading to the kitchen. Another scream sounded, beyond the hatch. I took a deep breath and slowly opened the door. It creaked and groaned as it shifted, dragging metal against tile. Standing in the kitchen was Impaled Meghan, the fence spike wedged through her body angling toward the back corner, where she stared. "Sorry," she muttered. "Didn't mean to be so dramatic. But that's just gross, even for us."

Beside her stood Half-Broken Hannah and Strangled Sarah. Hannah's hands, more gnarled and twisted than ever, were attempting to shield her eyes from whatever she saw. Sarah, bent and broken, raised an arm and pointed to the tall refrigerator against the back wall. The door was slightly ajar, spilling out cold air and light from the bulb inside. I walked slowly toward it until I felt a stickiness on the bottom of my shoes. The rubber peeled slowly off the floor and when I looked down, I saw I was standing in a pool of blood.

I gazed back at the three ghosts, who huddled together, almost holding each other. A strong tangy metallic smell hit me as I opened the fridge door, and a wave of nausea flooded my body. I let go of the door to cover my nose and it swung open, hitting off the counter. The ghosts gasped behind me. Meghan squealed.

Inside, on the top shelf, nestled between the reduced-fat mayonnaise and oat milk, was Gabrielle's severed head.

Rule #19
EXPECT A GROWING BODY COUNT

The breeze spilling in from the window shook the blinds, banging metal on glass. We shifted uncomfortably in the chairs that all faced inward in a circle, trying not to catch each other's eye. Olive sat beside me, her short shallow breaths momentarily distracting me from the stares of the others. Rochelle and Annabelle were positioned opposite us, their forced sniffling drowning out the ticking of the white-rimmed clock on the wall behind their heads. Next to them were Headmistress Blyth and Mr. Gillies.

    Hannah stood mournfully in the corner, either looking out the window at the trees and the cliffs or staring at her own ghastly reflection, while Sarah glowered at Rochelle from the chair beside her. Meghan balanced on a desk at the back of the room, practicing her vocal scales with a combination of strange high-pitched sounds and the odd line from a West End show. She occasionally stopped to give herself a jaw massage.

HOW TO SURVIVE A HORROR MOVIE

My head throbbed and pulsed, a reminder of how little sleep I'd managed to get last night after everything happened. I had of course shut the party down and alerted both Eden and Harrogate staff, much to everyone's dismay.

"Charley—" Ms. Blyth started again, her tone laced with fatigue and annoyance.

I cleared my throat and continued, "Headmistress, I'm telling you, she's dead. I saw her *head* in the fridge."

Annabelle squeaked, grimacing in disgust.

"And I'm telling you that Mr. Gillies didn't see anything in that kitchen when he arrived." I glanced at Mr. Gillies, who glared darkly at the remaining Elles. Blyth continued, "Frankly, I'm more upset at learning that my girls have been sneaking out and . . . and . . . doing goodness what with those boys at Eden!"

"If it wasn't Gabrielle, then where is she?" I called out, throwing my arms in the air.

"I told you, we had a fight last night and she stormed off," hissed Annabelle. There was suddenly a coldness in her eyes that I hadn't noticed before. A slight hardness to her jaw when she talked. Maybe Archie was right.

I turned to Blyth. "You can't seriously think Gabrielle is sulking somewhere on this island? Where did she sleep last night? I didn't peg her as having an interest in wild camping." I quickly glanced at Annabelle, whose eyes hadn't left me.

Blyth nodded. "I admit, at this time Gabrielle Harrison is *missing*."

SCARLETT DUNMORE

"Missing? She's dead!"

"It's not yet been twenty-four hours. Then an officer will come across from the mainland to draft a missing person report, which will be most unfortunate for Harrogate's reputation."

"I think Harrogate has bigger problems," I scoffed.

"How long do we have to sit here for?" Rochelle asked, wiping a fake tear from her cheek. "I'd like to go out and help look for my best friend. Plus, I've got a French assignment due tomorrow."

"You take French?" Olive said, scrunching her face up in confusion.

"Oui." Rochelle grinned.

"Right, girls. This has taken up too much of everyone's time already. I don't know what happened last night, or if this is just a hoax—"

"It's not a hoax!" I wailed.

"But it's time to get back to our day. We'll continue searching for Gabrielle as planned, with Eden's assistance."

Annabelle shrugged. "She's probably at Eden right now."

Blyth frowned. "So, we'll check in again with Eden and make it very clear that if Gabrielle doesn't return to Harrogate immediately, she will be suspended indefinitely."

Olive gasped dramatically. To her, suspension was worse than death.

I looked up at the headless corpse that banged and bumped into every wall and desk as she tottered about the classroom in a black-and-white leather dress and blue heels. It seemed Dead Gabrielle was every bit as stupid as Living Gabrielle. "She's not at Eden. You're wasting your time when the person you should be searching for is the killer."

Rochelle rolled her eyes, while Annabelle sneered. Beside me, Olive slid a little farther down in her seat, avoiding my stare.

"Charley, we've already discussed your vivid imagination. Let's not get into that conversation again, please," Blyth said, her eyebrows going up.

A deep sigh escaped as I slumped against the back of the chair. It was pointless. No one believed me. This was exactly what the killer wanted, for everyone to think I was crazy. Why else would they go to the effort of cleaning up the severed head before anyone else found it? And how did they know I saw it? They must have been watching me. Just like that first night, outside my window, the killer had been watching me this whole time. I had run out of the kitchen straight after seeing the head, barricading it to stop others from going in, for their own sakes, but now I'd realized I should have left the doors wide open, let everyone be witnesses. In the time it took me to call for help, the killer had come back and cleaned up the scene, which meant two things: first, Gabrielle's head was kicking about somewhere on this island—gross!—and second, this seemed to be about *me*. Maybe there was a reason that *I* was finding these bodies, and that *I* was seeing ghosts. This really did give me the starring role. I was Jamie Lee Curtis in *Halloween*, except I would make sure there were no sequels. Michael Myers would not be returning in my movie.

"You're probably right," I said firmly. Everyone in the circle slowly turned to me, eyes wide. "I mean, I'm tired, exams are coming up, this is a new school, new life, and all that. Who knows what I saw?" I shrugged, sliding off my chair. "And Annabelle's right—"

"I am?"

"Gabrielle Harrison is probably at Eden as we speak." Blyth squinted at me. I was not fooling her at all. "We should get back to our dorms. Rochelle needs to finish that French paper." Rochelle snapped her head between Blyth and me, her eyebrows furrowed in confusion. "And Olive and I need to get to the library," I quickly added.

"OK," Blyth said slowly, inspecting me. "Let's talk on Monday if Gabrielle hasn't reached out to anyone."

"Good idea," I quickly said, grabbing Olive and yanking her out of the chair.

She stumbled alongside me out of the classroom and down the hall, the stares of other students following us all the way through the wing along with the ghosts. "Um, Charley, the library is that way," she said, pointing down the other hallway.

"We're not going to the library."

"We aren't?"

"We've got other things to do."

HOW TO SURVIVE A HORROR MOVIE

"We have?" She looked up and stopped, her eyes widening, her breath hitching a little.

Striding down the hall toward us in an expensive designer suit, firmly clutching a long, sharp, inky-black umbrella in one hand, was Dr. Pruitt. I also froze. Something about him, his presence, made the hallway feel tight, like the walls were moving closer together, pressing in on us.

He stopped when he saw us, his jaw tightening. "Girls, do you know where I would find your headmistress?"

Olive nodded, but no words came out, just a squeak.

"She was just down in the literature and languages wing, room 13. I can show you if you like?" I immediately regretted the offer. I bit my lip waiting for his reply.

He waved me off. "No need. I know my way around here." He scanned the hallway, his upper lip curling in disdain, then strode past us. His black loafers echoed down the corridor—*thud, thud, thud.*

Olive and I both shivered at the same time, exchanged brief glances, then walked on. We crossed the courtyard, the drizzle dusting the tops of our heads and shoulders. The rain tickled the rim of the marbled fountain in the middle, where on a dry day, students balanced on the edge reading textbooks or talking with their friends. Today the courtyard was empty. We crossed over to the Edith Wing and pushed open the door to our dorm. Inside, the floor was still strewn with potential outfits for last night's party. Eyeliner, lip gloss, and face powder still sat open on the dresser, their lids lying off to the side. A large bristly face brush lay on the floor with a small scattering of orange on the carpet that we'd need to clean up before we left for Christmas break.

Pop. Snap. Crack.

I knew I didn't need to, but I held the door open for the three—no, now *four*—ghosts to follow me. They bypassed it and wafted in through the wall instead. Headless Gabrielle bumped into an annoyed Impaled Meghan, who turned her body and allowed the fence stake to smack Gabrielle in the hip as she stumbled around. Strangled Sarah tried to laugh, and instead broke into a wheezing, choking splutter. Half-Broken Hannah remained in the corner, quietly looking at her hands.

The room was becoming a bit tight for space these days.

"That didn't go well," snorted Meghan, crossing her arms so they rested on top of the fence spike.

I slammed the door shut and quickly toed out of my sneakers. I pinned another sheet of paper over the last one, taping it up, and began hacking at it with a black marker, almost taking the felt point off: <u>SUSPECTS.</u>

"What are you doing?" asked Olive, still standing in the middle of the room, her back to the four bumbling ghosts.

"I'm making a list of suspects that we can narrow down . . . Oh, and thanks for sticking up for me back there," I muttered, turning back to the paper.

Olive grimaced and sat down on the edge of her bed.

"Sorry. I wanted to say something, I really did. But I didn't see anything. You went in alone. One minute we were standing there with a kayak at our feet, and the next you were just gone. Then you appeared from the kitchen, screaming something about a bloody head, and suddenly the whole pool house was in chaos!"

"I think they were more scared about being caught at a party," I added, drawing a vertical line down the middle of the page.

"I couldn't get to you. I couldn't see for myself. Sorry."

I stopped and turned around. "It's OK, really. I get it. The most important thing is that you believe me . . . You believe me, right?"

"Of course, I do. You're my best friend—"

"Only friend."

"You're my only friend. I believe you."

"Thanks." I smiled. "Will you help me make a suspects list now?"

"Sure, on it!" She jumped up, grabbed a pen, and marched over to the list. "Who should we add first?"

"Rochelle," we said in unison.

I started scribbling her name on the left side of the line. "Rochelle used to date Archie."

"Really, it was *Archie* she was seeing?"

"Yes, and he cheated on her with Sarah," I said, pointing to her ghost. Olive glanced at the blank wall, tilting her head quizzically. I stopped pointing. "Rochelle got so mad she broke into Eden and destroyed his room. Along with Annabelle, who I'm also putting up on this list. That girl is hiding a whole lot of crazy underneath all that hairspray."

"How did they get into Eden?"

"Exactly what I wondered. Archie suspects Rochelle has keys to both Eden and Harrogate, which would explain how she gained access to the rooftop to throw Meghan off. Maybe Mr. Terry did lock it. And we know Gabrielle fell out with the other two Elles at the party, then conveniently disappeared. And Rochelle has a motive for killing Sarah and Gabrielle!" I jumped up excitedly.

"You're enjoying this a bit much," Meghan remarked.

I stopped jumping and looked at Sarah's and Gabrielle's lifeless corpses. "Sorry," I muttered. I started pacing around the rug that sat in the center of our dorm room, separating our beds. "So, we've established Rochelle was jealous and angry at the party on Saturday—"

"And drinking!" added Olive, putting her hand up like she was in class.

"And drinking, yes. So, she has a motive and a means."

"Where does Annabelle fit into all this?"

"Maybe they're working together?"

"But what about the lights? How did she or they turn the lights off without anyone seeing?"

"I doubt they know *how* to turn the lights off," Meghan piped in.

"They must have snuck out at some point, or one of

them did," I said as I scribbled furiously. The tip of the pen scratched deep into the paper, the ink blotting and bleeding out. "Now, who else had an issue with Gabrielle?"

Meghan sighed and glared at her fumbling ghost, which was now waving her arms around. "Other than the *entire* sixth year?"

"I'm going to add Dr. Pruitt," I said.

"You really think he wants Harrogate that badly?"

"Don't you think it's odd that he knows his way around the school? That means he's been here on many occasions."

"Maybe he and Blyth have another way to pass island time." Meghan winked.

I scrunched up my nose. "Gross."

"What's gross?" Olive asked.

"Never mind."

"We could add Archie," Olive suggested.

"Good idea!" Strangled Sarah suddenly appeared between the white sheet of paper and my hand. I retracted the marker. "Or not."

Olive continued, "He had a connection with two of the victims—I mean, girls."

"Motive?" Meghan questioned.

Sarah circled around me, her bent, crushed neck twisting and snapping, sending an ice-cold shiver up my spine.

"I suppose he has no obvious motive," I pointed out. "If anything, others had motive to kill *him*." Sarah croaked and coughed angrily. "But let's not cross him off just yet."

"OK, then who else?"

"Since we're adding Pruitt, we have to add Mr. Gillies." I waved the marker around.

"Mr. Gillies?" Olive repeated slowly.

I started counting on my hand: "One—he's been acting suspiciously for weeks. Two—we bumped into him around the time of Sarah's death. Three—he was nowhere to be found when Meghan died and came late to Blyth's office soaking wet. And four... um, four... he just creeps me out sometimes. Even if he does appreciate my woodworking efforts."

"Add him. We all know he wasn't a fan of Gabrielle. And the other two Bitches of Eastwick."

"Bitches of Eastwick," snorted Meghan from the back of the room, as Headless Gabrielle continued bumping and banging into my dresser.

"Ever notice that Gillies is missing the tip on his right pinkie finger?" Olive waved her pinkie at me.

"No, I don't think I have ever stared longingly at his hands." I snorted.

"Woodworking accident," she continued.

"That doesn't inspire confidence."

"Apparently Gabrielle has very poor hand-eye coordination. Almost took his whole hand off with a band saw, had he not moved in time. Just caught the fingertip."

"Ouch. That would make me murderous too." I hoped it wasn't Mr. Gillies. His class was the only one where I was actually getting a decent grade. Why couldn't it have been Ms. Evans? I was already failing English.

"Adding him." Olive nodded, taking the pen from me and writing on the poster.

I took a step back and looked at the list. "Now what? We follow all these people around for the rest of the school year? We listen in to their conversations, go through their trash?" I sighed and collapsed on the bed.

Sarah paced in front of the poster while Meghan examined it, her hands on her hips. Hannah curled up into a ball in the corner of the room, hugging her knees and softly wailing. Gabrielle had somehow ended up on her knees, her arms stretched out across the rug, her fingers wiggling around like worms.

"Nothing here is ringing a bell. Any of these people could have pushed me," Meghan said, running a finger down the list.

I flung myself back onto the quilt in a starfish position. I wondered if the killer was here in this building right at this moment, plotting their next move, their next victim. Who would be next? And why?

Olive lay down beside me, her head lightly touching mine. "You know, there's a quicker way to learn people's secrets—one that doesn't involve rifling through someone's trash bin." I sat bolt upright. She leaned in. "Headmistress Blyth keeps a record on every student and staff member in her office," she whispered.

SCARLETT DUNMORE

"Olivia Montgomery, you're a genius!"

"Yeah, I kinda am." She grinned, the deep dimples in her chin curving inward. I jumped up off the bed and began yanking out dresser drawers. "Dig out your camouflage, Montgomery. We're going in covert!"

Rule #20

CONDUCT CLANDESTINE OPERATIONS IF NECESSARY

"I said camouflage, Olive, not . . . this."

Olive stood in front of me in a pair of green polka-dot jersey pajamas, her bushy hair squeezed tightly into a bun. "I don't own anything camouflage. I'm not in the military," she argued. "And what are *you* wearing?"

I gazed down at my black skinny jeans, sneakers, and the giant garbage bag over my torso, with cutouts for the arms. "I thought because it's nighttime I'd dress in black to blend in. It's better than *polka-dot pajamas!*"

"Is it really?" she quipped.

"OK, let's do this. Flashlights?" I asked, showing her the small silver one that came in our welcome packs alongside letter paper, envelopes, and printed Harrogate pens to write home with; a bottle of spring water; and a copy of the school handbook. We got flashlights so we didn't trip and sue anyone, a reminder of the rules so we wouldn't break them, and ways to write home to tell our tuition-paying families what a fabulous school Harrogate was. I wondered what came in Eden's welcome bag—an iPhone? A hardback book about horrendous modern architecture?

"Let's go."

We inched open the dorm door and slipped out into the dark hallway. The other students were already in their beds. The darkness swarmed me, and Olive immediately yawned. I didn't tend to sleep well and was used to staying up late watching movies on the sofa, waiting for Mom's late shifts to finish, whereas Olive was definitely not a night owl, preferring a strict 9 p.m. bedtime on weekdays.

I elbowed her to keep her awake and coaxed her down the hall of the wing, past the other dorms and the shower rooms, where the faint smell of coconut conditioner and floral body spray wafted out. The door to the courtyard creaked open. Outside, cold air settled around our warm bodies and started pressing in. A thick mist rolled in from the cliffs, a dense wave of it tumbling into the courtyard. It was so quiet, the crack of ocean on rock was audible from here, and it danced around our footsteps as we crept to the other side of the yard.

Pop. Snap. Crack.

I turned around and put a finger to my mouth to hush Hannah, then immediately remembered that only I could hear her. Gabrielle floated through the fountain, her blue heels stumbling along. She bumped into Sarah on the other side, who shoved her out of the way.

HOW TO SURVIVE A HORROR MOVIE

The door into the Elizabeth Wing popped open. The hallway beyond was blanketed in nighttime silence. Our shoes were quiet on the flooring, but I grossly underestimated the noise of a black trash bag as it crinkled against my arms.

Olive turned to me, frowning.

"Sorry," I mouthed silently. I yanked it over my head and made a mental note for next time—no trash bags for undercover investigations.

Meghan floated a bit in front of us, peering around the corners and waving us on. Having a ghost for a lookout was actually quite handy. The library was locked, but the moonlight that streamed in from the stained-glass windows trickled out under the doors, casting thin shadows of green, red, and blue. We stepped over the strips of color like they were lava and tiptoed past the infirmary to Blyth's door.

The darkness pushed against the glass window of her office as we all hovered outside, the ghosts behind the living girls. Blyth's name was etched in a gold font across the glass, the bottom of the *Y* slightly chipped away. I resisted reaching up and picking at the rest of the gold paint with my fingernail. Olive looked at me, her face ashen in the moonlight. Our breaths were shallow, and I longed to take a deep, loud inhale back in the safety of our dorm. The handle was cold like the night and gave way when I pressed down on it. It opened, creaking with every

SCARLETT DUNMORE

inch, freezing the blood in our veins. We stepped inside and closed it behind us.

"Why is it unlocked?" I whispered.

"Because no student in their right mind would break in here."

The headmistress's office looked different in the night, more menacing and uninviting. The sharp edges of cabinets protruded into the dark like claws, and the metal chair legs glistened like knife blades. Everything we touched screeched like nails on a chalkboard. It was impossible to stay quiet in here. "Shh!" Meghan hissed.

"Shh!" I repeated to Olive.

"I can't help it, every drawer squeaks!" she muttered.

We fumbled in the dark to the big gray cabinet in the back corner by the window. When I pulled at the handle, it didn't budge. "It's locked. This must be where the records are kept." I sighed. "I can't believe Blyth doesn't trust us."

Olive put her hands over mine and tugged. Unsurprisingly, still locked. "Maybe she keeps the key somewhere in here?"

We reluctantly pulled out our flashlights, angling the light down, and ran our fingers through Blyth's belongings. In her desk drawers were brown and white envelopes brought over from the mainland, addressed to Ms. Cornelia Blyth, and a copious amount of stationery, rulers, staplers, hole-punchers, pencils, erasers, sharpeners, and highlighters and pens in an array of colors to match the stained-glass windows in the library. The remaining drawers were filled with folders, a first-aid kit, batteries, and a large money box, also locked. Not that I was looking to steal from Blyth too. Breaking into her office was bad enough.

Olive poked and prodded along her windowsill, in a computer bag by the door, and even in a pair of slippers under Blyth's desk.

"Her slippers, really?"

"You never know. People hide things in the weirdest places."

I snorted and turned back to the desk, with its framed photos of students long gone, an aging Ms. Blyth the only one of them remaining on this island. Beside the frames was an artificial succulent, the rubber leaves slightly tacky under my touch. It was then I heard a gentle clink of metal. Buried at the root, stabbed into the dried fake soil, was a set of two small keys.

"People hide things in the weirdest places," I repeated, pulling out the keys and showing Olive.

We hurried over to the cabinet and thrust one of the keys into the top drawer, wrestling with it. It didn't move. The other key slid in effortlessly and clicked as the drawer popped open. Olive shone her flashlight inside as I flicked through what looked like the staff records of everyone who had ever worked at Harrogate, Blyth included.

"Why would she keep a file on herself?" whispered Olive, opening it.

Beneath the files was correspondence. Letters from parents, some complimentary, and some not: complaints of teacher misconduct, unfair grading schemes, inflated tuition fees, and tolerance of bullying. Underneath was a paper-clipped stack of printed-out email exchanges. My eyes skimmed the words as fast as I could.

"What does it say?" Meghan asked.

"They're emails between Blyth and Pruitt."

"Told you there was something going on." She grinned.

"Listen to this one: *Harrogate may tolerate recreational drug use, but Eden does not. Any future incidents will be reported to the school board . . . I have decided not to contact the police regarding Eden's recent break-in; however, I have attached an invoice for all damages incurred.* Archie was right. Blyth did have to pay for a new laptop." I flicked through the other emails. "There's one where he and his benefactors offer Blyth a sum of money for the building and grounds. She refuses, of course."

"How much we talking?" quizzed Olive.

I picked up the folder, pulling it closer to the glow of the flashlight. A brown envelope slid out and hit the ground by Hannah's mangled feet. When I bent down to scoop it up, I noticed patches of charcoal all over her torn flesh. I scooped up the file and slowly stood up. Her eyes were dark, empty, void of the light I'd seen when she first appeared to me in the library.

"What's wrong?" whispered Olive, gazing around the dark office.

"Nothing," I muttered, opening the envelope. Inside were bank statements, with bold Harrogate lettering at the top. Red print and minus signs everywhere.

"Maybe she shouldn't be turning down offers. Looks like Harrogate's in financial trouble," I said, showing Olive the paperwork. "No wonder Blyth is so desperate to keep us quiet. All these killings could ruin her."

"I guess that pretty much rules out Blyth, then?"

"You're probably right. She's been here her whole life. If anything, she'd kill to keep it open. But it does move Pruitt a bit further up our list."

"Check the others."

The files for English and the sciences were practically empty, with only the CVs of the recent faculty, and letters of recommendation from teachers now gone. Math and languages were much the same. Arts and drama predictably had a couple of complaints from disgruntled parents who thought their daughters should have had the lead in school plays, and PE also boasted a few angry emails about missed opportunities and unsupported athletic dreams. The last record was for the technical arts, wood shop being the largest file.

I glanced tentatively at Olive and slowly opened the file. Beneath the standard staff evaluations, all giving Mr. Gillies the highest grade, an outstanding CV, and the odd email praising his "good Christian influence" on the students was a police statement. My fingers skimmed the embossed Department of Justice heading, all the way down to the summary, but where there should have been an explanation of why he was interviewed by the mainland police on May 19, 2015, there were only thick streaks of black marker. Everything had been concealed, redacted, censored beyond all recognition. I couldn't read a single word. Olive grabbed the file from my fingers and held up the statement, shining a flashlight at the back.

"Anything?" I asked her. Meghan, Hannah, and Sarah leaned in too.

She squinted harder, grimacing with concentration. "Hmm, the odd word... *investigation*... *lawsuit*... *provocation*... *attempted suicide*... whoever did this really didn't want anyone reading it."

"Suicide?"

"Attempted suicide, it says here."

"Sounds like he almost caused a student to take their own life. So, why would he still be working here, then?"

"He and Blyth go way back. There were rumors of him and her back in the day, you know."

"What? Really?"

"School gossip, probably. But they were together a lot. He

was one of her first hires. In fact, Mr. Gillies was brought on to be the assistant head teacher. Looks like he was demoted to wood shop after 2015, though. He and Mr. Terry, the boatman, have been here since the seventies. Harrogate is their life."

"A life given to ungrateful, self-serving rich kids like the Elles," I muttered, watching a headless Gabrielle wrestle with a filing cabinet.

"Better move Mr. Gillies up the list too."

"Mentally added."

We slipped the record back into the cabinet drawer, carefully positioning it between the F and H files. Then we dropped to our knees and slid out the bottom drawer.

"Student records. Now this will be interesting." Olive snorted. "Where do we start?"

"S for Smyth."

I yanked out Rochelle's file, not at all surprised at the thickness of it, and skimmed the first few pages. "Emails from parents, complaints from students, complaints from staff, nothing new. Ooh, she's flunking most of her subjects . . . or should I say, *was*." I turned the sheet to Olive, bringing it into the light. "See, her grades have been changed, crossed out, bumped up. Last year she got a D in Mr. Gillies's wood shop, but someone's crossed it out and given her a B."

"I knew it! I always wondered how she got a B. She hardly ever shows up, and when she does, she spends half the time leaning against the machines, chatting to her friends. And her project last year was a square plaque of her name, and she misspelled that. She forgot one L. And it was a rectangle, not a square."

I giggled and popped the file back into its place. Annabelle's was much the same, as was Gabrielle's. I shuddered as images of her head, all bloody and tissue-y, came into my mind again.

"Here's yours, Charley."

I reached over and stopped Olive from pulling it out. It was far thicker than Rochelle's. I hadn't anticipated seeing my own file there, but of course it would be. Blyth knew everything before I even set foot on this island. I had been fooling myself that Charley Sullivan was a real person, *could* be a real person, here. No, deep down I would always be Lottie Ryan. And everything in that file confirmed it. All the bad reports, failing grades, police statements, even that short time I spent in a detention center on the mainland. It would all be in there, and once Olive saw that, she'd know. And she might look at me differently. I liked who I was with her. I liked the person she encouraged me to be. Suddenly the thin gold chain around my neck felt heavy on my collarbone as memories of my time on the mainland pressed into my mind—that day in court, the last time I saw Sadie, and then that morning on the docks when I said goodbye to the person I was and got on the boat for Harrogate. Clenching my jaw until it throbbed and ached, I pushed my file back down, losing it in the sea of student records.

Olive frowned and opened her mouth to say something, but a soft bang from down the hallway startled us and we jumped to our feet. She glanced at me, her eyes wide like a terrified animal.

I jumped as I heard another bang, this time followed by a click, like a door closing. I bent down and quietly eased the drawer back in as my insides curled and twisted. The sounds continued, a shuffling at first. Then louder tapping, which soon became the distinct noise of footsteps. Suddenly Meghan's head floated in through Blyth's door. "Someone's coming!" she squealed.

As if she'd heard her, Olive started flapping her hands around, the wrist strap on the flashlight slapping in the air. I grabbed her shoulders and pulled her down, crawling to Blyth's desk. We pushed the chair back and huddled into the foot space, along with Meghan and Sarah. Hannah stood in the corner by the window, and Gabrielle was nowhere to be seen.

"Flashlight!" I mouthed silently to Olive as the office door creaked open.

She clicked it off and closed her hands around her mouth to stop any squeaks or gasps escaping.

The footsteps were soft, as if intentionally muffled, coming closer into the room. They stopped at the desk, blanketed by the darkness. Hands fumbled with the items on Blyth's desk, as if looking for something. I glanced down at the keys still in my hand, sharply pressing into my palm.

The person shuffled away. My chest loosened slightly. The room was still, shrouded in black, with only a sliver of moonlight staining the floor around us. Suddenly the squeaking of a drawer broke the silence, making my shoulders twitch. Then the footsteps moved farther away from us, closer to the door, then down the hallway.

We sat frozen, exactly where we were, not even moving to stretch our legs, for what felt like hours. Then we slowly uncurled ourselves and crawled out from under the desk. Meghan's butt jutted from Blyth's door while her top half must have been out in the hallway. She pulled herself back through and shook her head. "Couldn't see anything, sorry. The person was covering their face with their hood."

"I wonder who that was," Olive whispered, peering out into the empty hallway.

"Clearly someone who wants information like we do, but why?" I glanced over to the bottom drawer of the Student Records cabinet, still wide open. "I closed that, so whatever they wanted came from that drawer."

Olive and I knelt down and skimmed our fingers over the student files, going from A to G, H to N, then O to—

"Charley, your file is missing. They took *yours*," Olive gasped.

Rule #21
SECRETS DON'T STAY HIDDEN FOREVER

The Monday morning clatter of breakfast dishes, coffee mugs, and butter knives pounded my head. We hadn't gotten much sleep at all. Olive had managed a few hours until the alarm rattled on her wooden desk, but I had been awake all night, thinking about that file and whose hands it was now in.

"I just don't get it." Olive sighed, as she dropped her cereal spoon into her bowl. "Who would want your file?"

"There's not much in there apart from some old school reports, grade sheets, and maybe some recommendations from my teachers to get me in here. It's pretty boring, really," I muttered, my skin prickling.

Olive leaned in to say something.

"I think my entire application packet is in there too, doing nothing but taking up space," I said before she could speak, hoping that would be enough to account for the thickness of the folder.

Olive closed her mouth and sat back in her chair.

I exhaled loudly and gazed down at my breakfast. My toast sat untouched, the butter now glistening on the soggy bread, which stuck to the ceramic plate. My coffee mug had been drained, and I'd begged the cafeteria ladies for a second mug. Sixth years were allowed one hit of caffeine in the mornings; anything else was a vice, according to Blyth, who I had seen in the teachers' lounge hunched over her own coffee mug at all times of day.

Strangled Sarah sat opposite me with her bent, crushed neck, waving her hands through a coffee mug.

"I know," groaned Meghan beside her. "I need one too."

"So what now?" asked Olive.

I shrugged again. I knew I had more important things to consider, such as a crazy serial killer picking off us sixth-year girls one by one, but selfishly, all I could think about was my file. What would this person do with it? Who would they tell? I glanced around the room, wondering if any of them had it. And if the thief was here, had they read it yet? Of course they had. It made for good reading material.

A wave of nausea flooded my body. Everybody would know who I really was, and if they didn't already, then a quick internet search of my real name would give them all the information they'd need. I'd have to leave Harrogate, say goodbye to Olive, go to a new school, a new town . . .

"Charley, are you OK? You look as white as a ghost," said Olive.

I briefly glanced up at the ghosts, all red and tissue-y and . . . *crumbly*? Why were Hannah's hands beginning to blacken and crumble?

"Charley?"

I looked at Olive, whose eyes widened with concern and fear.

"I'm fine. I'm just feeling a bit under the weather with everything that's been going on. Do you mind if I go lie down?"

"No, go ahead. I'll clean up your breakfast tray, don't worry."

"Thanks," I mumbled, stumbling out of the chair. The dining hall was still busy, sounds of chaotic chatter and clanging cutlery reverberating off the old stone walls, where a tapestry from the old friary hung alongside lanterns and sconces. Rochelle and Annabelle sat huddled into what I imagined was their second or third coffee, the standard breakfast rules not applying to them. Their eyes darkened as I walked past them, eyes following me out the door. Were they our killers? Did they have my file? Surely if they did, the entire school would know the contents by now?

I skimmed a finger over my thin gold "S" pendant, then forced myself out into the bitter morning chill. Halloween was just a few days away, my favorite time of year, but I was far too distracted to enjoy it. Besides, I didn't need to read Stephen King or watch a teen slasher flick about a vengeful killer—I was *living* the horror genre.

"Cheer up," Meghan said beside me.

"Easy for you to say. You're not being targeted by a killer from a horror movie and haunted by his victims." I immediately bit my lip.

Meghan spun around to face me, the fence post jutting from her torso. "No, you're right. I was just thrown off a roof by the killer from a horror movie and now I'm one of the victims haunting you. Oh, yeah, I have it *so* easy."

"Sorry." I winced. "Sometimes I forget you're . . . you're . . ."

"Dead?"

"Yup."

"Yeah, me too." She sighed. "On Saturday I tried to go to Theater Club rehearsal, but I couldn't, obviously. Sucks."

I opened my mouth and then quickly closed it as a group of students hurried past me. If they saw me talking to myself, I'd be on a boat to the mainland for a trip to the hospital. I pushed open the door to the Elizabeth Wing, the warmth from the radiators thick and stifling. The walls were lined with framed awards and certificates—*School of Excellence, Highest Achievement in the Education Sector, 2022 Cultural Award, 2023 Sustainability Award.* Harrogate was a school full of overachievers. And then there was me. I saw my pale, tired reflection in the glass cabinets filled with trophies, plaques, and awards. I rubbed my eyes and stumbled on. Farther down the Elizabeth Wing was Blyth's office, tucked into a corner of the hallway, facing out onto the courtyard where students gathered and talked animatedly. Blyth probably saw and heard everything, knew all of our secrets.

As I crept past her office, I saw the door was slightly ajar and heard familiar voices. I snuck over to the wall and leaned into the room, careful not to cast any shadows across the door.

". . . Are you certain?"

"Yes, Martin. Someone has been in my office. I can tell."

"A student?"

"Perhaps."

"Pruitt?"

"If Pruitt has been here, it means he's getting desperate, which is not good. Not good at all." Blyth sighed, and I held my breath. "Tell Terry to be on alert. I want to know all Pruitt's movements on this island from now on."

"Will do."

Suddenly the door flew open and Mr. Gillies stood in the doorway, blocking most of the light from Blyth's office. I gasped. Meghan squeaked.

"Sullivan? What are you doing here?"

"I . . . um . . . I . . ." What was I doing there? What could I say?

Blyth's voice called out from behind him, "Charley?"

SCARLETT DUNMORE

I squeezed past Mr. Gillies, who glared at me. "Sorry to interrupt, but I was just wondering if there was any news about Gabrielle?" Phew. I had a reason to come by. Kind of. Gabrielle's headless ghost bobbed around in the hallway, her limbs shooting out, searching for a head. Meghan jumped over her leg like it was a skipping rope.

Blyth glanced at Mr. Gillies, her eyes wide and full of concern. Did they know something?

"No," Mr. Gillies said sharply. "Now shouldn't you be getting ready for first period?"

I nodded and fumbled my way out of the office, down the hallway, and through to the next wing, where I crossed over to get to my dorm. I checked behind me to see if anyone was following. Other than four ghosts.

"That was close," Meghan cried, floating down the hallway.

"Very close," I agreed.

"You better hope they don't trace the office break-in back to you and Olive. Otherwise, you're going to be on the first boat out of here, and we're all going to be stuck like this—haunting Harrogate's hallways."

"That has a nice movie title ring to it," I mused.

The dormitory hallway was eerily quiet at this time, with most students still in the dining hall finishing their breakfasts before first bell, and the squawking of the hungry gulls could be heard. I had heard tales of gulls pestering students in the courtyard on sunny afternoons as they sat by the fountain with their lunch trays. I had yet to see a seagull attack myself, and was happy about that. I didn't like birds. Sharp hungry beaks, snapping claws and wings. I tended to avoid horror movies where they were the antagonists.

As if they could hear my thoughts, one swooped at the window of the hallway, making me startle and squeal. I hurried on a little faster to my dorm. The door was stiff, like it was caught on something, perhaps the sleeve of a sweater lying on the floor or a corner of one of Olive's textbooks. When I thrust it open, I heard the crinkling of paper.

Beneath my feet, still partially wedged underneath the door, was a brown envelope with my name scribbled across it. I bent down and slowly opened it, tugging out a single sheet of paper.

I have your file.
Meet me at the friary at 8:30 p.m. Come alone.

Rule #22
CARDIO, CARDIO, CARDIO!

That evening, while Olive memorized the periodic table for her advanced chemistry exams, occasionally mumbling something about atomic numbers and symbols, I layered up in as many clothes as possible. Yet an icy cold set into my bones as I wondered who had put that note under my door. Was I about to come face-to-face with the thief who had snuck into Blyth's office?

For the second time that day, I had lied to my roommate and best friend. When she'd asked where I was going, I'd said I was meeting a tutor in the library. I couldn't tell her I was meeting someone to beg for my student file back because I couldn't risk her wondering why it was so important to me. And I certainly couldn't risk her tagging along and hearing any conversation about it. I needed a fresh start, a new life here, and whoever had my past in their hands was offering me a deal. I didn't have much money, and I certainly couldn't offer up my academic skills, but

I was so desperate that I had to hear them out. What did they want?

"I'm off now," I said to Olive, lacing up my sneakers. Survival skill: wear footwear you can run in.

"You sure you don't just want me to tutor you? I'm free."

"So is this one. Blyth set it up to help me pass English."

"That's unusually kind of her," she snorted, scribbling notes on flashcards. She glanced up and looked at me. "You're very overdressed for the library."

"That walk across the courtyard will be freezing," I replied quickly. "See you in an hour."

She nodded and went back to memorizing facts and formulas, and pacing up and down the room, while I slid out the door. The hallway outside was bustling with pre-bedtime chatter and the sounds of shower streams and shampoo bottles hitting tiles. I pushed open the door to the courtyard, the island wind slapping my cheeks. I bypassed the wing to the library, glanced behind to make sure no one was following me, other than the four ghosts, and continued on through the courtyard to the iron gates.

"Better hope you don't bump into anyone," Meghan warned, glancing around. Curfew was nigh, but the gates to the clifftops were open. I, too, scanned the courtyard for any movement, then headed through them, under the large iron archway.

I welcomed the sounds of the ocean as I headed up toward the friary. The chapel, menacing in the misty darkness, loomed over the stone walls and wings of Harrogate, keeping a close eye on us all. The stained-glass windows were dark, with the occasional flickering of a prayer candle from the altar within. At the back of the friary was a small thatched cottage, with thick walls and shuttered windows. It would be empty tonight. The minister, or whatever he was called, came only on the weekends for Sunday service, then returned on Mondays to the mainland, where he belonged. The island wasn't for everyone. Not even those who lived in solitude could spend their days out here, battered by the storms, bitten by the cold, haunted by the wails of the ocean.

October was much colder on the island than on the mainland, with temperatures occasionally dropping below freezing in the dead of night. The wind pricked at my fingertips, making me wish I had brought warmer gloves. I'd have to ask Mom to send out a pair in her next care package, assuming the school was still open by then. Even if the killer was caught, would Harrogate really be able to go on after this? Or would Blyth do her best to cover this up too? She could perhaps hide financial ruin and incidents of bullying, but surely not cold-blooded murder?

The crunch of my boots and the thrashing and crashing of waves kept up a steady rhythm, soothing me like a lullaby. But thoughts of my stolen file continued to whiz through my mind.

Pop. Snap. Crack.

"I still think this is a bad idea," Meghan said, floating next to me. Hannah beside her shook her head and looked at me longingly. "We *all* think this is a bad idea," Meghan added.

"I know, but I need that file back." I couldn't stay here if everyone knew.

Strangled Sarah marched on ahead, the moonlight illuminating all the cracks and bends and small fractured bones in her broken neck. Beside her Headless Gabrielle staggered dangerously close to the cliff edge.

"She's getting annoying," Meghan moaned. "Although I should at least be grateful that without her head she can't talk."

I snorted and carried on up the path, which rose to the stone steps of the friary. Its thick wooden door was padlocked. There would be no meeting inside, apparently. I tugged my coat tighter around my torso, huddled into the collar for warmth, and waited. Down below, the seas churned, the coastal fog rising up and pooling around my shoes until I couldn't even see my laces anymore. The deep murky blue waters crashed and rolled over the rocks, competing with the sounds of Hannah's bones as they cracked, popped, and snapped. It seemed louder tonight, more frenzied.

"It's freezing," I mumbled, my mouth pressed against the fabric around my neck.

"I'm toasty warm," Meghan remarked.

"How long have we been standing here?"

"I don't really keep time, being dead and all," she retorted.

I yanked my sleeve up, the cold biting at my exposed skin, and glanced at my watch. "It's been twenty minutes. Is this person coming or what?"

"Curfew's at 9 p.m.," Meghan reminded me.

"I know," I said, sitting beside her.

"You can't afford to be caught out here past curfew."

"I know."

"If you get expelled from Harrogate, what happens to all of us?" she snapped. I glared at her, briefly wishing she'd been impaled through the mouth.

She rolled her eyes and looked over to the cliffs. "She's a bit close to the edge, isn't she?"

We watched Gabrielle as she teetered on the rocks by the coastal path in her blue stilettos. Before I could call out, she disappeared over the edge, a glimpse of a tanned leg in the darkness.

Meghan and I shot upright and slowly turned to each other. "Did she just . . . d-die again?" I stuttered.

Meghan's eyes widened and she opened her mouth, then closed it and sighed. "Shit, she's back." She pointed to Gabrielle's headless body stumbling back up the friary hill toward us. "Knew she wouldn't be that easy to get rid of."

"So you all can't die twice—good to know." I nodded.

Suddenly, the curfew bell tore through the crashing waves and silent dark skies, startling me.

As it clanged and tolled, swinging to and fro, Half-Broken Hannah staggered toward me, her arms outstretched, her fingers blackened. Her joints twisted and curled as she walked, and she was trying to say something. The black I'd noticed on her feet only days earlier had spread all over her body, along her arms and up her back to her cheeks like something out of *Silent Hill*. She continued reaching for me, her fingers clawing the air. I screamed and staggered back against the stairs, bashing my spine on the stone. The black turned to ash, crumbling her broken limbs, until she was dust. Then she was gone.

A deep silence closed in around us as the bell stopped tolling. "What . . . what just happened?" spluttered Meghan.

"I don't know," I gasped. "Is she coming back too?" We gazed to the friary hill, where only moments ago Gabrielle had reappeared, but the hill was shrouded in an empty darkness.

I looked at Meghan, no longer feeling the cold. "I don't think she is."

Before Meghan could reply, I heard heavy footsteps behind the friary. I sucked in a breath and waited to see who it was, but the fog closed in and all I could see was darkness and mist. I resisted calling out, knowing full well from horror movies that saying "Hello, is anyone there?" only informs whoever is there of your presence and location.

Clomp—clomp—clomp.

These were definitely footsteps, and moreover, they were coming toward me. Suddenly my school file seemed trivial. Here I was, alone on a cliff edge, in the dark, past curfew, in the middle of a Halloween killing spree. Not even Olive knew I was here, which meant no one would come looking for me.

"I think it's time to go," Meghan urged, staring into the mist that surrounded the friary, as the footsteps became louder. Closer.

"Good idea." I turned and broke into a run, my sneakers catching on the small rocks and stones on the path, tripping me. My hands clawed at the mist, desperately trying to clear my path, but the sea fog blanketed everything the moonlight hit, and I stumbled. That was all it took. One stumble and they were suddenly right there.

A weight slammed into me from behind, then I was down. My head brushed against a stone, and I felt the world around me tilt. The weight was upon me, on my belly, my chest, pushing me down. Through the wet mist, I saw a glimmer of gold—a mask!

I bucked hard, lifting myself as far off the ground as I could. The figure on top of me fell over sideways. I saw black trousers and black boots, then I scrambled up and started running again. My thighs throbbed as I pounded the ground, sweat dripping and warming my skin. My legs felt weak underneath my jeans, and I cursed myself for ignoring a vital rule for surviving a horror movie: cardio! You can't run from the killer if you're huffing and puffing!

"Damn you, PE!" I howled as I bolted down, down, down, toward the Elizabeth Wing of the school.

I could feel them still behind me, gaining on me. "Run *faster*!" I heard Meghan shout to me.

The courtyard was almost there, almost . . .

The impact of whatever I hit next sent me tumbling to the ground, rolling off to the side. I hit the corner of the courtyard archway and howled in pain as a shriek pierced the air beside me. I flipped over and gazed back at the cliffs, but there was nothing behind me anymore, just mist. Whoever was chasing me was gone.

"What the hell?!" screamed someone from the ground.

I slowly turned to face whatever I had run into and saw Rochelle sprawled on the courtyard, her long dark curly hair covering her face. She swept it off to the side and glared at me. "Charley? Now you're in for it. I'm going to enjoy telling Blyth." She smirked, her eyes darkening.

Rule #23
KNOW THE FINALE

Headmistress Blyth tutted at me the next morning. "Charley Sullivan. I'm getting sick of seeing you in my office."

I sighed and collapsed back into my armchair, while Rochelle Smyth curled up in the one beside me, grinning.

"Do you want to explain to me why you were out last night after curfew?"

"She just barreled into me, knocking me right over. I could have been seriously injured," Rochelle moaned.

"Rochelle," Blyth chided. "I'm handling it."

"Of course, Headmistress." She smiled sweetly.

"What were you doing out there, Charley?"

I considered telling Blyth everything—that I was chased by a person in a mask, that the person sitting beside me and her friend might be the killers, or maybe it was even one of Blyth's staff, but I knew she wouldn't want to hear this story again. Also, I didn't want to give her that information just yet. I didn't fully trust her. We'd already ruled her out as our killer, given her desperation to keep Harrogate afloat, regardless of what it took, but what if she was also protecting someone—a student? An old friend?

I glanced back at the now three ghosts for answers, but they huddled together quietly, still reeling from last night. Gabrielle didn't seem to have noticed, but without Hannah, Sarah and Meghan looked . . . *lost*.

"Charley?" Blyth said.

"Um, I was out walking."

"Walking? In the fog?" asked Blyth.

"Creepy," Rochelle muttered. "She broke curfew. She might be new here, but rules are rules."

"Rochelle!" snapped Blyth. She got up from her seat and turned to face the window, looking out onto the courtyard, where clusters of students huddled together.

I glanced at the filing cabinet beside me, wondering whether she knew a student file had been stolen yet: *my* file. A ghost of a grin flickered across Rochelle's face when I looked over at her. Why would she send me that note? What did she want?

"Charley." Blyth sighed, turning back to me. "Curfew is there for a reason. We can't have students wandering around in the dark too close to the cliffs. And we've already had three tragic deaths this semester, possibly four now."

"Four?" I asked, my eyes shooting up to meet hers. "Gabrielle is no longer *missing*?"

"We found a handbag at the bottom of one of the cliffs, on a rock near the water. Gabrielle's bag."

Rochelle shuddered beside me, placing a hand over her mouth as if she expected to burst into tears. But no tears came, just theatrics.

"We're treating it as a tragic accident."

"Another one?" I muttered, trying not to roll my eyes. I must have imagined that someone chased me along the cliff in a mask like a scene from *Halloween*.

"I'm sorry, but I have to emphasize the importance of rules such as a curfew, for the safety of my students. I have no choice but to put you in detention for the remainder of the week."

"The week?" I wailed. Rochelle removed her hand from her face, from her fake tears, long enough to smirk at me. "What about her?" I added. "She was out too. Shouldn't she also be made an example of? For the safety of the students, of course."

Rochelle's face paled, then flushed red. "I couldn't focus on my French assignment. I'd just heard that my best friend had possibly fallen to her death, so I went for a walk."

I narrowed my stare. Had she been coming to bribe me or kill me?

Blyth cleared her throat. "Rochelle, Charley's right. I'm afraid it's detention for you too."

"I'm grieving!" she howled.

"You can grieve in detention," I snarled. "It'll be nice and quiet."

"Detention for both of you, starting today. Now, back to your classes."

Rochelle launched herself out of the armchair and pushed for the door, knocking me out the way.

"Oh, and Charley," called Blyth.

I turned back to see her perched in her chair, hands clasped tightly together, the rain behind her hammering at the glass.

"Try to stay out of this office for at least the rest of the week, please. I'm trying hard to keep this out of your file, for your aunt's sake," she warned.

I glanced at the bottom drawer of the cabinet, knowing my file was no longer there, and nodded quickly.

The hallways were quiet with most students now in their first class, having finished breakfast while Rochelle and I had been meeting with Blyth. I decided to skip English, because I had more important things to do that didn't involve heated debates about Mr. Rochester from *Jane Eyre*, and headed straight back to the dorms. It was quiet without the pop, crack, and snap of Hannah's bones, and an unfamiliar silence set in, spreading over the floors and furniture. I sat on the edge of the bed and took a shaky breath. Sarah and Meghan hovered by the sink, and Headless Gabrielle floated into Olive's laundry basket in the corner of the room.

"What happened?" I finally asked.

Sarah wheezed and gasped, desperately trying to talk.

"I don't know. We all thought we'd be stuck with you either forever or until you'd figured out who is behind all these killings," Meghan said solemnly. Sarah stopped making sounds and sat down on the bed beside me. "It was like she fast-forwarded through decomposition. One minute she was there, and the next she was a pile of ash."

"What do you mean? Is being a ghost *temporary*?"

"Maybe," she whispered. She sat, as if putting her weight on the bed, but the covers lay undisturbed next to me. "Where do you think she went?"

"Hannah's probably in a better place than here," I said, biting my lip.

Meghan shook her head. "You don't believe that."

"I do," I argued weakly. Honestly, I had no idea where Hannah was, but I couldn't say that. Not when it could be Sarah's or Meghan's turn next.

"You saw her." Meghan sniffed beside me. "She looked scared. She definitely didn't look like she was walking toward any light."

"She has to be in some kind of afterlife, surely. I don't think here, at Harrogate with me, is the afterlife? If so, then I hope I never die."

Meghan stood and began pacing, though her feet hovered just above the ground. "There must be some kind of timer on all of us, and while this carries on, while the killer is still out there, our timers go off, one by one."

"Don't say that."

"It's true. And I know you think so too."

I gazed down at the ground by my feet, not quite sure

what I thought now. Serial murders, ghosts, a school on a cliff edge in the middle of the ocean? My head was scrambled. Suddenly, I stood up. If Meghan was right, and they all had some kind of timer, then I wouldn't just sit here and wait for each one to buzz. We were a team—a very dysfunctional and paranormal one, but a team nonetheless. And even though I didn't do sports and dodged PE whenever possible, I knew you didn't abandon your teammates. We were in this together. "Well, if it's true, then we still have time to catch the person who did this to you all before—"

"Before we turn into a pile of ash and get sucked into some in-between world, or maybe even hell?"

"Yes, before all that happens." I winced, wondering if she would persist or give up. "Sorry, I'm not very good at pep talks."

Sarah gurgled and choked on words in the corner of the room.

I pointed to her. "She's the sports captain here. She should be doing this."

Sarah spluttered and wheezed some more, then rolled her eyes and gave up.

"I think that *was* her pep talk," Meghan said.

"Great job, we heard every word," I said to Sarah, plastering a vacant smile on my face in an attempt to boost morale. "Now, let's get back to it. We have a lot of work to do!"

Meghan stood beside me. "We better hurry up, otherwise

you'll only be left with that one over there since she was the last to die." We all glanced over to Headless Gabrielle, who was now crawling on the floor in her blue stilettos, her hands stretched out, still searching for her head. I immediately grabbed a marker off the desk and got to work.

By the time Olive came back from class, I had rewritten the list of suspects from the poster on the door, but this time added more names and faces, including *Lunch Lady with Crooked Tooth* and *Girl in English Class with Lazy Eye*. Suddenly, everyone was a suspect.

"How did it go with Blyth?" asked Olive tentatively, creeping into the room.

"I got detention." I shrugged. "Not my first time."

She gasped dramatically. "I've never had detention."

"Why does that not surprise me?" snarked Meghan from the corner.

"What are you doing?" Olive asked, coming closer.

"Looking."

"For what?"

"Something I missed the first time I looked at this."

"Like what?"

"Something that could tell us what the big game plan is."

Olive plopped down on the bed, unknowingly next to a ghost with a bent, crushed neck and another one without a neck, or head, at all. Her heavy shoulder bag fell to the floor with a loud thud. "If we're the horror movie experts, then shouldn't we know that?"

"She's onto something." Meghan nodded. "You both should know how this all ends."

"You're right!" I started pacing around the rug that separated our beds. "We need to work backward—what do we know about movie finales?"

"They're always set at night!" Olive quipped, raising her hand again like she was in a classroom.

"Yes!" I snapped my fingers. "The ending of slasher movies almost always unfolds over the course of an evening, like—"

"*Scream!*" Meghan squealed excitedly, clapping her hands like she was applauding herself in a performance.

"*After Midnight, Night School, Hell Night,*" I added, racking my brain for our favorite "night" titles.

"And there's always a costume, like a stupid mask to cover up their identity until the very last scene, where it gets ripped off or broken, just to make it extra dramatic so the audience gasps when their face is revealed," Meghan added, wagging her finger at the poster on the back of the door.

I nodded. "And the final scene is usually when a group of people get together, like they think safety in numbers is going to help them."

"*The House on Sorority Row,*" Olive chimed in. "And *Killer Party!*"

"Sometimes during a dance or school prom."

"*Carrie.*" Olive nodded. "*Prom Night.*"

SCARLETT DUNMORE

I nod enthusiastically. "And sometimes over a holiday, like *Black Christmas* or—"

"*Halloween*," Olive added.

I glanced at Meghan, then grabbed Olive's shoulders, my eyes widening. "That's it!"

"The Halloween formal!" the three of us shouted together.

Meghan bounced up and down. "I got it! I'm a film nerd too!"

"That's the end game!" I shouted. "That's the killer's last move. It's *Halloween*! Mike Myers is gearing up for the big finale! And we need to be ready."

"How?" Meghan scoffed.

I took a step back. "We need to stop the Halloween formal for a start, and not give the killer the backdrop for their final scene."

Olive shook her head. "Good luck with that. The party committee will kill you. I'd be more afraid of a committee full of hormone-crazed seniors who've been counting down the days to this formal than the masked Harrogate killer."

"Rochelle will just have to find another dance to wear her French maid costume to . . . assuming she's not the killer," I quipped.

Olive groaned. "She was probably going as a *Great Gatsby* flapper girl. She's definitely a Daisy Buchanan wannabe."

I raised my eyebrows. "Who?"

"Seriously, Charley, you can't just read Stephen King books all the time. No wonder you're failing English."

I waved her off. "Anyway, back to the task at hand. We're stopping the Halloween formal."

Meghan shrugged. "Then what?"

"Then we need to prepare everyone," I continued. "Source weapons, stuff like that."

Olive scrunched up her nose. "Weapons? What, like sharpened pencils and heavy textbooks?"

"I bet wood shop has some cool weapons," Meghan suggested.

"Wood shop! Yes! And if the Harrogate killer really is targeting us for whatever reason, other than we're easy to frame because of our horror and gore fascination, then we need to arm *ourselves*. Because we'll be their final targets."

Olive grinned. "The smug final girls."

"Seriously?" scoffed Meghan.

"The smug final girls." I nodded in agreement. "We're Jamie Lee Curtis. We're putting an end to Michael Myers once and for all." I stood and faced the poster on the back door, suspects circled, crossed off, highlighted. One of them was the killer, and we were going to find out who.

Olive shuffled up behind me. "You know, Michael Myers comes back. Like again and again and again . . . I mean, there are a lot of sequels to *Halloween*."

I put my hands on my hips and sighed. "I can't stop watching them, but I really hate sequels."

Rule #24

ARM YOURSELF, NOT THE KILLER

Detention came around fast. Classes whizzed by, and thankfully I had gone most of the day without seeing Rochelle Smyth again.

Until now.

By the time I reached the doors of detention, which was held in Mr. Gillies's wood shop classroom—much to his dismay—Rochelle was already there, perched on a high chair at one of the workbenches. She scowled at me when I entered and continued burning the scowl into my back as I walked to the other side of the room and found a chair as far away from her as possible.

"This is all your fault, you know," she snapped.

"No talking," I reminded her, flashing a wide grin.

"I should be grieving for my friend, not here with you. I'm trying to plan a memorial party for Gabrielle."

"Because nothing says *rest in peace* more than dance

music and sequin skirts. Oh, you are such a good friend, Rochelle," I snarked.

"What would you know about that?" she snapped. "You have one friend on this whole island, and that's only because she's your roommate. And I bet you have even less friends on the mainland. No one's exactly missing you back home. *Snitch*."

My blood turned to ice, my skin tingling with shock. "W-what did you just say?" I stammered, slowly turning to face her.

There it was. The truth. She *knew*.

The door slammed against the wall, jolting me out of my seat. Mr. Gillies stood in the doorway with a stack of papers and a coffee mug. "No talking in detention," he snapped, slowly making his way toward his desk and slumping into his big leather chair. He looked around at his machinery and craftsmanship. "And don't touch anything."

I glared at Rochelle, desperate to ask more, to find out exactly how much she knew about me and, more importantly, who she was planning to tell. And why? Was this all really just to know more about me? Was she that desperate to expose my past? Or was this the work of the Harrogate serial killer and now she was sitting behind me . . . in a classroom filled with hacksaws, hammers, and screwdrivers?

I stared at the workbench she was perched over as she stared mindlessly at the clock next to Mr. Gillies, her face still plastered with that smug satisfied smile, a hacksaw only inches from her hands. Did no one around here understand the stupidity of leaving such weapons unattended with a serial killer running about? Hadn't anyone watched a high school horror movie before?

The minutes ticked by slowly on the clock, each stroke excruciatingly long.

Tick.

Tick.

Tick.

Then commenced the gurgling and wheezing of a ghost with a bent, crushed neck. Meghan, Sarah, and Gabrielle hovered around the hand-drill bench, looking perplexed. I supposed they hadn't been wood shop students. Meghan caught my eye and awkwardly smiled. I gave her a half smile back. It had been a strange few weeks indeed. At least I now knew what came after this life. The in-between. I'd always felt a strange presence, especially after Dad died, but I didn't expect to be an actual ghost whisperer. Perhaps when all this was over I could get my own reality TV show as a medium or something, assuming I survived as the final girl, of course.

After pondering potential titles, eventually landing on *The Living Dead*, as an homage to Romero, I slumped back into boredom.

Tick.

Tick.

Tick.

HOW TO SURVIVE A HORROR MOVIE

I couldn't take this anymore. The classroom felt hot, stifling. I scratched at my collar, and pulled at my shirt, wafting a cold breeze up and under it. Rochelle didn't flinch, didn't show any signs of being uncomfortable or bothered at all. She just stared straight ahead, like a mindless killer. Could it really be her? Or maybe Olive was right, that was too obvious?

Tick.

Mr. Gillies drummed his fingers on the desk as he leaned back in his chair, his eyes inky and empty. Or was it him? Could he really be harming his students? He continued drumming, the rhythmic patter lulling me to sleep. I rested my chin on my hand, feeling a heaviness wash over me. I couldn't remember when I'd last slept through the night.

Tick.

The heaviness became overwhelming, pulling me under . . .

under . . .

under . . .

When I opened my eyes, I was sitting in the middle of a long line of cold metal chairs, the backrest stiff and hard against my spine. My sneakers had been replaced with shiny black shoes; my school uniform was a crisp pantsuit with a freshly ironed white shirt. There was a red poppy pinned to the collar of my blazer. I brushed a hand to my ear and felt the lobe bare, all the piercings removed. My hair was tightly knotted in a bun, secured with a thin band. I wore the gold necklace, the "S" pendant sitting at my collarbone, but she didn't come that day to see me.

A shuffling of feet and a murmur of voices brought my attention back to the courtroom full of people waiting for my statement. Lawyers, parents, relatives, social workers. They were all here. All waiting to see what I would say today.

I knew this moment well, as I often replayed it in my head at night while Olive snored beside me. This was the moment I turned against all of my friends. This was the moment I pointed my finger, named names, and showed evidence. This was the moment I threw everyone under the bus to save myself. Perhaps if Sadie had come to court that day, I wouldn't have said her name. Or perhaps I still would have.

I served six months in a detention center after that. Not everything I had done could be forgotten. And then I was allowed home, my record wiped. I was no longer Lottie Ryan. I needed to be someone else, and I couldn't be that someone else in this town. I had to leave, go somewhere new, somewhere isolated, where I could pretend. Mom showed me a leaflet for Harrogate School for Girls the day I was released. The day someone threw a rock at our front door. I would have said yes to anything.

A voice danced at the edges of my mind, telling me that this was a dream, but I couldn't break free, couldn't find my path back to reality. When I glanced up, I saw my mom sitting in the front row of the courtroom with our lawyer and social worker, dressed in a pantsuit similar to mine that she'd borrowed from a friend. She still wore her wedding ring and the pearl earrings Dad had given her for their last anniversary. She sold those only a few months later to pay the registration fees at Harrogate.

I watched her, the courtroom silent, voices once again muffled. She wiped a tear from her cheek and glanced at me, her cheeks suffused with a warm red shade.

Suddenly, gloved hands appeared around her neck, sliding over the skin. When I looked up, I saw the Harrogate killer, dressed in black, masked in glimmering gold. I opened my mouth to scream, to warn Mom, to save her, but the words choked me like hot burning bile. Then I saw the hacksaw, rising up and up, aimed at her neck. Her perfect white neck. It sliced slowly through the skin, the vein gushing, blood soaking through her clothes, spilling onto the floor around her and inching closer to where I sat. Her head bobbed to the side, held on by a sliver of remaining flesh. The masked killer turned to me. He wiped the blood on his sleeve and began walking toward me—

"Wake up, Charley!"

I jumped, the wood shop classroom coming back into focus, dotted with stars that flickered in my vision. The three ghosts stood silently at the workbench. I slumped to the side and felt arms around me, maneuvering me back onto the chair. When I came to, I saw Mr. Gillies and started.

"You fell asleep," he said. "Detention is over." His tone had a crispness to it. A sharpness. Like a knife.

I exhaled shakily and inched away from him. I looked over to where Rochelle had been sitting, but her chair was empty. We were alone.

He didn't move toward me, didn't lunge for the hacksaw beside him, didn't pull out a gold theater mask. He simply stepped back and gestured to the door.

"Sorry," I murmured, easing off the chair but keeping my eyes on him. My legs felt alien to my body and buckled. I grabbed the bench to steady myself.

"Are you OK? Do you need me to walk you back?" he asked.

"No!" I snapped. I didn't want to show Mr. Gillies where my room was, making it easier for him to return if he was the killer. Although maybe he already knew all of our dorms, and even all of our secrets too. "I mean, no, thank you, Mr. Gillies. I'm OK to walk back myself." I staggered toward the doorway.

"Charley," he called out, and I turned around. "Be careful." His eyes darkened, and I rushed out into the hallway.

The Rose Wing was empty, classes long ended and students long gone. Rooms were darkened, doors closed. The gentle humming and buzzing of tablets, laptops, and projectors was gone, and all that filled the halls was the ticking of clocks and the distant chattering of students from outside in the courtyard, making their way to the dinner hall.

When I got back to the dorm, Olive was perched at our dresser tying her shoelaces. "You're back." She smiled. "How was your stint in jail?"

"What?" I spluttered.

"Jail as in detention," she said slowly. "That's what I call it, anyway."

"Oh, right, jail," I scoffed, shaking off the paranoia. "Fine, I guess. I slept through most of it."

"Doesn't sound too bad to me. I'd love a nap." She shrugged. "Dinner?"

I swallowed hard. "I'm not hungry. I don't think I can stomach anything tonight." The image of my mother getting her head hacked off was still etched in my mind. It may have been a nightmare, but it felt real. Too real.

"No!" she wailed. "I have to sit alone?"

"Sorry, I just have a queasy stomach. If I smell short ribs tonight, I'll throw up everywhere."

"Now I'm craving short ribs," moaned Meghan from the corner.

I gathered up my shower caddy and towel, which was still a little damp from the morning. "I need a hot shower, I think."

"You can't shower alone, remember. It's one of our rules," Olive argued.

"Right." I sighed, sinking back down on the bed.

SCARLETT DUNMORE

"But I'll eat quickly and meet you at the shower rooms at seven?" she suggested, grabbing a textbook about diatomic chemistry elements off her bedside table. I gazed over at the stack of Stephen King books on mine, all with dog-eared pages, some with coffee stains.

"Seven," I agreed, collapsing starfish-style onto my bed. I rolled over onto my belly and slid the book *It* off my nightstand, diving into the first chapter even though I'd read it numerous times already. I had a modern studies paper due next week, but after the day—no, the month—I'd had, a novel about a murderous fanged clown appealed to me more than a textbook about government practices.

I nestled into the bedcovers and kicked off my sneakers . . .

And by 7:20 p.m., I was five chapters in and Olive had not returned. Unsure of whether we'd agreed to meet here or at the shower rooms, I folded down the page of my book, tossed it onto the bed, and undressed. I wrapped a green Harrogate towel around me, scooped up my shower caddy, and headed out into the hallway.

"Don't worry, we'll be your shower buddies," Meghan cooed, following close behind me.

I gripped my towel tighter and walked quicker to the shower rooms. When I got there, sounds of chatter and gossip were trickling out from the cubicles, and I glanced around one more time for Olive. I padded into the middle cubicle and yanked the shower curtain across, hanging my towel and caddy on the hook inside. The showers here took

HOW TO SURVIVE A HORROR MOVIE

a moment to heat up, so I stepped back into the corner and waited for the wafts of steam to rise and billow. Then I let the water soak slowly through my hair and run in rivulets down my shoulders, arms, hips, and legs. It was wonderful.

The nightmare flickered in my mind again. My mother's face as the saw hacked through her neck. The blood, the flesh. The gold mask the killer wore as they walked toward me. I rubbed my temples and forced away the dream, instead trying to focus on the snippets of trivial conversation that floated through the shower steam from other students.

"—and I've not heard from him since then. I don't even know if he's getting my notes."

"—I can't believe exams are in a month!"

"—Halloween formal is in three days!"

"—Don't worry, I'm sure he's just busy with schoolwork."

"—Is it true they never found Gabrielle Harrison's body?"

"—and then she just freaked out! Started evacuating everyone out of the pool house, screaming something about a head in the fridge!"

I froze, the water trickling down me. I focused on that last snippet of conversation, straining to hear through the curtain.

"Don't you think it's odd that the suicides started when she got here? I'm telling you, there's something suspicious going on."

I was torn between feeling offended at her insinuations and relieved that there were other students questioning all these "accidents," so I crept closer to the curtain to hear more. But the voices all blended together, everyone talking over each other. Sounds of running water and shampoo bottles being kicked around drowned out the words, as did Meghan's voice as she loudly sang Taylor Swift outside my cubicle. I sighed and closed my eyes. Of course people were talking about me. I freaked out onstage at the academic challenge. I got a party at Eden shut down. I alerted staff to underage drinking, broken curfews, and improper use of school grounds after hours. I was found running around outside after dark in the fog and got detention.

I was as talked about here on this island as I was back home. I rubbed my neck, trying to banish images of Gabrielle's head in the fridge, of Sarah hanging from the beam, of Hannah's broken splayed body, of Meghan's vacant eyes as she slumped over the fence with a spike through her body. And of the night Hannah crumbled to ash before our eyes and disappeared forever.

When I finally opened my eyes, I realized Meghan had stopped singing. "Hello?" I called out. I turned the valve, shutting off the shower, and stood still, waiting for the cacophony of Meghan's singing, the running water, and the gossip from my living peers. But all I heard was the beating of my own heart. "Meghan?" I whispered.

"Shh!" I heard her hiss from the other end of the shower room.

Heavy footsteps thudded as someone entered. I waited, wondering if it was Olive. But no voice followed. She'd surely call out to me to check if I was here.

The air around me suddenly became very still and very quiet. My heart started racing.

A neighboring showerhead dripped, cutting through the silence. I slowly crouched down to see under the curtain. Black leather boots stood in the middle of the room, the tip of a hacksaw resting on the tiles. I shot back up again. Nope, definitely not Olive.

Meghan and Sarah appeared beside me, and Gabrielle's blue stilettos poked out from under the adjacent shower curtain.

"Charley, I don't want to freak you out or anything, but there's a person with a very large weapon outside your shower," Meghan cried, her eyes wide.

I grabbed my mouth to stifle a scream and curled into a small ball, hugging my legs in tight. Each step the person took, the saw dragged beside them, scraping the tiles like Freddy's talons in *Nightmare on Elm Street*. The dragging, scraping, screeching noise continued as the dark figure, likely masked in gold, circled around the room. Then I could hear the quick pull of shower curtains as they made their way down the cubicles, one at a time.

Rule #25

HAVE MORE THAN ONE ESCAPE ROUTE

I hadn't considered what my death would be like. I just knew that death would visit me, as it eventually would all those around me. My dad knew he was dying, so how and when he died wasn't much of a surprise to him, or us. The cancer had taken decades off his life, and the chemo treatments only gave him a few months back. Six months to be exact. Not enough time to get things in order, financially or emotionally. But his death was scheduled, and we were the spectators at the event. The specialists said he would likely die that winter, and he did. He was always a punctual and predictable man.

But as I cowered in the corner of the shower cubicle, naked, wet, and shivering, I realized that my death didn't have to be today. Unlike my dad, I had a choice—a chance. A slim one, sure, but a chance all the same.

The serrated edges of the hacksaw continued scraping on the ceramic floor tiles, like razor-sharp claws. I swallowed hard and quietly wrapped a towel around myself. My breath hitched as I heard the dragging of the saw echoing through the steamy shower room. I swatted away a cloud of warm steam and contemplated my exit options.

I had none.

As the killer made their way down the row of cubicles, they stopped suddenly. I could hear the slow dripping of a shower on the opposite wall, then a scrape of metal on tile as footsteps crossed the room. I peered out from the curtain. The killer had their back to me. I now had an exit option.

I knew this scene. Many horror films had a shower scare scene: *The Grudge, Evil Dead, Final Destination, The Faculty, Nightmare on Elm Street 5*, and of course, who can forget the classic that started it all, *Psycho*.

I was not dying in a shower. Not today, anyway.

I inhaled quietly and dropped slowly to my belly, then I shimmied under the cubicle divider to the next one. Meghan gestured me on, popping her ghost head out to keep watch. I continued on to the next, then all the way along the row until I hit the last cubicle. My back seared with pain. I must have scratched it on the bottom of a divider. I bit my lip and muffled any sound as I touched my spine and felt the warm stickiness of blood. Meghan shooed me back, her arms waving frantically. I pressed myself against the wall, tucking in tightly behind the partially opened shower curtain. The hacksaw scraped along the tiles again as the killer crossed back and recommenced the shower scare scene, yanking open one curtain at a time.

SCARLETT DUNMORE

From this last cubicle I could see the door. In fact, it was right in front of me. I just had to get past the serial killer wielding a saw. Minor obstacle.

I needed a weapon of some sort, something to throw at them. I cursed myself for leaving my L'Oreal shampoo bottle in my cubicle. A towel would have to do. Begrudgingly, I removed my towel and crept out from the cubicle. The person was facing away from me, wearing a black hoodie with the hood pulled up, concealing the string of the mask. The tip of the hacksaw was still on the floor, poised for action. I glared at the exit.

"Really?" Meghan whispered doubtfully, following my gaze to the door. Sarah shook her head. She'd seen me in PE.

I could make it. Maybe. Sure, cardio was not my strongest trait. I was not fast or light on my feet, and I sweat a lot more than the average person. One bad decision could lead to a saw slicing into my flesh. But I couldn't stand here and wait for the alternative, either. Funnily enough, that scenario also ended with a saw in my flesh.

I tiptoed closer, the soles of my bare feet merely a whisper on the wet floor as I halted behind them. Everything around me was so still, silenced, waiting, poised like the tip of the hacksaw. The killer's shoulders tensed as if they could suddenly sense me, and I knew my time was up. It was now or never. I threw my towel over their head and pulled it taut across the mask. The plastic cracked and snapped like Hannah's bones used to.

The killer staggered back into me, dropping the saw and clawing at their face.

I pulled hard, yanking them backward until they lost their footing and tumbled. "Run!" Meghan screamed as Sarah flapped her arms wildly toward the exit.

My body lunged forward, my feet moving faster than I had ever seen them move before. I skidded at the exit on a puddle of shower water, grabbing the doorframe to steady myself. Whoever was behind me grunted and gasped as they tried to stand. I screamed and bolted out of the door, down the hallway. I ran until my bare heels throbbed and ached, and the breath threatened to explode from my chest and—

Thud!

I bounced off someone and landed hard on the ground.

"What the— Charley! Again!"

I looked up from the ground, where my legs were splayed open, destroying any remaining dignity I possessed. Rochelle stood over me, hands on hips.

"Why do you keep running into me?" she fumed, then stopped to gawk at me. "And why are you naked?"

"There's someone in the showers!" I howled, covering my body with my hands.

She balked. "Of course there is—it's a *communal* shower."

"No, there's someone in the shower room with a giant saw, trying to kill me!" I hoped that was a little clearer.

"Are you crazy?" she snorted.

"Why is she here?" Meghan argued, pointing at her.

SCARLETT DUNMORE

My shoulders tensed as I took a breath. "Yeah, why are you here? This isn't your wing, Rochelle."

"First, I can go into any part of this school I want to, and second, not that it's any of your business, but I'm going around personally inviting people to Gabrielle's memorial party. And guess what, that invite list doesn't include you."

"Well, I–I . . ." I glanced across at her shoes and the words immediately got stuck in my throat. I knew those black, round-toed boots. I had been staring at them only moments ago as I cowered behind the shower curtain.

"Rochelle . . . it's . . . it's . . ." I kicked at the ground and pushed myself back away from her, away from the killer.

"I knew it!" Meghan gleamed.

"What's wrong?" Rochelle asked, taking a step toward me.

"Stay back!" I screamed.

"You are so weird," she snapped, rolling her eyes.

I clambered up and started running again, past her, past the laughter, all the way back to my dorm room, where I barreled in through the door.

"Charley, you gave me a fright! Why are you naked?" asked Olive casually. She was sitting on the bed, reading a textbook.

I rushed over to the dresser and dragged it across the wooden floor. It was heavy. "Help me!"

Olive jumped up, her eyes wide, and started pushing

from the other side, until it barricaded the door, then she quickly turned to me. "OK, what's going on?"

I collapsed on the floor, pulling the blanket off my bed to cover myself, although I was pretty sure it was a bit too late for any semblance of dignity. "Where were you?" I gasped, panting for breath.

Olive's eyes widened and she clapped her hand over her mouth. "Oh, I totally forgot!" She knelt down beside me. "Charley, I am so sorry!"

"Charley," Meghan choked.

Strangled Sarah stood at the foot of Olive's bed, her neck bent and twisted, staring at her forearms as a dark dust spread over her gray skin.

Meghan walked over and took Sarah's hand. "It's happening again."

I glanced between the ghosts—who were waiting eagerly for me to solve these murders, to avenge Sarah before she, too, vanished—and my best friend, Olive, who was still here, alive. But perhaps not for much longer.

I couldn't take this anymore. Everyone depending on me, needing me to do something, to act. I didn't know what to do. The killer was after me too. I was next on their list, and probably Olive as well. I couldn't spend the rest of my days here at Harrogate dodging a maniacal murderer. Who was I kidding? I was no expert. I was scared. Same as everyone else. And just like before—like that day in court—I had to choose survival. Over everything else. Over friendship.

SCARLETT DUNMORE

I jumped up, the blanket still wrapped around me, and started throwing my things on the bed. Books, clothes, hairbrush, DVDs, everything. "That's it. We're getting off this island."

"What?" Meghan screamed. "You're leaving us?"

"I'm leaving *Harrogate*," I corrected.

"You're such a coward!" Meghan yelled.

"When?" asked Olive.

"Tonight."

"Tonight? We won't get a boat out tonight," Olive gasped, gazing at the darkness pressing against the windows. "If there is a serial killer on this island, then I'm not walking out to the pier in the pitch-black darkness! You may as well tape a sign to your forehead saying *Kill me next*."

"We have to go now," I panted, rushing around the drawers and the cabinets. How could I have accumulated this much stuff in such a short time?

"Charley, don't go," Meghan pleaded, pointing at Sarah.

Olive took a step toward me, blocking my path to the wardrobe. "Charley, listen to yourself. You're breaking all of your own rules."

I sighed and collapsed on the bed, my head throbbing. "Fine, tomorrow, then. We're leaving tomorrow. There's a homicidal maniac at Harrogate, and she's not going to stop until we're all dead! No one believes me. Everyone thinks I'm crazy. I'm done!"

"Me too." Meghan threw her arms up in the air and

then, in a blink of an eye, disappeared, along with the fumbling Headless Gabrielle and the now-fading Sarah.

"She? How do you know the killer is a she?" Olive wheezed.

"I think it's Rochelle," I said, throwing my vintage *Friday the 13th* hoodie over my wet hair. The damp strands clung to my spine, soaking through the material.

"Rochelle? Look, I've been thinking . . . she's evil, I'll give you that, and you haven't been here long enough to fully appreciate just how evil she can be, but a serial killer? I don't know."

"It has to be her! Prom queen is our killer! I know she took my file that night, and every time the killer attacks, she just happens to be hovering nearby. And she has the same boots. It's her! I know it is." I paced frantically in circles, occasionally tripping on the bottom of my joggers. "Tomorrow morning, we'll head down to the docks first thing—"

"Will we have breakfast first?"

"No, Olive. There's no time for breakfast. We leave at dawn." Olive's shoulders dropped. "And Mr. Terry will take us over to the mainland, where we'll go to the police ourselves. No more hiding this. If Blyth isn't going to do something about it, then I will."

Olive chewed on her bottom lip, her fingers wildly fidgeting in her lap.

"Are you with me, Olivia Montgomery? You're the only one I have left," I said, gazing at the empty corner of the room where I was used to seeing Meghan, Hannah, and Sarah. Now all I saw was a pile of Olive's dirty PE clothes and a half-folded zombie graphic novel. A twinge of guilt tugged at my insides, and I bit my lip. I wasn't abandoning them. As soon as I reached the mainland, I'd get help. Out here, I couldn't do anything. I couldn't help anyone. I just needed off this island.

Olive stared at the ground, shifting her weight on the bed. "Um . . ."

"Olive?"

"We're not supposed to leave the island. And it's in the middle of the semester. Blyth will kill us! Or worse, expel us!"

"There's a murderer on this island! I'm next, then probably you!"

"Me?"

"We're all targets. And if it is Rochelle, then she knows just how to get us."

Olive sighed and flopped onto her bed. "OK, but after she's carried off this island in handcuffs, can I please just get back to my studies? I'm taking seven subjects!"

"Deal." I finished stuffing my things into the yellow case I'd come here with and collapsed on the bed. "Try to get some sleep. It'll be an early start."

"Sleep? No chance. Not now that you've told me the school bully is also the school murderer, and she knows what dorm room we're in." Olive sighed.

When we lay down in our beds, she tossed and turned at first, the quilt loudly churning with her, but after a few minutes her familiar grunts and snores filled the room.

Now it was my turn to wrestle and squirm under the covers, sliding them on and off my body, feeling both chills from my recent brush with death and heat from the probability of another one approaching. Would the killer come here, to our dorm room? Would I wake to find a gold-faced figure standing over my bed with the same saw Olive used to accidentally slice through her bird feeder? I gazed over at her, sleeping deeply on top of her covers in her clothes, halfway down the single bed, her high-top Converses dangling over the end; then gazed at the back corner, but Meghan, Sarah, and Gabrielle hadn't returned. I wondered if, when they did finally reappear, having forgiven me for abandoning ship, Sarah would be with them still. A lot of thoughts spiraled through my mind that night. Yet somewhere between 2 a.m. and 5 a.m., I dozed off.

I awoke with a jolt. Darkness shrouded everything. From what I could see, Olive still lay curled up on top of her covers.

I sat up and willed my eyes to focus on the door again, pressing into the dark air. The wind howled at the window, pleading to come inside, and the raindrops thumped against the glass. By the time light crept into the room, staining the bedroom floor in warm amber hues, my head throbbed and pulsed with fatigue and fear. At around 5:45 a.m., I gently woke Olive, waited for her to throw some things into a backpack bigger than she was, and then we set off on our journey back to the mainland. We shifted the dresser together, scraping the feet on the wooden floor, and slid out into the silent hallways of a sleeping Harrogate.

The morning chill slapped our cheeks as we pushed open the back door and started making our way across the gravel paths, down to the pebble beach and the dock. Above us, seagulls squawked and soared. Hungry, waiting, slicing through the sky. I had forgotten my gloves at the dorm room, and the cold nipped at my fingertips, but I didn't intend to turn back. The wheels of my silly yellow suitcase caught on every shrub, every blade of grass, every stone, and I remembered the day I wheeled it through the courtyard to Blyth's office. She'd welcomed me to Harrogate, her tall, broad silhouette blocking the doorway, then sat me down to review my academic electives. She gave me a map of the school, before diving into the rules and formalities, after which she'd suggested I review them in the handbook waiting in my welcome bag in my room. I'd walked slowly to my dorm room, alone. The hallway was empty and quiet, except for the squeaking of my suitcase wheels on the floor. I'd whispered to myself, over and over again, until my hands touched the doorknob of my new bedroom, "I am Charley Sullivan. I am Charley Sullivan."

I didn't know if I was reminding myself of my new name

or reminding myself that my former self had been left behind on the mainland, back at the harbor where the city buildings rose high and the landscape was crammed with roads and streets and cars. I had been terrified that day, not knowing what to expect from Harrogate.

But not as terrified as I was today.

By the time we reached the cliff edge and started our descent, I was sick of dragging the case and considered launching it over the edge into the vast ocean. But then I remembered my entire retro horror film collection was inside plus my favorite Stephen King hardback and an unopened bag of Skittles, so I quickly changed my mind. Beside me, Olive's stomach gurgled and moaned for food. She rubbed her belly apologetically.

We stood on the edge of the pebble beach, the ocean unfolding in front of us, the mainland nowhere in sight. All I saw was water and space, a vast empty space. But I knew it was out there somewhere—civilization, *rationality*, home. "Come on," I said, gesturing toward the docks.

The school ferry wasn't much bigger than an old fisherman's trough, yet it was the only mode of transport off the island at this time. A larger vessel came in June and December to take us all home for the holidays. Another opportunity to mix with the boys of Eden.

We edged slowly toward the trough as it bobbed and swayed in the shallow water. "Hello? Mr. Terry? I know it's early, but we need you to take us to the mainland."

"It's an emergency!" Olive added.

The only reply was the gentle lapping of waves against the side of the boat and the tinkling of chimes.

"He's probably still sleeping." Olive shrugged.

"He's a fisherman. They're up at like 3 a.m."

We stood at the stern, our boots at the edge of the dock.

"Maybe he's at Harrogate, eating breakfast like normal people," she grumbled as she shimmied her giant backpack off her shoulders. It crashed like a boulder to the wooden dock. The sea splashed gently against the hull, making a gurgling sound much like her stomach. Overhead, the gulls became more feverish, squawking louder, diving lower. They were charged up about something.

Olive gazed up. "I feel your pain. I'm starving too," she said to them. I lowered myself over the side of the boat, gripping the edge tightly in case I fell.

"What are you doing?" she asked.

"I'm just seeing if he's in there."

On board were blankets and nets, old lobster baskets lying on their sides, and an overpowering smell of salt and fish. The floor beneath me shifted and bobbed, making my stomach churn and flip as I zigzagged through the bench seats across the deck to the helm. The bridge was empty, a weathered-looking yellow rubber raincoat hanging on a hook beside the wheel, with some green waterproof boots underneath. Inside the bridge, taped up above the wheel in the small cabin, was a photograph of a young boy standing on a beach with a red bucket.

"Anything?" called out Olive from the dock above me.

"He's definitely not here!" I shouted back, making my way across the deck to her. Suddenly a strong smell of sulfur enveloped me, and I started coughing. "Do you smell that?" I spluttered.

"Yeah, what is that? It smells like eggs . . . God, I'm so hungry," Olive moaned.

I made my way to the back of the boat, following that smell. In the corner, where black oil seeped out, was the engine. Or, what was left of it. Whoever had got to the boat before us had ensured its destruction. Thick puddles of diesel, torn cables, a ripped-out exhaust, and dented metal plates were strewn across the back deck. Even if we could miraculously rebuild the engine, the risk of fire from the ignition was far too high. We'd blow ourselves up before we'd left shallow waters. Whoever did this knew that. And knew there was only one way off this island.

I screamed into the air, swearing and cursing.

"Stuck here with the rest of us." Impaled Meghan appeared cross-legged on top of a white cooler box, smirking.

"Did you do this?" I accused her.

She grinned. "With my ghost hands?" She tried to pick up a cable, but her slim, manicured fingers brushed through it like a cloud. "If I could touch something, it would not be a boat cable, trust me."

"Gross." I snorted.

"Did you say something?" called Olive from the docks.

Meghan uncrossed her legs, circling her ankles. As she did so, I noticed the fervent buzzing of flies around the cooler where she was hovering. Crimson was smeared on the edge of the lid.

"Um, Meghan . . ." I started, pointing to the bloodstain beneath her.

She jumped off the cooler. The lid was slightly ajar, a familiar metallic smell seeping out. Hands trembling, I reached out, my fingertips grazing the cooler lid. It was cold under my touch, under the chilly October sky. I took a deep breath as I flipped open the lid. It sprang wide, as the gulls circled rabidly overhead and the flies swarmed my hands. Inside, nestled in a pool of sticky, murky blood, was Gabrielle's severed head.

I screamed and staggered back, gripping the side of the boat to stop myself from falling into the water.

Olive fumbled onto the deck, tripping on a torn cable as she hurried over. "What is it?"

"My head!" shrilled a voice beside me. Gabrielle stood in the middle of the boat carnage, cradling her newly found head in her arms, stroking the blood-clotted hair like a pet Chihuahua. "You found my head!" she squealed again.

Rule #26

TAKE PROOF TO CONVERT THE NON-BELIEVERS

"Um, Charley, are you sure this is a good idea?" Olive called from behind me as I staggered back toward the school, dragging my yellow suitcase with one hand and the cooler containing Gabrielle's head with the other.

"I'd like to see Blyth try to label this a suicide!" I laughed hysterically, sounding a little more deranged than I had intended. But this was what I was waiting for—*proof*. Proof I was not crazy, proof that there was a serial killer at Harrogate, and proof that we needed to call the police, the military, the SAS, the prime minister himself, whatever. And this time, the killer wasn't going to clean this up and make it disappear.

The cooler bumped over rocks, grassy masses, and clumped balls of sand, and I could hear the severed head bobbing around inside. It slightly concerned me that I wasn't as grossed out as I maybe should be, but for me this was merely grisly discovery number five, and I was getting used to the blood and the gore. Maybe I could have a career in medicine after all.

Gabrielle sauntered beside me, still hugging her head, which hadn't stopped talking since we left the docks. She was alternating between panicked sobs and animated chatter, half-finished sentences and random bursts of giggles. Dead Gabrielle apparently had been desperate for some social interaction.

"I'm so happy I can finally talk. It's been killing me not being able to hear my own voice . . . I can't believe I'm really dead . . . ! Did they find my handbag yet? It's really expensive leather . . . Were there a lot of people at my memorial? Like more than the others . . . ? Seriously, who would kill me? Why? What did I ever do . . . ? Will I still get to graduate . . . ? If you find out who killed me, will I come back to life . . . ? Oh my God, I'm dead! Am I really dead . . . ?"

Finally the tall gray stone monastery came into view, and we all sighed, Meghan especially. So far Gabrielle had not given us any new information—or any information at all. She could only remember dancing at the pool party; everything after that was a blur. She also remembered drinking a lot of the neon punch.

The skies opened up with a sudden deluge. The colors from the library's stained-glass windows shimmered through the rain, which was pelting so hard it bounced off the ground. The rain and salty ocean mist dampened my hair, plastering it to the sides of my face, and when I got to the courtyard, I scooped it up into a ponytail and marched across the cobbled yard, past the fountain, into the Elizabeth Wing, and straight into Blyth's office.

It was barely eight o'clock, but she was there, sitting at her desk holding a mug of coffee with the words "Aspire to be the Best" written across the white ceramic.

"Charley, what are you doing?" she said, straightening up. "At Harrogate, I teach my girls to knock."

"Sorry, I couldn't knock, Headmistress. My hands were full," I panted, heaving the cooler onto her desk, knocking over a cup of pens.

She pushed her chair back, a look of disgust crossing her face. "Charley! Get that dirty box off my desk. You've got sand all over my papers."

"Will do. Just wanted to show you one thing first." I reached over and popped the lid open, releasing about half a dozen flies. I didn't know I had trapped them in there, but they certainly added to the effect.

She stumbled backward, her spine hitting the window that looked out onto an empty courtyard, then bent over to vomit into her trash can.

"Yep, that was the reaction I had when I saw my first dead body here at Harrogate."

Blyth staggered to her feet and took another look at Gabrielle's open-mouthed lifeless head floating around in the crimson pool. Then Blyth let out a small squeak and slid down the wall. Her eyes rolled to the back of her skull and she collapsed to the floor, her brown heels sticking out from under the desk.

"And that was the reaction Olive had," I added, while Meghan covered her ears with her hands to drown out Gabrielle's wittering.

———

She eventually came to, after some medical attention from Ms. Clare. We huddled in her office as the rain and the wind battered the stone courtyard and fountain beyond. On hearing that his precious vessel had been trashed, Mr. Terry had rushed down to the docks, more affected by the destruction of wood and metal than the discovery of a severed head. Mr. Gillies had taken the cooler down to the basement to make sure no students would stumble across it, and I had watched his every movement trying to ascertain whether there was a killer living inside him. He had been oddly calm, avoiding looking inside the box.

"I just don't understand," Blyth wailed, tears streaming down her face. "Who would do this? Poor Gabrielle!" She blew her nose on her blazer sleeve, and I resisted turning away. Even after all the gore and the blood and the body tissue and the broken bones, *that* was gross.

Gabrielle smiled gleefully at the chaos that had erupted over her bobbing decapitated head.

"And you—" Blyth pointed a thick finger at me. "Why would you bring this here?"

"I'm sorry, Headmistress. I just needed to show you, to prove that there is a serial killer here at Harrogate."

"Those other girls took their own lives." She sniffled.

"Those girls were killed, just like Gabrielle. It was *murder*," I corrected.

"Murder?" Gabrielle repeated slowly, as if her tongue could not get around the word. Her bottom lip quivered like she was about to start crying again. Beside her, Strangled Sarah's hands and limp fingers grew dark. She gurgled and wheezed and gasped. I was running out of time. We all were.

Mr. Gillies reentered the office, glancing briefly at me before returning to Blyth's side. A drop of blood stained his sleeve, near his wrist, and I wondered how it had gotten there if he'd never opened the cooler. Mr. Gillies and Rochelle were currently vying for first place on my suspects poster.

Blyth turned to him. "Call the mainland police, cancel classes, and proceed with emergency lockdown procedures."

"Lockdown procedures?" queried Mr. Gillies. Clearly Harrogate had none of those, as such.

"Fine, then use the emergency storm procedures: Years one and two to the hall, years three and four to the common room, years five and six to the library. Divide the staff to cover all locations. When the police get here—"

"No, we need to evacuate now!" I jumped in. "We can't

sit in a library all day and wait for the police to come. It's the day before Halloween! We're approaching the big finale!"

"The what?" asked Blyth.

"It's the final battle between good and evil, survivor versus slasher!"

"Charley, this isn't the time for that nonsense." Headmistress Blyth sighed.

"Look outside," I continued. "The weather is getting worse. We need to go soon."

"And how do you suggest we leave now that the ferry is destroyed?" asked Mr. Gillies, his expression cold, vacant.

"You have blood on you," I said flatly, pointing to his sleeve.

He glanced down, then his eyes widened. He rubbed the sleeve down his trousers in a quick, sharp stroke. When he looked back at me, his eyes were burning.

"Eden School has rowboats? Or we could all swim? How far can it be?" I suggested to Blyth. She frowned at my suggestion.

Blyth picked up the receiver on her desk, her fingers hovering above the digits. She slowly put it down, picked it back up again, and lowered it. "The phone lines are down."

I jumped up, almost lurching through Impaled Meghan, who had her arm protectively around Sarah. "Of course they are. Like I said, we're coming to the movie's finale."

HOW TO SURVIVE A HORROR MOVIE

"Martin, will you go to Eden and let Dr. Pruitt know exactly what's going on. Try their phone lines too. And until the coast guard comes, he should probably follow similar lockdown protocols, just in case."

"Shouldn't we all stay together?" I suggested, glancing suspiciously at Mr. Gillies, who was shoving his hands roughly into some black leather gloves.

"Shouldn't we warn Eden too?" he replied, yanking on a long black trench coat. He pulled the hood up until it partially covered the top of his head. I shivered.

"Maybe Pruitt already knows," I muttered, scanning the courtyard beyond the window. Was he out there? Watching us?

"What was that, Charley? Speak up," Blyth scolded.

"Um . . . I was just saying that Eden boys aren't being targeted. This is about Harrogate. This is about the sixth-year girls."

Mr. Gillies cleared his throat. "I should get going." He lightly brushed past me, a faint metallic smell from his sleeve lingering in the air between us. Blood? Boat fuel? My head was throbbing with all the possibilities.

"Charley, Olive—I want you girls in the library as soon as possible."

"Can I grab my textbooks?" Olive asked, causing me to whip my head around and stare at her. "What? It's exams soon. Every moment is precious study time." She shrugged at me.

"Quickly, please," snapped Blyth. "And, girls, I don't want you to mention this to the other students."

"Why? The sixth years have a right to know there's a killer after them!"

"Fear causes chaos, and if everyone is hysterically running around this island, then it just makes finding the person responsible more challenging. I want to know where my students are for the rest of the day. And I want everyone to be calm. Staff will guard the hallways and report back."

"But—"

"Charley, I just need you to trust me on this, for once, OK?"

I gazed at Olive, who was staring at the ground by her feet, and nodded reluctantly. When we left, I could hear Blyth moaning inside, loud sobs pressing against the door, spilling out into the hallway. After this, Harrogate was finished. The school would almost certainly close now. The doors padlocked, windows boarded up, dorm rooms gathering dust and cobwebs. Perhaps it would be torn down, bulldozed, and made into a memorial garden where victims would be commemorated by Blyth's surviving Italian basil and lemon thyme. Maybe Dr. Pruitt would make a ludicrous bid for it, turning it into a golf course or a spa for Eden's finest. Assuming *he* wasn't our maniac.

And as for us—Harrogate's surviving students—where would we go? What would happen to us after we left this island?

Rule #27

DON'T ENGAGE IN A
FOOD FIGHT WITH THE ENEMY

Back at the dorm, Olive packed a bag for the library that included every textbook she could physically carry, a hoodie, a blanket, and whatever snacks she had stashed in her bedside drawer. I wheeled my bloodied and half-broken yellow case back inside and took only a blanket, some strawberry licorice I had been saving, and a Stephen King book. An assigned library day was Olive's dream, but for me it sounded like torture. We trudged slowly down the hall, Blyth's voice booming from the speakers overhead. "Due to the severity of the incoming storm, years one and two are to report to the assembly hall, years three and four to the common room, and years five and six to the library. Immediately. Please sign in with a staff member so all students can be accounted for. Bring only what you absolutely need."

I hid the licorice in my coat pocket.

Outside, the courtyard was chaotic with students,

umbrellas flipping inside out and the odd paper whizzing past in the wind, having escaped from a student's grasp. The rain was fierce, the wind even fiercer. I huddled into my hood and hurried across, past the fountain. The water inside churned and bubbled with the rain hammering down. The hall outside the library was even busier. Students with soggy textbooks and dripping hair were all fumbling through the doors. The librarian frantically yelled, "Mind the books!" to those who got a bit too close to the bookshelves in their wet gear.

Mrs. Briggs stood with a clipboard, checking off names, her glasses slipping down her wet face. "Hi, Olive." She nodded, marking her on her board. She looked up at me, squinting, trying to place me. I was not one of her advanced physics students, funnily enough.

"Charley Sullivan."

She checked my name. "Go find a spot, girls."

Inside the library, the fifth- and sixth-year girls congregated in the center by the computers and search catalogs, each friend group choosing an appropriate aisle. The athletes chose biology and physiology while the Creative Writing Club had philosophy and social policy. The Theater Club of course chose poetry and romantic literature. I knew it was futile searching for a horror movie section, so I aimlessly ambled after Olive as she made a beeline for anthropology and linguistics. Meghan hovered cross-legged on a stack of textbooks on the librarian's desk, while Sarah desperately attempted to shake off the black ash that was now creeping up her legs. Gabrielle tried to communicate with everyone and anyone.

"Hey, Charley."

I spun around quickly, wet matted hair whipping with me, smacking Saoirse in the face. She giggled and wiped rainwater from her chin.

"Oh, sorry." I grimaced.

"That's OK. Bad storm this time, huh?"

"Yeah, it's bad." I bit down on my bottom lip to stop myself from saying more. I don't know why, but suddenly I wanted to spill everything out to her, to let the words tumble out about the murders, the ghosts, my undying and rather dramatic love for her.

"Charley, over here!" Olive called, having found a corner spot at the end of the aisle.

I bit my lip harder and passed Saoirse instead, the aroma of oak and lemon floating in the space between us.

"Um, Charley?"

I turned back, a spatter of rain from my hair hitting the shelf beside me.

"It's a shame the Halloween formal will likely be canceled."

"Yeah, sucks," I agreed.

"It would have been fun." She smiled, her eyes lighting up. Then her cheeks flushed coral. She tucked a strand of red hair behind her ear and walked back to her friends.

I stumbled in a daze over wet boots, soggy umbrellas, and

overflowing bags. When I reached Olive, I slid down the book stack and collapsed onto the ground, my heart racing.

"Why are you smiling?" she asked, her eyebrows going up.

"No reason." I grinned, glancing again at Saoirse, who had nestled down beside the other fifth-year girls from the Alexandria Wing. A flash of dark brown curls and pink lip gloss suddenly caught my eye from across the aisle. Rochelle and Annabelle sat with their legs straight out, nonchalantly, staring at us. A shiver ran up my spine as I thought about the other night in the shower rooms, those boots, *her* boots. I cocked my head, trying to find another spot to move to, anywhere I didn't have to look at them, but the aisles had filled up fast.

"Just ignore them. If it is one of them, then they can't do anything to us here, and it's better to have them in our sights than not know where they are," whispered Olive.

"True. I'm not taking my eyes off those two."

"There you are!" Gabrielle's head squeaked, still cradled in her arms. She fumbled over to the other Elles and immediately launched into conversation.

"Oh my God, I have had the worst week," she ranted to Rochelle and Annabelle, who were huddling on the library floor. "Hello? Can you hear me?" She waved a hand frantically in their faces, almost dropping her head at the same time.

"They can't hear you!" Meghan called out to her from down the aisle.

HOW TO SURVIVE A HORROR MOVIE

Olive dug through her bag. "I only brought nine textbooks. Do you think I should have brought more?"

"No, Olive. Hopefully we won't be here for that long."

Olive glanced around at the groups of chattering students invading her once sacred space of silence and study. "Is it bad that I'm wishing we were sheltering in Eden's wide-screen movie theater right now and not here?"

"Yes, if Dr. Pruitt's our killer."

She whipped her head around. "You're on to Pruitt now?"

"Honestly, I have no idea," I said, gazing at Rochelle, who twirled and twisted her hair while glaring at us.

Gabrielle bounced up and down, her decapitated head now tucked under her arm like a rugby ball. "I don't think they can see me!" she yelled to me. I ignored her and instead tried to focus on the chills and scares of my novel, but the shrill caterwauling of the wind—and of Gabrielle—made it impossible. Olive frantically scratched away at index cards with her pen, testing herself periodically, and scolding herself when she got an answer wrong.

Occasionally I glanced over the top of my book, monitoring Rochelle's movements. Her scowls burned a hole in the front cover of my book from across the aisle. She whispered animatedly to Annabelle, glancing in my direction as she did. Was she really the Harrogate killer? And Annabelle? Seeing them, with their designer handbags and fancy raincoats, which probably did little to protect them from the rain, I just couldn't believe it anymore. Was Rochelle Smyth smart and elusive enough to evade being caught until now?

"Ignore them," repeated Olive, flicking through her index cards of potential test questions. She was the only person I'd ever met who would review for an exam two months ahead, and during a murder rampage. But I suppose that's why she had her grades and why I had mine.

I dug deep in my novel, searching for sentences and words to draw me in, to immerse me in the chilling story world, anywhere but here. But Rochelle's chattering got louder, drawing people's attention.

"I think they're talking about you," Meghan muttered as she stretched her arms up behind her head and tried to lean back against the bookcase. She instead went right through it, her white sneakers sticking out from the base.

I tried hard to zone out, to dull the murmurings of the two living Elles, but their voices carried through the aisles, wafting over the musty bookshelves. "That's it." I tutted and threw my book down, hitting and almost knocking over Olive's textbook tower. I crossed my arms and glared at the two Elles.

"Got something on your mind?" Rochelle called to me, smirking wider.

The words sat on the tip of my tongue, but I couldn't say them, not without provoking her to talk about the contents of my file, and this was not the place to discuss them.

"Rochelle, if you have something to say, then just say it," Olive boldly challenged.

Olive, no!

"I'm taking your advice," Olive whispered. "You know, standing up to bullies."

"I do have something to say, actually," Rochelle said. "All these deaths, all this trouble, only started after your roommate arrived. Trouble just follows you everywhere, doesn't it, Charley? Or should I say Lottie?"

"What's that supposed to mean?" Olive demanded, glancing between her and me.

"What? Your own roommate doesn't know?" Annabelle piped up.

"Know what?" asked Olive.

"It's nothing, just ignore them like you said," I muttered, tugging at Olive's shirt.

"You're living with a criminal," Rochelle blurted out.

A heavy silence fell upon the library, everyone putting books down to listen in. Meghan stopped yawning and eagerly sat up straight.

"Rochelle, please stop—" I started.

"Don't want everyone to know your secrets, *Charley*?"

"Rochelle, I'm sorry about Gabrielle, I really am." Her jaw tensed like I'd just struck her. "But all this isn't because of me. There's a serial killer at Harrogate; none of us are safe here." The words spilled out before I could stop them.

SCARLETT DUNMORE

"Here we go again." Annabelle tutted. "A serial killer? You're such an attention seeker."

"*I'm* the attention seeker?" I scoffed.

"As usual, playing the victim," she threw back.

"Is that how you got off those police charges?" added Rochelle. "By playing the victim? The grieving student who succumbed to peer pressure?"

I clutched my head, trying not to listen, but she wouldn't stop. It was just like before. It was happening all over again. I would never be able to escape my past.

"I knew you were hiding something, that Blyth was keeping your secrets!" she sneered, her eyes ablaze. "You marched in here at the end of the school year, acting like you were above us, like you didn't deserve to be stuck here. Some big-city girl. Rolling your eyes at every chance, making snide remarks about the school, the island, about us—"

"I never—"

"Now you're trying to scare us, shut this place down, when you're the one we should be afraid of! *You're* the criminal!"

"Rochelle, stop . . ." I begged.

"You had to change your name because anyone could google you and read the truth. About how you're a druggie screwup who broke into people's houses!"

The library was silent, deathly silent. Everyone had heard. Teachers, students, Olive, *Saoirse*. Now everyone knew the real me. The me I had tried desperately to get away from.

HOW TO SURVIVE A HORROR MOVIE

My head felt foggy. I staggered to my feet, falling back on the shelves behind me as images of interview rooms, courtrooms, and detention cells ran through my mind.

Rochelle continued, also rising to her feet, "Everyone should know that you're a—"

"Shut up!" I screamed, my voice reverberating around the library, threatening to shatter the windows and spray shards down on every single person here.

"Snitch!" Rochelle glowered at me, her face reddening, but not with anger, with delight. She was evil to the core.

My feet lifted off the ground and I lunged for her, my hands around her shoulders, wrestling her down. All the emotions from the last few weeks poured out of me—anger, fear, desperation. They coursed through my veins and out of my hands, which shook Rochelle violently. "I said, shut up!" I screamed, the rage making my own voice foreign to me.

Annabelle and Headless Gabrielle both squealed simultaneously, quickly moving out of the line of fire, while Olive tried to pull me off Rochelle. But I was unstoppable. The anger churned and bubbled like boiling water.

Someone yelled "Fight!" and the sounds of footsteps rushed toward us. I could feel the teachers' hands on us, pulling us apart.

"Get her off me!" Rochelle screeched. "This is an expensive coat!"

I finally let go and stumbled back against the bookshelves, but she sprang up and started running.

SCARLETT DUNMORE

Was she going to get my file? To show everyone? Before I could stop myself, remind myself that she was the school psychopath, not me, I began hurtling after her through the library, screaming her name wildly. She was fast and made it out of the library doors and down the hall. Whereas I walloped into Mrs. Briggs, almost knocking her off her feet.

"Girls, stop! It's a lockdown! This is not a drill!" she called after us, but it was too late. I chased Rochelle down the hallway, the clatter of the library fading behind us.

"Stop chasing me!" Rochelle screamed back at me as I pounded the tiled floor toward her.

"Stop running!" I screamed back.

Meghan floated alongside me, pumping her fist. "Fight, fight, fight!"

Rochelle ducked into the dining hall, and I followed, flipping on the lights. The room was lit by tiny teardrop bulbs perched on cast-iron chandeliers hanging from the ceiling. Rochelle was still running, toward the silver serving hatch, past it, then through the double doors to the kitchen. I ran in after her.

Thud!

I stumbled to the ground, landing hard on the heel of my hand. "Ow!" I howled. "What did you just hit me with?"

"I dunno, I think it's a colander!"

I pulled myself up and looked around. The kitchen was much larger than I had imagined, steel-top counters wrapping all the way around, a wide island with a stove in the middle, and a huge pantry in the corner. A clang made me spin around to face Rochelle as she launched another utensil my way. This time she missed. She bolted for the other side of the kitchen island as I positioned myself opposite her.

"How did it feel snitching on all your friends so you got off? Ever think they're rotting away in a cell while you're here, getting a new life, pretending to be someone else?"

"I'm going to kill you!" I howled.

"Psycho!"

"No, you're the psycho!" I yelled back. Wasn't she? Although I did just threaten to kill her.

A carrot hit my face, and I gasped. That hurt. Carrots were solid. Then a slew of food items started hitting me like bullets—mushrooms, peppers, onions, even a banana. Meghan stood with her arms folded over her chest while Sarah and Gabrielle dodged food that would have just gone through them anyway. As for me, I blocked what I could, the banana being the hardest to avoid, and launched whatever was in the white bowl beside me at her: something soft and stodgy, that smelled like cinnamon and autumn spice.

"Did you just throw churros at me?" Rochelle demanded as I landed another handful of sugary sticks on her. They didn't quite strike like I thought they would. I thought they'd be a bit denser and less bouncy.

"This is ridiculous!" I finally announced, stepping away from the stove. "We're having a food fight while there's a storm going on and a killer loose. There are more important things to worry about here! Rochelle, you're a bully. You're mean and spiteful, and you make everyone's lives miserable here."

She glared at me, her cheeks flushing a dark crimson, her lips slightly trembling.

"I'm done. I'm tired of trying to make everyone listen to me, and I'm tired of pretending to be someone I'm not. So, go ahead—keep my file, put notes underneath my door threatening to share it. You know what? Just share it, let everyone see—"

She pulled back and scrunched up her nose. "I didn't put any notes under your door—"

"Rochelle, I don't care anymore. You're not going to be at Harrogate forever. Good luck making a name for yourself off this island."

"Charley, wait—" Her voice wavered, catching in her throat at the end.

But I didn't wait. I turned and walked out of the kitchen, leaving her there, alone.

Strangled Sarah stood in the dimly lit hallway beyond, her neck still bent and folded and twisted, her legs and arms now visibly decomposed. Above us the dull light bulb flickered and spluttered, while the winds wailed and the sky cried outside. The corners of my eyes stung and watered. "I'm sorry I failed," I whispered as she crumbled to ash and disappeared forever.

Rule #28
DON'T IMPLICATE YOURSELF

I awoke a lot earlier than anyone else in the library. The rain had paused, but the wind was still hammering against the walls and windows. The storm would find a way in, sooner rather than later.

Today was October 31.

Halloween.

If anything was going to happen, it would be today. My fingertips tingled and my belly churned. I gazed out over the mass of sleeping bodies scattered around the floor. Olive was snoring loudly beside me, as usual not disturbed by anything going on, and Rochelle had thankfully moved to a different campsite in the library. Annabelle was still curled up in our aisle, her head resting on a couple of leather-bound books she would likely never read. Gabrielle's head sat beside Annabelle's designer handbag, while the rest of Gabrielle loyally lay next to her friend. I was pretty sure ghosts didn't sleep, but I wasn't in the mood to question anything this morning. Meghan hadn't spoken a word since Sarah had vanished, and now she solemnly stared out the window at the dark. A wisp of guilt crept through the fabrics of my layers and tickled my bare skin. I pulled the blanket tighter around my shoulders and tried not to look at Meghan.

I couldn't stop shivering with the cold that trickled through the old bookcases and crept over the sleeping students. Mrs. Briggs sat slumped in a chair by the door, the clipboard still gripped in her hands. Beside her were the biology and chemistry teachers. Apparently, the whole science department was here. I considered waking her to let her know I was popping across the hall to the bathroom but decided to let her sleep after having caused complete chaos the previous night with all the shouting and running and churro throwing. No doubt word would have gotten back to Blyth and I'd be punished for it today.

The hallway outside the library was washed with an early-morning glow, illuminating the framed photos of old students and retired staff members. A glass case sat beside the bathroom, gold trophies on narrow shelves boasting of Harrogate's academic and athletic achievements. I wondered how much bigger Eden's collection was. I hauled a chair from beside the case into the bathroom, the wooden legs dragging on the floor, and after searching every cubicle, I wedged it under the bathroom door handle so no one else could enter while I was in there. I didn't fancy being murdered while sitting on the toilet. Squatting down, I started my business, counting the tiles on the floor to distract myself. Taking a deep breath, I leaned back on the seat, momentarily closing my eyes. When I opened them, a pair of legs stood in front of me—legs that were not Meghan's or Gabrielle's.

My shriek echoed around the bathroom, bouncing off the cubicle walls. I slowly followed the legs up to the torso, which looked more like a dartboard with several knives protruding from the chest, then the neck, and finally the face.

Another shriek pierced the air. But this time it wasn't mine.

The ghost of Rochelle Smyth stood in front of me, apparently as freaked out at seeing me as I was at seeing her. Soon we were screaming together.

"Ew, why are you on the toilet?" she finally spluttered, turning around to face the cubicle door.

I roughly yanked up my cords and crawled up onto the toilet seat, tucking my knees in. This cubicle was not meant for two people, especially two people who disliked each other.

"Oh," breathed Rochelle. "I'm sleepwalking again!" She started laughing, shaking her head. "What an idiot I am!" She turned around and tried to slide open the latch on the cubicle, but the metal passed through her fingers. "What the—?"

"Um . . . you're not sleepwalking, R-R-Rochelle," I stammered.

"Am I dreaming? Ugh, why are you in my dream?" she moaned, trying to grab at the latch again.

"Not exactly. But you will be seeing a lot more of me."

She waved both hands over the handle this time, clawing at the door, which was like mist to her touch. "Why can't I get out?"

"Rochelle?"

"This is so weird," she muttered, still trying.

"Rochelle?"

"What?" she snapped, turning back.

"You're . . . um . . ." I pointed to her chest, the words getting stuck in my throat. "Um . . ."

She gazed down at the handles of the knives and started shrieking again.

Suddenly Impaled Meghan appeared, making the space even more crammed. She groaned loudly. "You have to be kidding."

I leaned through the ghosts and unlatched the door, releasing us into the sink space. We tumbled into Gabrielle, who held her decapitated head out to Rochelle like she was offering her a cup of tea. "Rochelle! You're dead too, yay! Now we're dead together!" she sang.

Rochelle screamed even louder.

Perhaps because she always did what Rochelle did, Gabrielle started shrieking too. I put my hands over my ears and tried to block them out.

"Oh, for goodness' sake, we'll be here all day," yelled Meghan, waving her hands. She grabbed Rochelle by the shoulders and shook her. "Rochelle, you're a ghost!"

"Wh-wh-what?" she gasped.

"You're dead. Like D-E-A-D. Dead!" Meghan shouted again.

"OK, that's probably enough for now," I said to Meghan. Normally I would welcome her brutal honesty when directed toward Rochelle, but right now it seemed wrong. The girl had just been stabbed to death with kitchen knives.

"No, no, no!" she howled, pacing around the room. "I am not dead!" She squeezed her eyes shut and grimaced.

"Rochelle, I'm sorry, but—"

She vanished. Meghan and a head-carrying Gabrielle glanced from side to side.

"Where did she go?" I asked.

"Why didn't she take me with her?" Gabrielle wailed.

I rushed over to the door, yanking the chair out from underneath the handle. "Now where are you going?" Meghan said, throwing her hands up.

I hurried out into the quiet hallway, trying to step quietly. "I can't just let dead Rochelle float around out there by herself."

"She can't go far from you, remember."

"Trust me, that fact is burning a hole in my brain right now. But I need to worry about that later," I muttered.

SCARLETT DUNMORE

My thighs burned as I hurled myself out into the howling courtyard, the wind sweeping me across the stone ground.

Rochelle stood just beyond the cast-iron gates, partially blanketed by the thick fog that crept in over the cliffs. The storm would return soon. A gush of ice-cold air hit my shoulder, and when I turned, Rochelle was beside me, her eyes still closed. She slowly opened them and saw me.

"Oh, come on!" she gasped. "I'm trying to get away from you!"

"You can't! That's what I'm trying to tell you," I shouted over the wind.

She shut her eyes again, and again she vanished into the moist air, before quickly reappearing beside me. She screamed and began stomping up and down. "Why can't I get away from you?!"

I shrugged. "You can't. We're in it together, *friend*."

"That's it," she said, snapping her fingers. "I know where I'm going wrong—I'm not picturing where I want to go." She closed her eyes again and brought her hands up into some sort of yoga posture. She started chanting to the clouds.

"Are you OK?" I asked her, pulling my hood up, trying to shelter from the wind that slapped against my ears.

"Shh! I'm meditating. I'm picturing a safe space. A place of comfort, happiness—"

"Home?"

"No, the Starbucks on Russell Street." Suddenly she started running toward the edge of the cliff. "Take me there!" she howled into the sky as she leapt off the rocks and vanished into the mist.

A heavy silence wafted in along with the fog, blanketing everything around me in stillness. My eyes widened and I gazed around. Had she actually done it? Was she standing in a Starbucks somewhere trying to order a skinny macchiato?

"Nooooo!"

I spun around and saw Rochelle sobbing on her knees.

"Took you right back here, eh?" I nodded, crossing my arms. "You had me there for a second."

"I hate you," she groaned, rolling onto her back.

I took a slow and cautious step toward her. "You know, there's a reason you're stuck with me."

"I know—I'm obviously being punished for something I did, although I don't know what."

I paused, wondering whether I should respond now and risk standing here on a clifftop for the next ten hours. I eventually shook my head. "We'll discuss that later." I took another step toward her. "Rochelle, first, sorry, because I actually thought *you* were the killer."

"As you can see, I am clearly not!" she snapped, gesturing to her chest filled with knives.

I continued on, "I think you're here with me because we have to work *together*."

"If it's to help you improve your life, I don't have time for that, and that's assuming I have infinite amounts of time."

"No." I clenched my teeth. This was giving me a headache. "You're here to help me catch the killer."

She sat up. "What?" She pulled herself up to her feet and marched past me. "No. Absolutely not. No way. Not a chance in hell. N-O." She waved her arms wildly like she was trying to signal air traffic.

"So, that's a no, then?"

"You want *me* to help *you*?" She snorted. "*You're* the person who killed me!"

"Technically *I* didn't kill you. The Harrogate Halloween killer did."

She marched toward me, pointing a heavily manicured finger in my face. "*Technically*, I wouldn't have been there in the first place if you hadn't chased me."

"I didn't chase you," I argued.

"You chased me!" Her eyes were wide like an animal's, and for a moment I could tell that she wore colored contact lenses to make her eyes brighter. I knew it. Another thing fake about her.

She waved her arms around like she was participating in a bad game of charades. "You . . . you . . . chased me into the murder kitchen!"

"You ran!" I fired back. "And you provoked me! You outed me in front of everyone! You called me a snitch!"

"Ha, so you did kill me!"

"I didn't kill you!"

"You might as well have!"

"Ugh!" I screamed, then I turned and walked away. "Fine! Keep trying to get to Starbucks—good luck with that!"

Suddenly Meghan's impaled figure appeared before me, blood-smeared fingers pressing me back. "Charley, as much as I'd love to watch Rochelle jump off a cliff all day—in fact there've been many times I've considered pushing her myself—we don't have time for this. I'm not going to live out the rest of my days, or maybe even hours, watching that girl try to teleport herself back to the mainland!"

"We don't need her. We can find the killer without her," I snapped, brushing past her and Gabrielle.

Meghan called after me, "Charley, we need her, you know we do—"

"Are you guys talking about me over there?!" Rochelle shouted from the cliff edge.

I shook my head. "We don't need her. Rochelle has nothing to offer us. She doesn't have the brainpower—"

"I definitely heard my name!" Rochelle continued. "You know I don't like it when people talk about me."

"She's another victim," pleaded Meghan.

"I certainly wouldn't call Rochelle Smyth a victim," I argued.

Meghan stood in front of me, blocking my path back to Harrogate. The fence post grazed me slightly, the icy cold piercing my skin. I resisted the urge to try to touch it.

SCARLETT DUNMORE

"We're running out of time. *I'm* running out of time," she reminded me. "Unless you want to bolt again?" She raised an eyebrow and scowled.

"I didn't—" I exhaled loudly. "What I mean is that . . . I . . . um . . ."

"Hmm?" She'd really perfected that theatrical scowl.

"I'm sorry," I muttered.

"I know." She nodded, the frown slowly fading from her face. "I'm scared too."

Up above the sky crackled and popped, bolts of lightning slicing through the dark clouds. I shuddered and gazed back at the iron gates and stone walls. She was right—we didn't have much time. We were also standing on the edge of a cliff while a killer was on a murder spree, which probably wasn't a great idea, for me at least.

"I think it's going to rain again," Rochelle called to us, gazing up at the charcoal skies, which were empty of soaring, diving gulls. She stroked her tight curls. "Can my hair get wet when I'm dead?"

I sighed loudly, then stomped over to Rochelle as she tried to shield her head from the raindrops. "Rochelle," I said calmly, plastering on my sweetest smile.

She looked at me and furrowed her eyebrows. "Why do you look like you're about to kill me *again*?" she said, backing up.

I dropped the smile. "Rochelle, it pains me to say this, but . . . I . . . I . . ."

"I hate when you stutter like that."

"I need you," I said slowly.

She raised her eyebrows, then crossed her arms over her chest, trying to avoid the knife handles. "I didn't quite hear you. It's a bit loud out here." She smirked.

The sky split open and heavy drops pelted down around us. "I said, I need you!" I shouted over the rain.

"Charley, you're really going to have to speak up."

"I need you!" I screamed into the air, tearing through the storm.

She rolled her eyes. "Fine. There's no need to shout." She touched her hair gingerly. "Hey, look at that. My hair's still dry." Then she flicked her dark curls over her shoulder and marched past me. "Come on, no dilly-dallying. I may not have places to be anymore, but I can't stand slow walkers."

I sighed loudly and trailed behind her back inside, my hands pretending to throttle her neck. Was it possible to kill someone who was already dead?

Back at Harrogate, students were waking up as we tiptoed down the corridor. The doors to the dining hall were still closed from last night and the hanging chandeliers were dimly lit, casting an amber glow. Usually by this time the long oak tables would be set with ornate jars of silverware, nestled beside salt and pepper shakers and a sprig of dried lavender in a single glass vase. But the dining room was empty and the kitchen beyond was shrouded in darkness.

My hands trembled above the door handle, knowing that inside, only a few meters from where I stood now, was another dead body.

"Well?" urged Rochelle. "Are we just going to stand here or go in? Everyone will be getting up soon."

I slowly pushed it open, the door creaking and cracking like it would break any moment, and gasped. Rochelle softly squeaked beside me. There she was, right where I'd left her last night. But rather than standing on the other side of the kitchen island, her hands in the ingredient bowls as she prepared to launch carrots and onions at me, she was splayed across the floor, eyes wide open to the sky, knives protruding from her chest. A lot of knives. The killer must have been here, waited until I left, then done this. This could have been me if Rochelle had walked away first. As if I could feel each stab wound, I rubbed my chest.

Rochelle stiffened beside me. "Oh. My. God."

"Yup." Meghan nodded, circling around her corpse. "Like I said, you're dead."

"Take them out of me!" Rochelle cried, waving at the knives and then gesturing to her chest.

"I don't think it works like that. You'll still be dead," I said quietly.

"Charley! Please!"

"OK, fine." I bent over, her body starfished on the blue

kitchen floor. I hesitated, then pulled my sleeve up over my hand, using the fabric like a glove.

"What are you doing?" balked Rochelle.

I tutted. "Trying not to leave fingerprints. Obviously." I gripped the handle of the biggest blade, but it was stiff and didn't budge.

"Hurry up!" Rochelle ordered.

"It's really wedged in your rib cage." I spluttered and panted, now using both hands to pull it out. This was really going to stretch the fabric of my hoodie, unfortunately.

"Put some muscle into it, come on!"

"I'm trying!" I threw my foot against the kitchen surface and used it push myself back. I felt the knife shift and loosen and slowly slide out.

I stumbled backward, knife in hand. "There." I grinned, quite pleased with myself. A stifled cry from behind me startled us and slowly we all turned to find the lunch lady standing in the doorway, her eyes fixed on the meat carver in my hand and Rochelle's dead body on the ground beside me.

"This is not what it looks like . . ." I quickly said. I took a step toward her, knife still in hand. But she bolted, screaming and howling all the way out of the kitchen, through the dining room and out into the hallway.

"Well, this isn't good." I sighed, dropping the knife. The metal tip clanged on the floor.

Rule #29
LIGHTS-OUT MEANS TROUBLE

The thin threads on the armchair pressed into my spine as I sat in Blyth's office gazing out at the howling wind and torrential rain that continued its attack on Harrogate, and the island. I had already been locked in here for two hours, unable to free myself from this room, which smelled like stale coffee and powdered sugar. I had kept trying to plead my innocence, to no avail. I fit the profile, just like the headmistress and all the teachers said: new girl, loner, troubled past, a conveniently missing student file, and a fascination with the blood and gore of horror films. It didn't help that about a hundred eyewitnesses had seen me chase the now-deceased Rochelle from the library, and it most definitely didn't help that I was literally caught with the murder weapon while standing over her dead body.

After an hour of begging and pleading, I was eventually locked in here, for "the safety of the other students," according to Blyth. The phone lines were still down, there was no word from Eden, and Mr. Gillies was now "missing"—as in either dead or running around the island killing Harrogate students. From what I could hear through the door, an evacuation to Eden on the coastal paths was out of the question due to the dangerous weather conditions. Blyth had already lost five girls; she couldn't really afford to lose any more. And due to Rochelle's recent murder, students couldn't be trusted to remain in the library when told. Everyone was now to be moved to the assembly hall, bringing all years together for the first time, much to the younger students' dismay, as even they had caught on that it was the sixth-year girls who were being picked off one at a time. Of course, the gym was off-limits due to the final decorations for the Halloween formal having just gone up this week. I was seriously beginning to question Harrogate's priorities.

I sighed and leaned back in the chair, gazing at the harsh overhead lights until tiny warm dots appeared in my vision. I rubbed my face and started biting my fingernails again. The lights above me flickered and shut off, leaving only faint afternoon light, further muted by the storm.

"Great," I murmured, squeezing my eyes shut. I knew this scene well. Lights go out. Killer appears.

I marched over to the door and started knocking loudly. "Hello? Headmistress Blyth?" Silence pressed against the door. "The power's out!" I yelled. "This is the part where we all hide!" Stillness, a vast emptiness beyond the door. "Hello? Anyone?"

The wind scraped the window glass, making my shoulders tense. I turned around to walk back to the armchair I was supposed to remain in for the duration of a murder spree, a storm, and now a power outage.

I froze, my skin taut, tiny goose bumps quickly spreading all over. In the window stood a dark figure, dressed in a green fisherman's raincoat and a gold theater mask, the comedy section worn over their face, the tragedy section sticking out awkwardly to the side. In their hand was a large, thick hammer. My eyes flicked between the theater mask and the hammer and back again. Then I spun around and started clawing at the door handle.

"Help! Ms. Blyth! Anyone?!" I howled, shaking the door in its frame.

The window behind me fractured with a violent splintering sound. I grabbed a stapler off the cabinet and desperately tried smashing the door handle, which I'd seen in a movie. It didn't work. In fact, the stapler split in half and tiny silver staples spilled out all around my feet. The window glass continued clanging and splintering like a broken chime.

I threw myself at the door and staggered back, my shoulder throbbing. I'd also seen that in a movie. I turned slowly, my heart thumping wildly, and saw the final shards of the window being hammered out. The killer climbed through the window, pulling down the final remnants of glass with a black-gloved hand. Their boots crunched, crushing glass into carpet as they walked toward me, the hammer swinging by his side. I launched the broken stapler at them. And missed.

High-pitched shrieks from the corner of the room almost knocked me off my feet. Rochelle and a head-carrying Gabrielle huddled against the wall, hands over their faces, screaming and howling as if auditioning for a role in *Friday the 13th*. They continued hysterically shrieking as the killer trudged toward me, raising the hammer. I joined in, not quite at the same level of theatrics, but close. Soon all the ghosts were at my side, screaming with me.

Then Rochelle stopped and put her hands on her hips. "Oh, I just remembered I'm already dead. He's coming for *you*, Charley. Phew!"

"Duck!" Meghan shrieked.

The hammer swung at my head, and I felt a slight breeze as it skimmed my hair. I ducked and backed up into Rochelle, feeling a blast of icy cold air float through my body.

"Ew" was all she said as she came out the other side.

The killer walked slowly toward me.

"Mr. Gillies, don't do this!" I yelled.

The masked figure stopped and cocked their head to the side, taking me in.

"Mr. Gillies, is that you?" I asked shakily. My voice sounded distant and unfamiliar.

The killer strode toward me again. I swung a leg and kicked over the armchair in their path. They stumbled over it. I turned and frantically pulled at the stubborn door handle. Nothing.

The only way out was through the window.

I lunged for the desk as Meghan screamed, "On your left!"

I dived and collided with an elbow, knocking me down onto the floor.

Meghan tutted. "Your other left."

My head pounded but I rolled onto my belly, narrowly avoiding another hammer swing. I clawed my way to the desk. Then I saw it. A flicker in my peripheral vision at first, but then it scuttled toward me on its fingertips like a crab. When it scurried across the desk, I could see all the details—the grayish skin, the fingernails, the wiry dark hair on the back . . . the missing right pinkie tip. Mr. Gillies couldn't be the Harrogate Halloween killer because his ghost hand was currently beetling across Blyth's desk.

Mr. Gillies was dead. And apparently all that remained of him was a severed hand.

When it landed on the ground, Rochelle shrieked and stamped at it like it was a rodent trying to bite her ankles. Gabrielle soon joined in, accidentally dropping her head in the recycling bin as she danced up and down.

"Charley," Meghan warned, pointing to the killer, who stood on the other side of the desk, chest heaving in and out as they gasped for breath. The theatrical mask had shifted slightly, and now the tragedy side covered their face. If it wasn't Mr. Gillies under there, then who was it? Dr. Pruitt? Annabelle? Someone else?

With every ounce of strength left in my body, I grabbed the edge of the desk and thrust it forward, right into the killer's groin. They stumbled backward, their back cracking off the fallen armchair. I spun around and edged myself out the window, avoiding the spears of glass that still protruded like shark teeth from the frame. One nipped at my jeans, slicing through the denim like a surgical knife. I howled as rain battered me, instantly soaking my clothes.

The courtyard stones were slick, and I fumbled and slid a few times making my way across to the door on the other side. I glanced back—Blyth's office was empty. The killer was gone. On the move, perhaps. Coming for me. I threw open the door from the courtyard and catapulted right into something soft.

"There you are!" gasped Olive as she stood over me in the hallway.

"Why do you always run into people?" Rochelle groaned, appearing beside her.

Olive reached out a hand, but as I slowly went to grab it, a chill snaked along my spine. My best friend's face was pale and expressionless, her eyes dark. Everything about her suddenly felt foreign to me, unfamiliar, *wrong*.

"Maybe she's the killer." Rochelle shrugged, looking at Meghan and Gabrielle. "Did anyone ever consider that?"

My eyes frantically flicked between Rochelle and Olive, until my temples throbbed.

Olive?

No, she couldn't be the killer. Why would she be? She was my best friend, my only friend. My partner in crime. The person I often slept beside when one of us had nightmares, the person I ate with every day, and the person I snuggled into for Slasher Saturday every week. Olive had become a sister to me. But I hadn't confided in her about my past and why I had come here, and if I held secrets from her, then what secrets did she keep from me?

Her hand hovered in the air, waiting for me to take it. "You OK?" she questioned.

"I-I—" I clambered up to stand, facing her.

She trembled slightly and glanced around the empty hallway, looking right through the ghosts. Mr. Gillies's hand scurried around her shoes. "Why are you out here?"

"Why are *you* out here?" I countered, sweat pooling around my hairline and the back of my neck. It was so hot in here—why was it suddenly so hot in here?

She gazed down at my hand, which was still smeared with blood from where I'd cut myself climbing through the window, and took a step toward me. Her eyes grew wild, feral, her lips parting. Was she going to say something? Was she going to *attack* me?

This was it. My fight for survival on Halloween. The last scene between Laurie and Michael Myers (before the next sequel). I curled my hands into fists and took a deep breath, readying for the final battle sequence . . . then bolted for the door. I ran away, out to the courtyard, looping around the fountain and through the archway to the main grounds. And I didn't stop. I kept running. I ran and I ran, the rain still blasting down, until I reached the hill leading up to the friary, where my progress became more of a pathetic limp.

"Coward," said Rochelle, floating up.

"Easy for you to say—you're already dead!" I yelled back, the wind pushing me back a step. Suddenly, a scream erupted, piercing through the wind and the rain. Blood-curdling, spine-tingling, and knife-sharp. I spun around, not knowing where it had come from. Beside me the waves thrashed, reminding me that I was trapped. Another scream ripped through the air, this time from the direction of the friary. The doors burst open, wildly swinging in the storm. A strand of rich auburn hair floated through. Then came the rest of her, staggering out the old chapel doors, clutching her side as blood seeped through her fingers and dripped onto the stone steps.

Rule #30

SAVE THE LOVE INTEREST

Saoirse screamed again when she saw me, her voice slicing through the air. Her hands stretched out and reached for me. I ran up the hill, my thighs on fire, not stopping until I held her. She hurled herself into me, blood and rain dampening her clothes. I pulled her in, holding her firmly. Even outside, with the salt air and the storm, she still smelled of lemon and oak.

She whimpered, clutching me tightly. "Charley, they're inside."

"Who?"

"Whoever did this," she cried, raising a bloodied palm to the sky.

I gazed wide-eyed at the open friary doors. Was it not Olive, then? Or was Olive just really fast and had gotten there before me?

"Charley!" Saoirse cried, her fingernails digging into me as she howled in pain.

HOW TO SURVIVE A HORROR MOVIE

"We have to go!" I grabbed her by the waist and helped her down the hill. We couldn't go back to Harrogate. It wasn't safe. Nowhere was safe. Or maybe there was one place. "We need to get to Eden!" I yelled over the wind.

She gazed down at the blood that had soaked through her shirt. "I won't make it that far," she sobbed.

We dragged ourselves away from the friary, away from Harrogate and Eden, going deeper into the wild. With every step we took, the storm swiped at us, driving us closer to the cliff edge. The cacophony of the ocean and the wind drowned out the voices of the ghosts as they called after me, warning me not to go any farther along the cliffs. Eventually they all disappeared, evaporating into the storm, much like the eroded corners of the island. The salt thrown up from the tumultuous seas stung my eyes. I rubbed them and continued on, until we found the coastal path. The gravelly trail jutted out slightly, over the ocean, with nothing but a thin railing to protect students from plummeting to the rocks in the waters below. Who would build a school on an island like this? It was just asking for a psychopath to kill everyone.

The weather and the ocean pressed against us from all sides. I collapsed against the railing, defeated. "I don't know where to go," I cried. I hated this island. I hated the cliffs, the rocks, the salty seas, and the stupid squawking birds.

Saoirse spun around, staring at the open friary doors still swinging in the breeze. When she turned back, her freckled face was ashen. "We can't stay out here. We're too exposed." I leaned over the railing. The beach below was a sandy mist. "There!" she yelled.

I followed her pointing finger to a large rock canopy that jutted out above the entrance to a cavern. The tide was low and would not be rising until the early evening. I hoped to be far away from the island before then.

She wrapped an arm around me as I shouldered her weight down the steps to the beach. Each mound and stone in our path felt like a mountain to climb. The rain battered our faces and washed the blood from Saoirse's hands, though her top was stained red. When our soles touched the sand, we sprinted for the cave, desperate to escape the storm and the masked murderer. I glanced behind to make sure no one was following us, but all I saw was mist and rain and Mr. Gillies's hand scurrying across the wet sand like a crab looking for a rock to shelter under.

We reached the rocks, and Saoirse hurled herself over the first boulder, screaming in pain. I scrambled to her, then helped her over the next one. The rocks were slick in the rain, and my sneakers slipped and skidded. When she got to the entrance, she fell onto the ground, crying.

"I can't walk anymore!" The cave towered above us.

"Yes, you can!" I yelled. I grabbed her by the waist and dragged her over the final rocks.

Inside, the air was much calmer, and our cries and whimpers reverberated through the cavern. It was damp, and dark, and the walls were slimy with seaweed and salt water. Above, stalactites protruded from the ceiling like claws. We staggered over to the wall and rested on a rock. My heart thudded and my insides churned as I recovered from the buffeting of the storm.

"We'll be safe here," I panted, trying to convince myself. Saoirse gripped her side, where the blood stained her top.

"Let me see."

She shook her head, still weeping. "What do we do now?"

"We can't go back to Harrogate. Everyone thinks it's me," I spluttered, my teeth chattering. "They think I'm the killer."

Saoirse trembled beside me. "I don't. I saw the killer, Charley, and it's not you."

I grabbed her arm. "Did you see their face?"

"No, whoever it was had a mask on."

"A gold one?"

She shuddered.

"Why were you in the friary?"

"I wasn't. I was at school, and someone turned off the lights in the girls' bathroom. When I came out, I saw a person standing in a black hoodie and that gold mask. I ran and ended up outside. I didn't know where to go, so I ran up the hill, and that's when I saw the friary doors were open. But the killer was already there. I almost didn't get away," she whimpered. "Who do you think is doing this?"

"I think . . . I think . . ." I didn't know if I could say the words. "I think it's my roommate, Olive."

"Olive Montgomery?" she gasped. "I know her. Not well, but we're in the same scholarship cohort. What makes you think it's her?"

"She's been there with me the whole time, finding the bodies, helping to piece this together. She wasn't with me at the pool party when the lights went out the night Gabrielle was killed, she conveniently 'forgot' to meet me in the shower rooms right before I was attacked in there, and she knew I was locked in Blyth's office when the power failed. And she convinced me to wait until morning to go down to the docks, and then we found the ferry destroyed. I fell asleep in the early hours, which would have given her more than enough time to get down there and do it."

"I just can't believe it."

"I can't believe it either. To think my only friend here on this island might be a serial killer . . . it's just crazy! But she certainly fits the profile." I sighed defeatedly. "Classic tale of a straight-A student gone berserk, *Carrie*-style."

"What are we going to do?" Saoirse asked again, another tear falling down her cheek. This time I brushed it away. I had no words for her; nothing I could say would reassure her that we were going to survive this.

The seas outside the cavern rocked up and down, and side to side. A crisp chill had set in as the rain started to soften its attack. I sighed and gazed down at the friendship bracelet Olive had given me back in summer. I traced my fingers over the sodden braided strands, and touched the small metal heart looped through one end. Was this really the end of Harrogate for all of us? Would I never again walk the halls, sleep in my dorm, feel the warm salty breeze on my face as Olive threw bread to the gulls?

Olive.

Was it really her, my best friend?

Rule #31
AVOID ROOMS WITH MANNEQUINS

Evening descended quickly, any trace of a sunset completely blotted out by the storm. The seas battered against the rocks and inched slowly toward us. Soon the tide would rise and the cavern would be submerged under the dark water. We couldn't stay here.

I glanced down once again at the bracelet on my wrist and felt the churn of sadness. With everything that had been going on, Halloween night had crept up on me. The formal was supposed to happen tonight. Olive had hung her Freddy costume up on the door of the shared wardrobe, having finally decided to replicate the infamous slasher's talons with knitting needles she'd borrowed from her math teacher. She'd woven them into the sleeves of her costume and taken great care to close up the ends inside so she didn't stab herself during the course of the night while serving bloodred punch to her peers. Tonight was supposed to have been a few hours off from all the drama of high school. A night when Olive and I could revel in our favorite hobby: the horror genre. A night when people didn't make fun of us for our obsession. It was a night when we could celebrate the great horror kings and pay homage to them: Romero, Craven, Cunningham. It was *our* night. Olive's and mine.

But the formal was just one more thing that had been taken from me.

At least I'd get to go home and see my mom. Right now I didn't care if people recognized me, called me a snitch, threw bricks through my living-room window again. Anything was better than this. I was cowering in a freezing cave (with my epic crush) on an isolated island, in soaking-wet clothes, not sure whether we'd drown, die from pneumonia, or perish at the hands of a serial killer stalking sixth-year girls. If I had a choice, I didn't know which I'd opt for. Pneumonia?

Saoirse slid off the rock beside me and walked slowly to the entrance of the cave. "The tide's rising. This whole cave will be submerged within an hour, maybe less."

I nodded. "We should go. I think if I carried you, we could make it to Eden. I'm not particularly strong or athletic, but I could try?" She didn't say anything, her dark green eyes just staring out to sea. "No, I can definitely do it," I continued. "I watched a movie once where the main character gets all this strength to defeat the villain because of the adrenaline. I think I have that—adrenaline, I mean."

Saoirse didn't say anything, she just kept gazing out. Was I talking too much? Was I not talking enough?

SCARLETT DUNMORE

"Saoirse?" I softly called out. Was now a good time to ask her if she liked me?

"I had roommates when I first arrived here on this island. I was scared, homesick, but they made it all better. We did everything together. We were best friends."

"That's nice," I said, a slight smile creeping onto my face. We were connecting, I thought. The classic overshare scene between the remaining victims, right before the big finale sequence. Sometimes, there's a kiss. Not that I was putting pressure on this moment. But a kiss would certainly follow the formula.

She continued talking distantly to the thrashing seas in front of her, like I wasn't there. "And then it became more. For me, anyway. I fell in love with one of them, and she became everything to me."

Oh, that sucks. Was Saoirse with someone already? Did I miss those signs?

"When she started having a hard time, she came to me," she smiled, color coming back to her cheeks. My shoulders sagged a little. I wanted to make her smile like that. "When Rochelle and her friends targeted her, for no reason at all other than they were just bored, she ran to me for help. But girls like Rochelle and Annabelle and Gabrielle rule this school—"

Rochelle floated out from behind a rock. "Why do people always talk about me behind my back?" she snapped.

"When families like hers pay big money to keep Harrogate's doors open, Blyth turns the other way," continued Saoirse.

"Student incident reports don't get filed, grades get changed, allegations are ignored. It was like that for years. It will always be like that: even when girls like Rochelle graduate, someone else just comes and takes their place. And the cycle repeats. That's how it works, isn't it? Money gives people power, and they take advantage of those who have none—"

Rochelle turned her back. "Oh, come on, do I have to listen to this?"

"Yes," Meghan said, raising her eyebrows scoldingly.

"Am I really that bad?" Rochelle argued.

Meghan scrunched up her nose and nodded.

Rochelle sighed. "My parents always told me you need to stay on top, whatever it takes..." She played uncomfortably with her hair, tugging at the tight curls, then finally looked up. "Maybe I took it too far."

Saoirse continued, "After a while, the bullying just got too much for her. Her grades fell, and she got kicked out of all her after-school clubs. Her parents requested a transfer, and Blyth was happy to sign off. So, she left this island, and me."

Saoirse exhaled deeply, mournfully. "I wrote to her for a while, but she didn't always write back. And when she did, she said she'd started at a new school and had met someone." She clenched her jaw and turned slowly to me. Her eyes were dark, empty. She smirked slightly, and cocked her head. "You don't recognize me, do you, Lottie?"

A cold shiver tickled my spine. *Lottie?*

"Who is this girl?" Meghan asked me.

SCARLETT DUNMORE

"I-I-I don't know?" I spluttered.

"Even if you don't recognize me, I recognize *you*."

"Me?" I gasped. Saoirse and I hadn't met before—had we?

"Yes, *you*," she spat out. "It was you she met, you and your group of friends! Soon she was sneaking out to go to parties with you, drinking and taking drugs because she thought that's what you liked. Doing whatever she could to impress you! And then that night happened."

"What night?"

"That night you convinced everyone to break into that old guy's house."

I swallowed hard and touched the gold "S" pendant around my collarbone. "It's Sadie you're talking about, isn't it?"

Sadie.

"Yes, Sadie. At least you remember her name," Saoirse scoffed.

"Of course I remember her name. I loved her."

"Liar!" she screamed. "*I* loved her. You used her!"

My stomach flipped as fractured images of that night twisted in my mind. I had been so stupid, trying to impress my older friends, make them think I was cool. I had been so broken after my dad died, I didn't care about anyone. But I had loved Sadie. Or at least I thought I had.

That night, she had run away with the others when the police had come. It was only me who got caught. I was never fast or athletic, even back then. All I had to do was keep quiet. I was going to juvenile detention regardless. But when they offered me a reduced sentence in exchange for names, I didn't think about her or the others. I thought about my mom, and then I saw my dad, or a flicker of an apparition. I thought it was a sign. Maybe it was, but I misinterpreted it. Deep down I always knew that my decision to tell on everyone came from a selfish place. I had a choice: five months in a juvenile center or five years. Maybe more. That's what they told me, anyway.

"Sadie," I murmured, my eyes stinging and watering.

Saoirse gazed up at the dark sky, at its absence of gulls. It was so quiet.

"She got two years after you snitched on her. She didn't even last six months."

I rose slowly from the rock I was perched on, my blood turning to ice in my veins. "What happened to her?"

"She hanged herself. She'd thought Harrogate was bad, but in there, she was an easy target."

I fought for breath, collapsing against the cavern wall, my body shaking. "I didn't know."

"You're lying," she whimpered, clutching her fists by her sides.

"I swear, I had no idea. I wrote to her, but she never replied. I thought she was still angry with me. Saoirse, please—" I rushed toward her, but she spun around. The knife in her hand glinted in the silvery moonlight that pushed through the stormy skies. I staggered back. The ghosts gasped, the sound echoing around the cave.

"I did not see that coming," Meghan choked out, still clutching her chest dramatically.

Saoirse continued, waving the knife around as she spoke. "I saw you that day in court, Lottie. I was there, but you obviously don't remember seeing me. I watched Sadie being sentenced, being taken away. I remember how much she cried. How she begged me to help her, like I did before. But I couldn't do anything. I can still hear her sobbing." She scrubbed away tears with the back of her hand. "I wrote to her every day she was in there, promised her that I'd be waiting for her when she got out. But apparently that wasn't enough."

"Saoirse, I am so sorry—"

"This island, this school, those girls in sixth year—and you! You all killed her!" she screamed, her eyes wide and feral.

I gasped, unable to catch a breath, and grabbed a rock to steady myself. "*You* killed those girls? *You're* the Harrogate Killer?" I spluttered.

"They all deserved it. The Elles were the ones who made her life hell here, Meghan kicked her out of Theater Club, Sarah took the title of hockey captain from her—"

"And what about Hannah? What did she do?"

"Hannah . . . that was an accident," she muttered, shaking her head. "Annabelle had paid her to do her English essay, and Hannah went to her dorm to drop it off. I was waiting there for Annabelle. But when Hannah came in and saw me dressed like that with the gold mask and the knife, she ran. I didn't want to hurt her. She wasn't part of the plan. *Annabelle* was supposed to die that night, not Hannah."

Poor Hannah. She wasn't part of this. I wished she could

have known that before she disappeared. But if Hannah were here now, if she could hear us somehow, then I was sure she wouldn't want anyone else to die. Not by Saoirse's hand. I balled mine into fists and took a breath, then I started to edge closer to the entrance. All I had to do was keep Saoirse talking long enough to distract her, then I could run.

"What about Mr. Gillies?" I asked.

"He stumbled upon me in his classroom. He knew it was me. He caught me with the mask. He would have told everyone. And I couldn't have that. I needed to finish my plan."

I inched along the wall, just a bit closer to the opening. "So you killed him."

"We fought, and I pushed him onto the table saw. It took me ages to clean up," she scoffed.

This was not the Saoirse I knew—or thought I knew. This was a different person. A deranged and broken person.

"And what about me?" I asked. "How do I fit into all of this?"

"The tide is almost here. Your body will be washed away, and I can tell everyone you were the killer. I'll be the only one of your victims who survived."

"No one will believe you. Olive will know you're lying."

Olive. All this time I thought it was Olive. How could I ever have blamed her for this? I missed her so much. She'd know what to do. She'd know how the final girl escapes the killer at the end.

"They'll believe me." She nodded. "You found all the bodies, remember? That can't just be a coincidence. You wouldn't believe how much planning that took. I was going to take you into the kitchen at the Eden party. I knew you'd come with me. But then you went in there yourself. Gabrielle's head was also particularly hard to clean up."

"The police will see right through you."

"No, they won't, especially when they find out who you really are. Plus, everyone knew you had a crush on me. I'll tell them you were obsessed."

"Harsh." I thought I'd been playing it cool.

Gabrielle appeared on the other side of the cave, stroking her hair as she cradled her head in her arms. "Sorry, I wasn't paying attention. What did I miss?"

"She's the killer"—Rochelle pointed at Saoirse—"and Charley's about to die."

"Got here just in time, then," Gabrielle cooed, plopping down onto a rock, her blue stilettos sticking out.

"You also missed a poorly performed monologue," Meghan added.

"You're the perfect killer," Saoirse continued as she started to pace. "A troubled past, a loner obsessed with horror movies, no friends—"

"I have friends!" I protested.

"One," snorted Rochelle.

I edged closer to the opening, the tide already washing over the floor of the cave and onto my sneakers.

"Harrogate won't be able to weather the scandal, and it'll close once and for all. And I might just finish Blyth as a final gift to Sadie." Saoirse smiled.

I was almost there, almost at the entrance. The ocean tickled my ankles, then my calves. "You'll have to be a bit quicker than that," Meghan piped up.

"Is she going to try to run?" squealed Rochelle. "Have you seen her in PE?"

"And I'll have avenged Sadie's death," Saoirse added, turning to face the murky waters that flowed into the cave.

It was now or never. I had to run. I breathed in quietly, crouched slightly, then bolted for the entrance. The water tugged at my legs as I ran. I was a lot slower than I thought, and Saoirse grabbed me before I got to the opening. She yanked my hair and pulled me backward. I stumbled into the water, the cold hitting me everywhere.

"Get up!" yelled Meghan.

Saoirse towered over me, knife in hand.

My body tingled, my insides turning to mush. I was about to die. In a cave, with only ghosts for witnesses. I backed up, trembling. "Saoirse, wait, please. I won't tell anyone. I don't blame you for what you did after everything you went through. You were angry. You didn't know what you were doing."

My mind began to fade, my thoughts slipping away, as I struggled for what else to say to her in these moments. I didn't know how to beg for my life. My whole body trembled as she walked toward me, the blade raised. This was the moment I was going to die. My mom's face popped into my head suddenly. Her long golden hair that curled around her chin, her almond-shaped green eyes, that way she talked about my father like he was just in the kitchen. Would she talk about me like that too after I was gone, like I was just upstairs in my bedroom? How would she live, without my dad and now me?

I closed my eyes and waited for the strike, the pain, the blood.

"Kick her," Rochelle said loudly.

I opened my eyes and squinted at her.

Rochelle rolled her eyes. "Put all your strength in it and kick her."

I turned to Saoirse, clenched my jaw, and kicked wildly, only succeeding in tapping her on her shin. She looked down at her leg, then back at me. "That was it?" she scoffed.

I shrugged. Then lunged at her, waving my arms around and screaming like a rabid woodland creature. Saoirse startled and stumbled back, dropping the knife into the water. Waves flowed in, filling the space, washing it away. She cursed and searched the darkness for the blade. I ran.

Suddenly all the ghosts were moving with me, shouting, cheering me on. The ice-cold seas took control of my body, seeping in and pulling me down to the depths. I spluttered and sucked in salt water, coughing as I clawed my way to the sliver of shore that remained on the other side of the cave. I heaved myself forward, every stroke one step closer to land, to safety, to Olive. The soles of my sneakers finally touched something solid, and I clambered onto the pebbly shore. I bolted up the dunes, the dirty clumps of sand clinging to my wet jeans, and ran until I found grass, then stone.

The courtyard was silent, except for the rain splashing into the fountain. I grabbed the handle of the first door I could find and hurled myself inside, grateful for a moment of relief from the weather. The staff room was in darkness, and the surrounding classrooms were locked. I hammered on walls, calling out, but no one came. A faint light from the hall ahead glimmered across the tiles, and I jogged toward it. I shouldered the doors open, and gasped.

Orange and black streamers hung from the ceiling. Taped into every corner were white balloons with blood-spatter patterns, and a huge "Happy Halloween" banner looped through and around the lights. Long tables lined the walls, adorned with black tablecloths, and rubber stage props of gory severed hands and plastic knives coated in crimson blood. On the gym floor were outlines of crime scenes, fallen bodies, and quarantine signs from zombie movies.

But that wasn't what unnerved me.

Scattered through the entire hall were tall, creepy figures with vacant eyes and unnaturally positioned plastic limbs.

Mannequins.

I really hated mannequins.

Rule #32

DON'T DIE—BE THE SMUG FINAL GIRL OF THE MOVIE

A room full of creepily dressed mannequins. Hollow eyes. Towering statures. Long, skinny plastic limbs that appeared to be reaching out to me. My heart hammered as I tiptoed through a collection of expressionless plastic dolls, with large, empty eye sockets.

A thud of a door echoed across the empty hall. I gasped and knelt behind a mannequin that someone had dressed like the scarecrow in *Jeepers Creepers*. Thanks, Olive. When you put a horror-obsessed student in charge of Halloween decorations, this was what you got.

From down here, I could see Saoirse's soggy, sand-smeared sneakers as she stood in the doorway. I crawled quietly away. The air was so still and silent, I soon became aware of a *drip-drip-dripp*ing from my ocean-soaked clothes onto the cold, hard floor. I curled my hands into fists. I'd probably left a trail of wet footprints for her to follow. I should have thought to remove my wet clothes and shoes, although

HOW TO SURVIVE A HORROR MOVIE

I didn't fancy being slashed or dismembered while naked either. I had *some* dignity, so dying in an A-cup bralette and beige-colored boy shorts wasn't an option.

"Lottie?" she called.

I stopped crawling and bit down on my lip.

She sang my name as she skirted around the mannequins. "Lottieeeee."

There were plenty of other girls at Harrogate. Why did I have to fall for the psycho?

A cold shiver ran up my spine as her voice danced through the hall, through the black and orange streamers, balloons, and Halloween banners. I did not want to die, even on Halloween night. I inched away as she approached, turning to see Meghan and Rochelle hiding behind a mannequin dressed like the possessed murderous doll from *Annabelle* in a white dress with a red sash around the waist, with long braids tied in ribbons. Gabrielle's blue stilettos stuck out from under an orange tablecloth draped over a plastic table. Meghan whistled and beckoned me across the hall. The black dust was already gathering on her arms.

Saoirse continued snaking between the mannequins, calling to me, taunting me. The floor was cold under my bare hands, which had now turned a raw red from the freezing salty ocean. The exit was just ahead underneath the crimson "Happy Halloween" banner. The air was silent, except for a squeaking noise behind me. It sounded like

SCARLETT DUNMORE

a rusty knob trying to turn . . . or perhaps a mannequin rotating on its metal base.

I slowly turned, my breath quickening. The last mannequin, which only a moment ago had been wearing a *Friday the 13th* hockey mask, now had on the gold theatrical mask. The expression of comedy looked down on me as I gasped and stumbled backward. The mannequin pitched forward, the gold mask cracking and splintering. Standing behind it was Saoirse, her face hard and tense, her eyes dark and empty.

I shrieked and scrambled for the exit, throwing it open to the dark hallways of the Catherine Wing. The dining room where I'd chased Rochelle to her death was shrouded in darkness. Saoirse's footsteps were just behind me, her warm breath on the back of my neck, her fingers reaching for my hair. She tugged at me, and I lurched backward, falling hard to the ground. I howled in pain as my spine hit the cold floor. I squirmed around and pulled myself backward, away from her. She dragged a hacksaw along the ground, the tip of the blade scratching the tiles. I cursed Mr. Gillies for keeping his woodworking tools so sharp as his hand scurried across the floor.

A flicker of silver caught my eye and I saw Rochelle standing beside Saoirse, the knives in her chest glinting. On her other side stood Meghan and Gabrielle, who had her head tucked under her arm. I thought about Half-Broken Hannah with her sad eyes and Strangled Sarah with her bent, twisted neck. Would I become a ghost too?

Or would we all instantly disappear when I died? If I was the last piece of the puzzle, the reason why we were all being targeted, then when the blade struck through me, would a bright white light appear for all of us?

I closed my eyes and waited for the impact, for the piercing of flesh and the fracturing of bone.

Clunk!

Thump!

I slowly peeled open my eyes and saw Saoirse groaning on the floor beside me. Olive was standing over her with the emergency axe from the assembly hall.

"Olive!" I howled. I had never been so happy to see her face, smiling down at me. She threw the axe to the floor dramatically and reached out a hand. As she heaved me to my feet, I wrapped my arms around her and pulled her in for a hug. "How are you here?" I cried, finally letting her go.

"I figured out who it was soon after you left. I've been searching everywhere for you!"

"You figured out who the Harrogate Killer was before me?"

"Duh! Who was the next obvious choice after the prom queen was bumped off?"

I rolled my eyes. "Of course, the love interest."

Behind her, Saoirse slowly rose to her feet, the hacksaw still in her hand. She winced, touching her back where Olive had gotten her, fingers coming away smeared thickly with blood. "Olive—" she panted as she glared at us, her eyes filled with fire and rage.

"Run!" Meghan shouted, gesturing to the door. Gabrielle bounced up and down in excitement beside her.

I pulled Olive toward the exit and thrust open the door to the courtyard, hurtling out into the rain. Heavy drops hammered down around us. Saoirse followed close behind, not letting us out of her sight. The sounds of the sea thrashing against the cliffs and fighting against the rain pierced the night sky as I wove around rock and stone, eager to feel sand underneath the soles of my shoes. The coastal path was illuminated, a dull amber glow visible in the distance. I hurried toward it, pulling Olive with me. She whimpered and looked back. "She's too fast for us!" she yelled over the rain.

I glanced back at Harrogate, at the sprawling estate, cursing myself for dragging us both out here, back onto the cliffs, into the elements of a storm. But I didn't want to die within the walls of that school. Soon there was sand underfoot, and the scent of salt and seaweed filled our nostrils.

"Where are you going to go? The tide's in," Saoirse shouted behind us. "There's nowhere to run!"

"Yes, where are we going?" spluttered Olive, trying to keep up with me.

"We're going to finish this."

"No sequels?"

"No sequels."

We ducked under the amber light of an old cast-iron lamppost that rocked in the wind and started stumbling down to the rocks. I could hear her behind me, smell her sweat, feel her rage burning.

Just a little farther . . .

Her fingers were on me, grasping at my clothes, pulling me down.

I skidded on the edge of the cliff, my shoes slipping on the mud. Olive tumbled from my grip as I fell backward, landing on sand and stone. Saoirse threw herself on me, pressing my shoulders to the earth as I fought and kicked and scratched and tore at her. She wrestled my arms to the ground and hovered above me.

"I need to end this, for Sadie!" she screamed, her eyes filled with bloodthirst and desperation.

Something pierced my side, and the world tilted around me, a deep silence setting in. I'd never felt anything like it before in my life, a pain that grounded me and yet knocked me out of myself. I gasped for air and squeezed my eyes shut. Nothing I had ever known, ever learned about surviving had helped me in the end. Because in the end we couldn't write our own finale, not like a movie. Because life wasn't a movie. Death wasn't a make-believe horror scene, people weren't actors, and blood wasn't Heinz tomato sauce.

This was real.

I gazed up at the sky, my arms splayed out, my body awaiting the next strike, the one that would end me. And I thought about how Hannah, Sarah, Meghan, Gabrielle, Rochelle, and Mr. Gillies must have felt when they were killed—scared, desperate, powerless. And as if they knew what I was thinking, the three remaining ghosts appeared in front of me, eyes filled with sadness because they knew I was about to die, and that I had failed them. I had failed to stop their killer, and now Saoirse would carry on, while the truth died with us.

Rochelle crouched down, her voice loud in my ear. "Get up, Charley. You're tougher than this."

I turned to her, her face soft and her eyes filled with an emotion I hadn't seen before—hope. I realized in that moment that they weren't haunting me because this was my fault or because I had killed them. They came to me because I was the only one who could end this. They wanted me to avenge their deaths, the way Saoirse was misguidedly trying to do for Sadie. I wouldn't let them down—not Meghan or Hannah or Sarah, not even Rochelle or Gabrielle. I would find strength somehow. Rochelle was right. I was tougher than this.

My hand clawed at the earth, and my fingers closed on a rock. I gripped it tightly in my palm and swung it at her head with all the strength I had left.

Crack!

She swayed backward, taking her weight off me. Before she could regain her balance, I kicked her hard in the belly, and she fell back out of my sight. Her screams shattered the silence, then ended abruptly as a loud crack tore through the night.

I grunted and swore as I clambered to my feet, Olive beside me. We peered over the edge of the cliff. Saoirse lay sprawled on the rock below us, her body illuminated by the dock lights and her long red hair spread across the stone. Her limbs lay twisted at an inhuman angle, much like Hannah's were when we found her. A slick of blood was smeared across the rock.

Her eyes were closed, her body still.

I heard the thud of Olive beside me as she fainted, face-down in the wet sand. The ghosts still stood before me, side by side, watching. I gazed over the edge at Saoirse's splayed body, straightened up, then staggered down the rocky cliff, holding my side where warm blood oozed out.

Rochelle scrunched up her nose. "What are you doing?"

"Making sure she's dead."

"Eh, I think she's well and truly dead." Meghan grimaced, staring down at the bloodied body.

"Don't you watch horror movies? Double tap."

"Double tap?" Rochelle asked.

"Double tap—another strike just to make sure they're dead," explained Meghan. "Like at the end of *Scream*, right, Charley?"

I nodded in approval. If Living Meghan had been anything like Non-Living Meghan, she and I could have been friends, perhaps. She could have joined Olive and me on Slasher Saturdays. We would have shared our popcorn with her, although maybe not our Skittles. Not in the beginning, anyway.

I edged down, one small steady step at a time, careful not to fall myself. At the bottom, I searched for a stone heavy enough to complete the job but light enough for someone of my size to wield, then gazed up at the ghosts who all stood with their toes over the edge of the cliff, looking down at me. Rochelle smiled. Warm tears pricked my eyes as I waved at her, at all of them, the faces I'd never see again. The voices I'd wanted so desperately out of my head in the beginning, but had now come to expect each morning, and sometimes look forward to. Come tomorrow, I'd miss them. I already missed the *pop, crack, snap* of Hannah's bones, and tomorrow I'd miss Meghan's vocal warm-ups and the wheeze of Sarah's twisted throat.

I looked down on Saoirse, sprawled on the rock, and tried not to focus on the tiny freckles across her nose, her flushed cheeks, and that beautiful mane of red. I tried not to smell the lemon and oak in her hair.

Suddenly her eyes shot open, furious and bloodthirsty still. The ghosts screamed. I raised my arms high and smashed the rock down on Saoirse's head until her skull cracked open and soft mushy gray fragments of brain poured out. Silence closed in, then the crash of the waves filled my ears. I threw the rock down beside her corpse and gazed up at the ledge above me. Meghan and Rochelle stared down, momentarily confused, as if they were waiting for something. Then Meghan glanced at her hand, which started to shimmer in the early signs of morning. Her skin glistened like sunlight had hit it. Then Rochelle and Gabrielle. Even Mr. Gillies's crab hand sparkled. They faded into iridescent dust, then disappeared.

HOW TO SURVIVE A HORROR MOVIE

I blinked. The ledge was now empty, nothing but sand and seaweed and bare rock. The ghosts were gone, and the salt air rushed into the emptiness. I pulled myself back up the rocks to the cliff edge, where Olive stood and gasped for air.

"That was gross," she panted.

"You know me: I hate a sequel," I muttered, limping back toward Harrogate, holding my side as blood continued to trickle out.

"Me too," said Olive, turning to follow me back to the school.

Scatterings of dusky pink and shimmering gold poked through the clouds. The storm had finally passed. It was over. Eventually boats from the mainland would come to bring us all home.

The early morning sunrays struck the tops of Harrogate's turrets, slivers of sunshine pouring out onto the school grounds.

"But do you know what I hate more?" Olive added.

"What?"

"Smug final girls."

Suddenly something struck me from behind, a deep and wet thrust to the back. I collapsed to my knees, the air in my lungs becoming short, shallow, and trapped. My ears pounded and throbbed, drowning out the sounds of the birds returning overhead. Gulping for air, I wriggled my hand up my back. There it was. Wedged deep beside my spine. A knife.

SCARLETT DUNMORE

My best friend had *literally* stabbed me in the back.

I took another sharp breath, then toppled onto the slick, moist grass.

"Sorry, Charley," said Olive as she stepped over me. "You were right the first time. I did hate the sixth-year girls for how they treated me and for what they did to Sadie."

"You knew Sadie too?" I stammered.

"Saoirse, Sadie, and I were all roommates. We lived together for years one to four. We were best friends, inseparable, much like you and I are . . . sorry, I mean *were*. It was all my idea. Saoirse was reluctant to go along with it at first, but she was so in love with Sadie and so devastated after her death that it didn't take much to change her mind. She ended up having to repeat year five twice, which worked out well because it meant she and I could pretend we didn't know each other. We probably would have ended the year the same even if you hadn't come here: graduated from Harrogate with a *bang*." Her eyes lit up. "But then you stepped off the boat that morning. We were so shocked to see you. We recognized you immediately. It was fate—you were the perfect suspect to pin it all on. And your infatuation with Saoirse was almost too well-timed!" She laughed, throwing her head back.

"Did she really kill those girls, or did you?" I spluttered, blood seeping out of me onto the wet grass.

"You know I'm too squeamish for that," she said, shuddering. She circled around me, stepping over my limbs. "I admit, I doubted Saoirse after the screwup with Hannah, but she did a good job after that. And she was good at handling all the icky parts. I couldn't have chopped Gabrielle's head off with the emergency axe. Not so clean through the bone like that." She swallowed loudly, her face suddenly pale. Then she shuddered and carried on circling me.

"Two villains?" I coughed, the heat draining from my body, the cold, crisp autumnal air washing over me.

"Of course! Wes Craven did it so well in *Scream*—the multiple villain thing. Did not see that coming," she sang.

"Why?" I groaned, the pain flooding my body, coursing through my veins.

"Because it was so unexpected!"

"No, I mean, why kill *me*? I would have told everyone it was Saoirse." I coughed and retched.

"Yeah." She nodded. "I could have let you walk." She sighed and bent over me. "But you know me, that's just too damn predictable."

She wriggled the blade in my back and I howled, my screams cutting through the air. I blinked slowly and watched her walk away, striding confidently toward Harrogate School for Girls. Up above me, the squawking of hooded crows suddenly grew louder, sharper as they hovered eagerly over my dying body.

Gliding.

Soaring.

Waiting.

Rule #33

ALWAYS PREPARE FOR A SEQUEL

A flock of ravens cawed as their wings pierced the wintery sky, peppered with the first signs of snowfall. There was a chill in the air, a sharpness that cut through the light mist that trickled through the branches of Glenbrook Road. Autumn had gone, and winter had crept in quietly. Or perhaps I just hadn't noticed its arrival, having spent almost two months confined to a bed in Wexford General Hospital.

Today I was discharged but it had been a long couple of months. Weeks of agonizing surgeries and post-op treatments to recover from the blood loss, not to mention the sleepless nights and endless nightmares of severed heads in coolers and splayed bodies on rocks. Thankfully Olive had missed my spinal cord, so any lasting physical damage was minimal. However, the emotional consequences of being almost murdered by my school crush and my best friend were about to be picked apart and analyzed in months of therapy that my mom had very kindly organized for me. Plus, there was the ghost thing. I had kept that part to myself, hoping to avoid a stint in Wexford's mental health clinic. I hadn't seen or heard anything since Halloween night, not since . . . since . . .

Meghan. Hannah. Gabrielle. Sarah. Rochelle. Mr. Gillies.
The blood.
The screams.
That gold mask.

Suddenly, I couldn't breathe. I sucked the crisp air, gasping and panting, as the screams of Harrogate's hallways flooded my mind, drowning me—

"Charley!"

I opened my eyes. My mom's red Fiat sat in front of me, the passenger window rolled down as she waved frantically. "Charley, come on. I'm in a no-parking zone!"

I shook my head, pushing the images of Halloween from my mind, and walked slowly to the car. It hurt to lean back, so I edged forward until my knees touched the dashboard and my belly squished into the bag on my lap. The tall glass Wexford hospital building shrank behind us as we started the short drive home. I hadn't been home in almost six months, not since the summer. What would I do now? Was I returning as Charley or Lottie?

We were to meet with the social worker in the new year to discuss my education options now that Harrogate had become a crime scene and was closed indefinitely. I couldn't go back there, and I couldn't go back to my old school. And with an unfinished sixth year and a criminal record, what university would accept me? And even if I did manage to gain a place, how would I be able to trust anyone again?

Suddenly a familiar song began to play on the speakers. "Red Right Hand" by Nick Cave and the Bad Seeds filled the car, vibrating against my legs. My mom hummed softly beside me, drumming her fingers on the clutch. I leaned forward and switched the radio off.

"I was enjoying that," she moaned.

"It's from *Scream*."

"And?"

"And I can't stand horror movies anymore."

"Since when?"

"Since Halloween." I sighed. "You know, when I was stabbed in the back? And that's figuratively too."

"Honey, you can't blame yourself—"

"Good, because I don't," I said, glaring at her, although a part of me still did, at least whenever I thought about Sadie. I touched my collarbone, hoping to find the "S" pendant, but I only found bare skin. I remembered I hadn't worn it since that day on the cliffs.

"What I mean is, try not to dwell on what's happened. Let's enjoy Christmas together, and we'll figure out the rest in January. It's a beautiful Saturday, and the only thing I have planned for us this weekend is lots of rest and some TV time. Sound good?"

HOW TO SURVIVE A HORROR MOVIE

"Sounds perfect," I said, my face softening.

She lightly squeezed my knee and flicked the radio back on. The Nick Cave song had finished and now Christmas tunes blasted out, penetrating our eardrums and pressing against the windows, likely spilling out on to the road around us. Thankfully the N25 was quiet at this time of day.

As we turned off into Whiterock, the roads began to fill up. Parked cars lined the streets, beside rows of whitewashed houses with small gardens and even smaller driveways. Hairdressers, nail salons, and quaint family-run shops were scattered among playgrounds and birch trees.

I closed my eyes and took a deep breath. "And we're home," chirped my mom.

I coughed on the last inhale and blinked open my eyes. Our townhouse sat in the shadows of the Greenstar recycling center and an industrial warehouse. I could see our Christmas tree lights twinkling through the windows. My chest began to loosen as a smile crept onto my face. I didn't realize how much I'd missed being here. I didn't care who remembered who I was before Harrogate or what I did. I was home. And I was alive.

I slid out of the car and walked slowly to the door. My mom rushed in front of me and unlocked it before I got there. The aroma of pine and juniper berries enveloped me as I entered. We had never been able to afford a real

Christmas tree so my mom filled the house with fragranced candles and plug-ins, anything she could find to infuse the rooms with the scent of an expensive balsam fir.

"Grab a seat. I'll put the kettle on." She smiled, plopping my bag down by the shoe rack.

I climbed awkwardly on to the barstool, perching on the edge again. The tightness of my back caused my spine to quiver. My fingers lightly grazed a bandage bulge under my hoodie. I shivered again and tried to distract myself with the mountain of mail strewn across the kitchen counter. Today's newspaper sat in front of me. I traced my fingers over the top headline: *Harrogate's House of Horrors*.

But it was the subhead that flooded my veins with ice: *Killer's Remains to Be Flown Home for Funeral.*

Since regaining consciousness, I had tried my best to avoid the papers and the media broadcasts, even when all I had for entertainment were the pale blue walls of my hospital room and the browning tulips on the table beside me. But it wasn't long before I heard snippets of staff conversation from the hallways, my mom dropped bits of information, and eventually I got the whole story from the detective who came to interview me after surgery number two.

It seemed that not long after Olive had plunged a knife into my back, leaving me to die on the cliff, she'd returned to Harrogate. Less than an hour later, a fire had ravaged the Edith Wing, leaving only burnt brick and a charred skeleton.

Some of the sixth-year girls said they saw her enter the Edith Wing with a bomb strapped to her torso and her arms out wide, like JD in *Heathers*. She did say she wanted to go out with a *bang*. Others said they never saw her at all, that she disappeared into the cliffs, hiding between rock mass and gull nests. But after several forensic tests, the authorities had finally identified her remains and according to this headline had now released her for a funeral send-off.

I tossed the paper down, watching it land in a pile of unanswered bills and final reminders, and slid off the stool. "I'm going to take a quick shower."

"Need a hand?"

"Nah, I'll be fine."

I headed down the hallway, past framed photos of Mom and me, of Dad, of our days spent playing on the coast or in the woods. My bedroom door was slightly ajar. I pushed it open and crept inside, my footsteps light on the wooden floor. The first thing I noticed was that the curtains were drawn tight, with only a sliver of light piercing through the window. The entire room was washed in darkness, except for the back corner where my old TV sat. Flickering on the screen were the opening credits of *Scream*—the crimson font, the ringing of a telephone, the sound of a woman shrieking in fear.

I staggered back, crying out in pain as my spine hit the doorframe. Had my mom put this on for me? When? We'd only just got home.

The movie continued, with the familiar opening of the naive young student answering the phone while popcorn danced on the lit stovetop and darkness pressed against the windows of a rural farmhouse. Miles from town. Miles from help. Then that face—that white howling mask, the black cloak, the sharpened knife—

I lunged for the light switch, my fingers trembling. When I turned back, I saw my mirror before me. I gasped as I read what was scrawled on the glass, in thick blood-red lipstick.

ACKNOWLEDGMENTS

First, I want to thank my incredible team at Little Tiger, including Karelle Tobias, Charlie Moyler, Lauren Ace, Jade McGrath, George Hanratty, and Jasmin Lindenmeir. To my editor, Karelle—it's been wonderful to share a love of the genre! Thank you for whipping this book into shape. I also want to thank the team over at Union Square for helping my book reach American readers.

To my agent, Silvia Molteni at Peters Fraser + Dunlop, thank you so much for your support, vision, and guidance during my writing career. You navigated me through the early drafts of this novel, and helped me find direction.

I have to give a huge shout-out to my family, the people I'd team up with in a horror movie any day. To my partner, my parents, and my siblings—thank you for your endless patience and support. And thank you for being clued up on the survival rules!

I first came up with the story idea in lockdown in 2020, drawing from those early memories of secretly watching scary movies with my brother. I have always loved the horror genre, having grown up reading the Point Horror collection, before moving on to Stephen King. Writing in lockdown was a challenging time for many authors. For me it was also a time I engaged with movies and television, particularly of the horror genre, which is where I found my inspiration for this book. So as an avid horror film fan, it wouldn't be right if I didn't acknowledge a few of the great horror directors that inspired some of the scenes in this novel, including Romero, Craven, and Carpenter. Thank you for giving me nightmares as a kid!

ABOUT THE AUTHOR

Scarlett Dunmore studied English and creative writing, eventually finding a love for YA literature. When she's not writing, she can often be found watching scary films or exploring abandoned abbeys, old cemeteries, and ruined castles in Scotland for inspiration.

@scarlett_dunmore